AROUSAL

A.C. ROSE

AROUSAL

Goddess Communications

Copyright © 2017 by A.C. Rose

Cover Design: Najla Qamber Designs

Editor: Victoria Miller

Proofreading: Marla S. Esposito at Proofing with Style

Book interior: Formatting Fairies

Paberback Edition 2017

ISBN-10: 1-941630-07-3

ISBN-13: 978-1-941630-07-5

PROLOGUE

The elderly woman called for her nurse and asked for help sitting up in bed. Frail and growing weaker, her days as matriarch and grand prophet for her clan were winding down. She had but one remaining goal before she left this world: to ensure her eldest grandson found true love. And that she passed her powers to him and his beloved. It was his birthright. It was her need. He had a tradition to uphold, and the family legacy must pass securely to him.

"Eloise," she said to her long-time, devoted nurse and companion. "Bring me my book of wisdom. I must give my grandson assistance. I will need your help."

The nurse picked up a leather-bound volume of handwritten notes on parchment pages and placed it on the elderly woman's lap. She brought over her reading glasses. Though unable to hold the heavy book, the woman opened the pages and found what she needed.

"I have seen her in my dreams, Eloise, and she is a beauty. They are fated to meet, but while he is so ready to love, she is afraid. There are walls around her heart. We may need to move things along. My time on this Earth is waning."

"But you know he doesn't like you to use your powers for such things."

"This is only for good." She smiled up at her nurse. Her blue eyes twinkled with conviction.

"Of course."

"An old legend tells us when two certain souls are created in heaven, an angel cries out, *Ves'tacha!* These two are meant to be. It is said that if these people meet and recognize each other for who they truly are, they will fall in love and become as one. Then together they will build a love that is a sanctuary and the foundation of their lives. A love that is so fulfilling that they may reach out to others with compassion and service. No hardship can alter the strength of their love. And everything they do will succeed because they are fated for each other."

"And you must help them meet." The nurse smiled and draped a shawl around the older woman's shoulders.

"Exactly. This marriage was arranged by the heavens, not by me. It just needs some help." She slipped on her glasses and perused the book.

"Which love prayer are you thinking of?"

"This one." The older woman pointed a wrinkled finger at a page that had been somewhat faded by time.

To help a man move heaven and earth for love, show him a ticking clock and tell him he has six dates to inspire a woman, to see she loves him, and to make her his. And repeat this prayer:

Bring these lovers together soon,
When the moment is opportune.
Let fiery passion them consume,
And bring consummation at full moon.
Stir arousal, so romance can begin,
Melt resistance and invite love in.
Give him strength to penetrate her shield;
Give her desire to fully yield.
Tho' she may not know they are meant to be,
Let awareness grow and become reality.

The elderly woman removed her glasses and gazed at her nurse. "They would bond naturally because they are meant to be. But, with this, they shall be immediately irresistible to each other. My grandson will have his true love—and our legacy will live on."

CHAPTER ONE
DAY ONE: TUESDAY

I may have been a little distracted as I searched the elevator control panel for Club Kismet, the new upscale private venue on the seventy-seventh floor of a Manhattan high-rise on First Avenue. I was heading to the launch party for the new, high-tech My Fantasy e-Reader. I'd worked for months as lead publicist to make sure this event would be a success, and it felt to me like a date with destiny. A great product introduction, with good press, would mean advancement for me. And it would put the company my father founded back on the map.

The elevator was like a hall of mirrors, and it was impossible not to look at myself—from all angles. I scanned my professional attire: black pencil skirt; slinky, white, tucked-in silk shirt; pearls on my ears and neck; and fashionable five-inch heels that gave my petite frame a boost. The outfit hugged my curves without being too revealing. My long, dark hair was neatly upswept off my neck with a barrette. I never wanted to look too sexy at a press event. People tended to drink a lot, and I didn't want to invite any touchy-feely behavior. Turning down an advance from a media hot shot was awkward as hell, but it was career suicide not to—so I kept my shirt buttoned to the top and played friendly but not flirtatious.

As I reached over and pushed the button for my floor, I noticed an errant strand of hair on my face. I turned toward the largest mirror in the center and as I was about to brush it off, a tall, golden-haired Adonis expertly karate chopped the air between the doors and stopped it from closing. He slid his long, lean body into the elevator and landed right behind me in the center of the car. The elevator door closed, but he didn't move; he stood there, as if he were meant to be so close. Something about him seemed familiar.

As the elevator ascended, our eyes locked in the mirror, which captured us from many angles and intensified his penetrating gaze. A slight tremor ran through me when his breath touched the back of my neck. I was mesmerized, unable to avert my eyes from his. We stood like this for twenty-seven floors and said nothing as we sped upward. It seemed that a strange magnetic force bound us together.

When the elevator unexpectedly halted at the twenty-eighth floor, we both turned toward the door. The unexpected stop gave me a chance to collect myself and pull to one side of the elevator. He went to the other, but his blue-eyed gaze stayed on me. It took me a moment to realize the elevator wasn't moving.

"Elevators," he said in a strong, sexy voice seasoned with an accent I couldn't place. "Sometimes they have a mind of their own." He turned to the control panel on his side of the car and pressed the open button. When nothing happened, he pressed for the seventy-seventh floor again. I anxiously waited to hear the churning gears of a moving elevator or the sound of the door opening. Nothing. That's when I began to panic.

Fear slid into the pit of my stomach. My breathing accelerated. I held on to the rails along either side of me with a white-knuckled grip.

He glanced over. "I am sure we'll start moving in a moment," he said, still calm and composed.

I eyed the red emergency call button and gripped the rails tighter.

"I ... I have a thing about elevators." Fright spread through my body and was now also settled in my chest. My blood pumped hot through arteries and veins. "Got stuck in one when I was young, with my grandmother. And—" It was getting harder to talk.

He reached his long arm to push the emergency call button. Nothing happened. Next, he slid his hand into his suit jacket for his cell phone.

"This is the worst day ever to get stuck in an elevator," I panted, staring at the buttons on the panel as if willing the car to move. "I need to get out of here."

He tried to make a call from his cell but shook his head and placed the phone back in his pocket. Apparently, the service was dead. He lifted his hand to his square jaw, with its slight cleft and perfect blond stubble beard, and rubbed it, as if giving deep thought to something.

"Stay calm," he said, his tone soothing. "Everything is going to be okay."

Those were the exact words my grandmother had said when I was eight years old and an elevator stopped in between floors. I could almost hear her voice and see her saying the words. I could feel my heart pounding.

"You don't understand; I can't be stuck. Not here. Not now. Not ever." I began to hyperventilate.

"Well then, there is only one thing to do."

Before I could blink, he came forward and closed the distance between his end of the elevator and mine. He was in front of me. Two strong hands brushed back a few lose strands of hair and reached for my face. "I won't let anything happen to you," he said, his breath against my skin—against my mouth—as he leaned in closer.

His lips came down on mine. Warm and soft, they issued an invitation that suddenly made me forget my panic. It happened so quickly, and powerfully, that my body responded in total surrender. My mouth yielded to his, and then opened as he pressed his tongue in deeply and passionately. It seemed impossibly intimate for two people who had just met, yet his mouth felt so good on mine.

He moved in closer, and pressed me against the elevator wall, his body touching mine. Arousal stirred inside me as his kiss grew deeper, more probing, and more possessive. My brain left the building and fear left my body as I was transformed into a tingling mass of nerve endings. The only thing that seemed to exist in that moment were our mouths, melded together, like a perfect, matching set.

Until the elevator started again. Abruptly. It moved so fast that my heart dropped into my stomach and my legs felt wobbly. He wrapped his arms around me and held my body firmly against his for support, but kept his mouth on mine. I moved my hands off the rails to grip his biceps. My chest was heaving and I couldn't tell if it was from the feelings he set off in my body, or my old elevator trauma getting set off by the weird stop and start of the steel box we were riding in.

When the elevator slowed, he pulled away, but held me in the moment with his soulful gaze. He seemed to want to linger, yet he ended the passionate moment by pressing his lips softly on mine and punctuating the intensity of his kiss with tenderness. Then he released me from his heated grip. His gaze stayed on me as he helped me stand up straighter. I eyed him inquisitively and noticed my pink lipstick streaked across his lips, and trailing to the side of his mouth, close to his light beard. Looking over his shoulder, I could see it all over my chin as well. He noticed too.

"You'll need this," he said, pulling a handkerchief from his jacket pocket.

"We both do."

"Being marked by a beautiful woman is a badge of honor," he said. A grin slid to his mouth and then reached his eyes. "I have nothing to hide, but if you insist."

I took his handkerchief and wiped my lip color from his face, admiring his square jaw and sexy lips. Then I patted the color from my face. It seemed more intimate than the kiss itself to touch him in that way. I tried to remove all traces of the unexpected passion from us both.

Placing his hand on my lower back, he led us off the elevator. Then he took my right hand, lifted it to his mouth, and kissed it European-style. His gaze was still on me as his lips gently brushed my knuckles. Those eyes. They were a striking and intense blue, yet seemed to change colors, alternating between hues of blue and green. Maybe it was the lighting.

Acting as if our amatory elevator ride was the most natural thing in the world, he released my hand, smiled, and tipped his head politely the way people do when they are about to take their leave. If there were proper etiquette for this moment, I had no idea how to invoke it. I simply held my hand out with the handkerchief.

"Hold on to it," he said, with the sexiest wink I'd ever seen. "You may need it again tonight."

I had no words. None.

"By the way," he added, "I hope elevators will be more pleasant for you now."

With that, he walked away. Into Club Kismet.

What the hell happened? My mind and body were still in some sort of hormonal daze. On wobbly knees, I got myself into the ladies' room, situated, thank goodness, just outside the venue. I imagined I was a disheveled mess on the outside because my insides seemed that way. Surely I needed to reapply my lipstick, fix my hair, and pull myself together.

It took a few moments to bring myself back to normal consciousness. And even then I was still on shaky ground. I thought I was done with elevator panic attacks that could bring me to my knees. And when did I ever allow a man—a stranger—to get under my skin with just one glance? Never. This is so completely unlike me. I'm not the girl who gets snogged on elevators or who finds herself in "situations." Yet he kissed me. And, worse, I didn't try to push him off. I didn't even want to. There was something irresistible about this man.

For a brief moment, I smiled, remembering his lips—until I came to my senses.

"Holy crap, he was heading up to Club Kismet," I said out loud. What if I just made out with a reporter or a TV producer? All I need is to start this event—the most important of my career—with a huge conflict of interest.

Plopping down on the plush chair in the ladies' room, I looked in the mirror and took stock. I seemed freshly kissed and needed new lipstick, but the rest of me had a healthy glow that belied the worry within. I closed my eyes and steadied my breathing, letting my insides settle so I could get to work. It helped. "Pull it together, Allison," I whispered to my reflection, as I got ready to rejoin the outside world. "Get your head out of your panties and get back into the game."

I put on my best smile and went into the club.

As I crossed the threshold into the large room, with its elegant décor and large chandeliers, my composure returned. I'd created this event! I headed to the press table my assistant had set earlier that day. Excitement rippled through me as I passed through party guests. They were talking and laughing. Thirty top media outlets had RSVP'd, and that in itself was a huge accomplishment. My night would be about talking up the e-reader, demonstrating it, and encouraging the press to try the product and write about it. My table was close to the bar, where media people tend to congregate when libations are free. That was a good thing; I may need a drink, too.

With so much riding on this evening, I could not afford to mess it up in any way. I had to block the hot guy from the elevator out of my head and avoid him at all costs. I prided myself on being a careful professional, and I especially never messed around with media or men in work environments.

I would pretend this never happened.

CHAPTER TWO

Thankfully, there was great interest in the new reading device, and I spent much of the first hour happily demonstrating it and securing media coverage. Truth is, I loved the product. It was a universal e-reader that allowed consumers to purchase romances from all the main sources— Kindle, Kobo, Nook, and iBook—and contained a database of photos and videos in an app we called, "Who Should Play Him in the Movie?" This was based on research that confirmed readers loved to select their own *look* for the characters in the books and enjoyed selecting photos of handsome men who might fit the bill. Once I started showing it off, I remembered what this night was all about.

It was so interesting how one's perspective could quickly change depending on the influences of the moment. I entered the building with nothing but business on my mind. I freaked when the elevator seemed stuck. The moment became about a desirable stranger randomly and passionately kissing me. Then I was back to normal, doing my job and focusing on my priorities.

Until I spotted him again.

There he was, the man from the elevator, surrounded by men who hung on his every word and women who gaped at him adoringly. He was clearly a center of influence in the room.

He stood out from the after-work crowd in a light gray suit with a white shirt, open at the neck, sans necktie. His golden hair was combed back, and looked very *GQ*. And those eyes—intense, exciting. I remembered how they connected to mine in the elevator. This man was physical perfection, really, and so self-possessed. His strong, captivating presence had everyone around him mesmerized. Me included.

I stole a glance. I had to. But my breath caught in my throat when my secret longing overpowered me. From afar, I could see how he could steal a kiss and get away with it. I almost couldn't believe this was the same man from the elevator. He belonged to the room now. He owned the room.

I noticed some of the young women from my office standing around in a cliquey circle, ogling him from a distance, and I wandered over to them. It was as if Chris Hemsworth was standing there shirtless, the way they were all gawking. My good friend and colleague, Aisha Vinay, an associate publicist at Berke and Monroe, was among them.

"Who is that?" I asked her, trying to make it seem like a randomly curious question. It was bizarre that I had no clue.

"That, my dear, is our new client, Nicolai Petre," she said, pretending to fan herself with a glossy copy of the product brochure. "He's C.E.O. of Petre Investments, the firm that funded our e-reader. Not to mention, he is also on my short list of hot billionaires I'd like to marry. He's thirty-three, has never walked down the aisle, and appears to be completely single, no girlfriend in sight—on Google anyway."

Holy crap.

"He's our client?" A feeling of dread gripped my stomach, accompanied by a wave of nausea. When a server passed by with a tray of cocktails, I grabbed a glass of wine and took a swig. And then another. "Our client! Why have I never seen or heard of him before?"

"Allison, you are so focused on work that you don't pay enough attention to hot, gorgeous, rich bachelors," she said, flipping her beautiful and shiny mane of hair off her shoulders. "I know of every wealthy, available man in the New York Tristate area. That's what I do on the weekends: research."

I was aware Aisha's conservative Indian parents took arranged marriages very seriously, and they were searching for a mate for her. She was actively conducting her own exploration because she worried her parents would match her with the "wrong boy." As a second generation Hindu, born in the United States, she joked that she wanted a romance novel character, not an IT specialist or accountant from New Jersey.

I took another sip of wine. Actually, it was more like a gulp. "But why hasn't he come to any of the client meetings? Why weren't we told?" I hoped Aisha did not detect the growing panic in my voice. I made out with a client, the worst possible thing to do. *Ever!*

"He has more important goals to focus on, so he sends his staff, Cal and Gina," she answered, a perky smile still on her face. Clearly, Aisha, like everyone, was enjoying the view. "I heard he likes to keep a low profile, but I guess he is here to, you know, represent. Yay."

"Out of the blue? Tonight?" Remembering what I had done earlier in the evening, wildly fluttering butterflies filled my stomach.

"This is a huge launch for the company because they are, as you know, going up against the biggies in the market place," she said. "I guess Sheila has been keeping him close to the breast, I mean, vest. We all learned he is involved only fifteen minutes ago."

"It's so odd I didn't know about him," I said, about to sink into an anxiety attack over my faux pas. "I've never even seen his name on a memo."

That's when my boss, Sheila Riley, interjected herself into our conversation. Now Vice President of Berke and Monroe, she'd once anchored the evening news in the New York Metro market and never let anyone forget it. She'd also dated my father's partner, Dan Berke, and maneuvered herself into the company as an executive when my dad had gotten sick. When he passed away a year ago, his partner had left *her* in charge, and she was constantly trying to edge me out of the picture. Dressed in a skin tight, low cut Donna Karan dress, and wearing so much makeup she looked like a caricature of herself, she pressed her skinny, underfed body between Aisha and me and maneuvered herself so she was standing in front of us, as if to block our view.

"He has specifically requested not to be the public face of this launch," she said, her false eyelashes fluttering in displeasure. "And, furthermore, I deal with him, directly and privately. There is no need for you to concern yourself about him or even talk with him. I will give him anything he needs."

She punctuated her statement with a glare that made her message even clearer: she wanted him all to herself.

"Understood," I said, silently thankful I didn't have to deal with him. That would be the epitome of awkwardness. Jeez.

In general, I tried not to give Sheila any reason to make my life a living hell. I loved my job, took my work seriously, and tried to do what would make my father proud. I'd worked so hard to make this launch a success, and if things worked out well it could be my ticket to a new position. I'd always thought my father was grooming me to take over for him, but Sheila constantly knocked me down a peg. At twenty-eight, success in the firm my father built meant everything to me. I didn't want anything getting in the way. I was not one of those women who competed with other females in the work place. Sheila, however, was. She was a cranky—because she never ate—overbearing, and non-supportive boss who just wanted to focus on her own career and had no qualms squelching others who got in her way. Her efforts to steal my ideas and undermine me over time had been annoying, to say the least!

I was excruciatingly aware that the best way to handle Sheila was to do what she asked because she was not beyond a tantrum or a direct verbal attack when I did not follow her precise orders. That's why a part of me wanted to get out of the general vicinity of Mr. Elevator Kiss, knowing Sheila would fire me if she had even the slightest inkling that the client had intimately explored my mouth on the ride up here.

Aisha glanced over at me and rolled her eyes. She had no idea about the elevator indiscretion, but she knew that Sheila was not fond of me. She'd often said my boss viewed me as a triple threat of beauty, brains, and willingness to work hard—and that she was threatened by my place in my dad's legacy. I didn't see myself that way, but clearly she resented my family connection to the company. I was careful to stay away from any work drama that could put my job in danger, or could thwart my plans to get my father's company back some day. It was like walking on eggshells with her, but I was used to it.

I headed back to my post, excited that big media people—*The New York Times, Huffington Post*, and *CNN*—were in attendance. I wanted things to go smoothly. Just then, a well-known columnist from *Publishing World Journal* approached me for a product demonstration. I opened a sample kit and began to show him all the details and explain how it worked.

"Say a reader loves a scene with a handsome hero in a tux." I enthusiastically clicked through sample images. "She probably has an image in her mind of how he looks. So, she can peruse our database of thousands of photos of movie stars and models donned in evening wear and pick the one who represents the character. The photo can be moved to the reader's homepage as a screensaver, for every book read. We know romance readers love having a visual to go with the written word. This is the first time this particular coordination of image and written word has been done."

I smiled warmly, but professionally, and asked him if he had any questions.

"Yes, why don't women just wait for the movie version of the book?" He laughed out loud and swigged his drink.

"This is more immediate," I said. "It's instant gratification for having the story you love, and the images that help the story come alive."

"Look, I have more questions, but I need a refill." He slugged down the last drop in his glass and looked at me with flirty eyes. "Join me at the bar. Help me understand."

"Gee, wish I could, but I can't leave my post," I said, gently brushing him off. "My suggestion is take a media loaner device home, let your wife use it for a week, and see how she likes it. Or ask some of the romance readers in your office to try it and give you feedback."

The columnist shuffled off to the bar alone, and I busied myself with restacking product boxes and press kits. With that done, I raised my head to look around the room again just to see what was happening.

And there he was, Nicolai Petre, now in a different circle of people, closer to me than before. He seemed indifferent to the chatter of those clamoring around him and was, instead, watching me. More than that, he was drinking me in.

He met my glance with an intense, soulful stare, holding my gaze with his from the distance. It was so intimate. I am not sure how it is possible, but I felt him from across the crowded room. A surge of energy tickled my spine, and then all of me buzzed with electricity. *Turn away now*, said my rational self. *Do not engage!*

I swallowed nervously, sure the sound could be heard echoing around the room. Memories flooded back, and I could almost feel his hand on my face, pulling me in for a kiss. My only recourse was to disengage. I looked down for a moment and took a deep, centering breath. When I glanced back up, he was gone.

Thank God. All I needed was for Sheila to see me having an eye-fuck stare-down with a client she clearly said is off limits. I should have felt relieved that he removed himself, but instead, my heart was beating fast. I was suddenly overheated, tiny prickles of sweat beading on my neck. At twenty-eight, I was too young to be having hot flashes and heart palpitations, so I chalked it up to some sort of odd reaction to this desirable man. Not wanting to sweat through my new silky white blouse, I had to get some air.

I asked my assistant to hold the fort and headed outside to the huge terrace that surrounded the upscale venue atop a Manhattan skyscraper. We'd selected this place for the stunning view. Tonight the waxing moon hung in the sky, casting a glow on the city. Surprisingly, the majority of guests were inside, drinking, so I had most of the area to myself except for a few people gathered at a table off to the side. I made it to the railing to collect myself.

A slight wind blew across the patio inspiring me to let my hair out of the barrette. I let it fall to my shoulders. Placing the clip in my pocket, I planned to put it back up later.

From seventy-seven stories above, New York City was a beautiful sight to behold. Watching the traffic move like illuminated toy cars below and catching sight of all the twinkling lights around me, my pulse slowly restored to normal. A panoramic view of New York always calmed me. I inhaled the beauty of the moment and steadied myself.

That's when I felt a presence. And heard a voice coming from behind me. "It is a beautiful evening," he said, the familiar accent carried on a soft breeze to my ears. "Even more beautiful with you here."

Turning around, pulse racing again, the energy I'd felt from across the room was now closer and stronger.

He moved toward me slowly and purposefully. He wasn't shy about looking directly into my eyes as he made his way over. Then, he was right in front me, so close I could smell sweet cherry and a hint of vodka on his lips. My heart rate accelerated as it became clear I would have to talk to him. Finally, I sucked in enough air to send some oxygen to my rational brain.

Snapping into professional mode, I extended my hand to shake his. Warmth emanated from his palm as he took my hand.

"Nicolai Petre," he said, that sexy, subtle accent reaching my ears like a pleasant melody. "Perhaps I was rude not introducing myself earlier."

"Allison Monroe," I said, trying to be cool, calm, and collected. I ignored his reference to "earlier."

He brought my hand up to his lips to kiss. Something close to a shiver ran up my arm as his warm mouth brushed against my flesh. He slowly disengaged his lips, and let go of my hand but stood close.

"I wanted to see how you are doing." His gorgeous blue eyes appeared to change color beneath the moonlight, blue from one angle and greenish from another. Whatever the hue, they were like refreshing pools of water and I wanted to fall into them. "I hope you did not mind the impertinence of my actions. I was concerned and wanted to help you calm down."

"Wait … you kissed me to calm me down?" Suddenly I wanted to smack him, the way I should have in the elevator, yet part of me wanted to press my lips against his again. It was devastating to hear it was a mercy kiss.

"You needed a distraction," he said, shrugging his shoulders. "A kiss releases dopamine, oxytocin, and serotonin, and it makes you focus on your lips instead of your fear. It stopped your hyperventilating, didn't it?"

"Yes." I hated to admit it. "But, so would breathing into a paper bag."

"If I had a paper bag, I gladly would have given it to you," he said. "I used my lips instead. Was it not a pleasant kiss?"

It was a remarkable kiss—although forward and inappropriate—and was the kind of kiss that woke up my whole body. But now that I knew he was my client, I wasn't about to tell him that.

"We need to forget *that* ever happened."

"Actually, I was thinking the opposite—that you are a woman I'm meant to spend more time with."

"Well, apparently, you're correct. I *very recently* discovered you're my client." I was trying to keep it professional. But those eyes—they were melting my resolve.

I was worried about being out here alone with him. What if it happened again? What if I didn't try to stop him again? My body quivered slightly from nervous energy. This didn't go unnoticed.

"Are you cold, Ms. Monroe?" he asked. "May I offer you my jacket?"

"I'm fine, actually." But tremors ran through me. My nervous system was going haywire due to his proximity. It was as if my body were remembering his touch.

"You seem to be trembling." He took off the jacket and draped it over my shoulders. It was huge on my frame, but I felt slightly protected by pulling it tighter around me. His chivalrous act meant I had a full view of his gorgeous form and all that had been hidden beneath his jacket. In his fitted shirt, his chest looked wide and his abs hard. His pants fit snugly and low on his hips. So many women at the party were looking at him with longing and desire. I did not want him to think he had the same effect on me—but he did.

"Take a walk with me," he said, placing his hand, again, on the small of my back and guiding me forward. I liked the way his hand felt—really liked it—but I was worried he would make a pass at me and I wouldn't be able to resist. A voice in my head screamed, *He's a client! This is so dangerous! Your father would not approve!* My dad used to say, "We only get into bed with clients and media to fill their business needs, not their biblical needs."

"I'm working tonight, Mr. Petre," I said, making a solid attempt not to wander off with him to a dark corner.

"I know," he countered. "But I would consider the time you spend with the client to be work, no? Although I hope my company is more pleasurable than work."

The sexy, seductive sound of his voice melted my plan to pretend we hadn't shared a moment in the elevator. I allowed him to move me along. He walked us to a completely deserted area of the terrace, behind a huge outdoor plant.

He stood quietly for a while and took me in. Was he waiting for me to say something first? I bounced nervously from heel to heel and looked away—out on the city—to relive the intensity of the moment. With my eyes averted, I blurted out what was on my mind. "I had no idea you were our client, Mr. Petre. I am so sorry. I never would have…" I lowered my head, not wanting to face him.

"Look at me, Ms. Monroe," he finally said. "Please don't turn away."

His words were so completely unnerving. Yet I felt them in my body, running through me and landing between my legs like a soft, sensual vibration. I looked up and let my gaze connect with his. Something seemed to pull us closer.

He stepped forward and took my right hand in his. The contact hummed with a subtle sensation that left a charge on my flesh. With him so close, the delicious, fresh scent of his skin traveled through my senses where it registered as enticingly familiar. Maybe I was seduced by pheromones. For a moment, I allowed myself to believe a sexy stare down with this gorgeous man, who happened to be a client, was the most normal thing happening on this terrace tonight.

"You are a beautiful woman," he said, punctuating his statement with another intense, intimate look into my eyes. "I know you have beauty and strength inside, too."

"That's very kind." What else could I say? "But how could you know who I am inside? We don't know each other." I pulled his coat around me tighter.

"Sometimes you can tell something about a person in a glance," he said. "And sometimes you feel it in a kiss."

I brushed two fingers across my lips, remembering.

"You would have to have a lot of confidence in your own instincts to get so much information at first glance," I challenged. "Or even from a kiss."

"I do have complete confidence in my instincts," he said, asserting his opinion into the air around us. "But even if I were a complete buffoon, with no intuition or emotional intelligence, I doubt I would have missed the electricity between us in the elevator when we first set eyes on each other, or how my kiss calmed you, or the way that energy rose up and traveled across the room when our gazes touched again. And how could I possibly ignore the force that continues to pervade the space between us. You feel it too, don't you, Ms. Monroe?"

"No." Yes, I did, all over my body, but his direct approach was disarming. "You don't mince words, do you?"

"Where I come from, people speak openly about emotions and they do not feel compelled to deny physical attraction," he answered, smiling. "There is a strong force between us, no? I kissed you in the elevator to take your mind off of your fear, and, maybe, because I found you irresistible. I followed you out here because I had to meet you again. I am hoping you're glad I did."

As much as I was relieved to know I was not completely imagining that there was this "force between us," the conversation was trouble on so many levels. Force or no, I had a job to do, and I could get fired for kissing and swapping sexy glances with a client, especially one my boss specifically told me to stay away from. I had to politely extricate myself.

"I'm so flattered, Mr. Petre." I did feel it but stopped myself from admitting it. "But you're a client and it's not meant to be. It's complicated. I guarantee my boss would not appreciate me being out on a terrace alone with you."

"I will manage your boss."

"I don't need you to manage my boss for me, nor do I need a rescue. What I need is to get back to work."

"You didn't seem this offended in the elevator," he said. "Now you are dismissing me the way you dismissed that reporter who looked like he wanted to have you for dessert."

Damn, he saw that.

"This is different, but it is the same principle." The strength of my conviction on this point helped me stay strong even though he made my knees weak. "I don't flirt with the press because I want to represent my clients in the most professional manner. And I don't get into romantic encounters with clients for the same reason. It is a bad practice, and I won't endanger our business relationship. I had no idea who you were in that elevator. Regardless, you were a stranger. I never should have kissed you. I have never ever done anything like that in my life. It was wrong."

He listened patiently, but the way he cocked his eyebrows told me he did not agree with my assessment that it was wrong.

"Are you finished, Ms. Monroe?"

I nodded.

"Do you believe in fate? That some things are meant to be?"

"I am a born and bred New Yorker." I laughed. "So, no, I'm not trusting enough to believe in fate."

A thoughtful expression crossed his handsome face. He took a deep breath before speaking. "Although my mother was American, my father was Romanian, and I was raised with a strong connection to an ancient folk culture that has a deep respect for Providence," he said. "I was taught some things are pre-ordained."

"That's a lovely philosophy for life," I answered politely. "But I am a big fan of free will and I don't believe that our paths in life are mapped out by the hand of fate."

His eyes lit up. "But you do believe there is a hand of fate? A possibility?"

"I guess," I said, biting my lip and wondering why he was waxing philosophical. "But fate is not as reliable as taking a proactive approach to life, is it?"

"What if they are not mutually exclusive? What if you could take a proactive approach to *establishing* something that is meant to be?"

"I guess anything is possible," I said, shaking my head. "It depends on what one considers or defines as meant to be. And how important it is to the individual."

"What if you *considered that* we met in that elevator for a reason?" He was unyielding about making his point. "And what if everything that occurred was part of a bigger plan?"

"What if you came up with a normal pick up line?" I was agitated now. "You're turning a random, accidental kiss, into some big cosmic occurrence. You could more easily sell me on the idea of having spontaneous sex with you on this terrace. "*Oh, fuck.* I didn't mean for that to come out of my mouth.

He laughed. Then he moved in closer and took my hand.

"Well, that's good information to have, Ms. Monroe," he said with an amused grin. "And, as a man who appreciates your charms, I'm not opposed to the idea. But I am hoping you will want *more* than my body."

I swallowed hard on his last words and had to reclaim my personal space. Slowly, I extricated my hand from his to lean on the railing, a safe distance away. He followed my lead, leaning his long, muscular body alongside mine. We both looked out at New York's twinkling lights and grabbed a moment of silence. High above the city, removed from stress and strain, there was a great peace. His arms were twelve inches away from mine, and he seemed to be respecting the space between us. But my body was literally swaying in the breeze, sometimes moving nearer to his, as if the wind were plotting to bring us closer.

Just when I was starting to settle in to the moment, he pushed off from the railing, stood to his full six two height and turned toward me. The look on his face said he was mulling something over. I assumed he would try to kiss me—and that I would then have to decide if I would risk my job for another kiss. My breathing slowed in anticipation of his next move.

"We may not always understand the concept of fate," he said, sounding like a voice-over on the History Channel or someone delivering a Ted Talk. "Discovering the truth can sometimes, at first, seem impossible or improbable. But it can change us quickly—it will change us quickly—and move us to where we need to go."

"I am not exactly sure what you mean," I said. Actually, I had no idea what he was talking about, but his voice was lulling me into some sort of trance.

His next words snapped me out of it.

"I believe we have a destiny together, Ms. Monroe."

"Excuse me?"

"I want to marry you."

CHAPTER THREE

Holy crap! I gripped the rail for extra support and tried to stay calm, but my heart sank because now I had to confront the idea that this very hot man was, quite possibly, delusional. Why couldn't he just kiss me or back me into the railing and tell me he wants to fuck me? *Destiny? Marriage?*

"Is this a joke?" I felt myself unraveling as I flung the question at him.

"I would never joke about a marriage proposal." He was completely self-possessed.

"How could you possibly say something like that to me and not be joking?" I was shaking my head. "I've known you for, what, two hours? Do you need a green card or something?"

"No. I assure you, if I did, this wouldn't be the way I'd obtain one."

"Is this an old European custom? Because in this country, a marriage proposal is a very weird thing to speak of to someone you've just met."

"You don't have to agree to anything tonight."

I stared at him in disbelief. "I most certainly am not going to agree tonight, or any night. On top of this being utterly ridiculous, you're a client and even having this conversation with you is putting me at risk on so many levels."

"Anytime the heart is involved, there is risk. But your job, that's not the risk you will face."

"Look, I'm here to launch your product." It felt like my head would explode from anger. "I am sorry if I misled you. I have no interest in anything other than doing a good job. I've put my everything into this product. Your product! I haven't had a weekend to myself in three months planning this event tonight and cajoling media to be here. I'm not here to make out with the investor or entertain marriage proposals."

I folded my arms across my chest, as if it could shield me from any feelings of attraction for—or from—him. Somehow, they did not go away.

"Haven't you ever heard of love at first sight?" He looked at me like *I* was the slightly crazy one.

"In movies and wedding toasts." A gust of wind swept across the patio and lifted my hair, as if on cue. I placed a hand across the top of my head trying to stop my locks from looking like something out of a high fashion photo shoot.

"Maybe it happens for real." He got that serious look on his face again, determined to debate me.

"Maybe, but if you are talking about this evening, I think you are confusing a sexual attraction for love." *Why did I even mention the word sexual?*

"Okay, fair enough," he said, reaching over to place a loose strand of hair behind my ear. "But isn't sexual attraction a symbol of love? Or a doorway to love?"

"I think sex hormones sometimes blind us from seeing the truth." Now I felt like I was the one reading to him from *Cosmo Magazine*. In fact, I wished I had some hard data to back my point of view because he was so insistent about his.

"Or," he persisted, "they might also help us see things we would not have noticed before. Arousal might just open your heart, or help you see someone in a different way."

"Honestly, it would have been hard *not* to notice you, under any circumstances." I sighed. He had to know he was gorgeous and that women could not take their eyes off him. "But this," I pointed to him and back to myself, "is off limits." Looking at him made every part of me feel alive. Standing close made me want to be closer.

That's why I had to get away.

"Things can happen very quickly when they're meant to be," he said, speaking gently now. "And when we allow them to unfold."

"Okay, Mr. Petre, I can't do this." I put my palm up in a talk-to-the-hand gesture. "I can't have *this* discussion with you, my client. If I can assist you with your business needs in any way, please let me know. I have to get back to work."

I pulled his jacket off my shoulders and shoved it back in his hands and turned to leave. He looked oddly amused more than offended.

"Ms. Monroe," he called after me. I did not want to turn, but I did. "I don't believe this discussion is quite finished."

"Oh, yes, it is," I answered, trying to cut him off from saying anything else. I went back to the party, but my head was spinning and my chest felt tight.

"Fate does not always intervene on a convenient schedule." He called after me as I exited. "And it often arrives with an expiration date."

I hated that he got the last word.

CHAPTER FOUR

I returned to the press table, relieved to be out of his range. Something about his immediate proximity caused me to feel things I should not be feeling.

What the hell was he talking about? Fate? Expiration dates? He must have been playing me. He was rich, gorgeous, and powerful, so he could play with women all he wanted. Maybe he took pleasure in rattling people with weird declarations of meant-to-be. I'd felt something between us, but I had to chalk it up to lust. What else could it have possibly been?

Busying myself with the work at hand, my equilibrium returned by having something to focus on other than the crazy episode on the terrace. I was back in my element, talking to media people again, when out of the corner of my eye I caught Sheila having a conversation with Nicolai. She twirled her hair and pressed herself toward his body with a big, fake smile. *Dear Lord.* Next thing I knew, he said something that made her look over at me, and she started walking over. Nicolai was with her, with one of my press kits in his hand. He eyed me as they approached. *What the fuck?* Maybe he told her what happened, and now she was bringing him over to accuse me of the crime of disobeying her directives. *Jeez.* Before I could even think of disappearing, they were standing in front of me.

"Allison Monroe," she said, not even bothering to hide the tone of disdain and condescendence in her voice. "This is Mr. Nicolai Petre. His company is responsible for the product we are launching. He wanted to meet the person who is handling the press tonight. And, by the way, in his culture, men do not greet women with handshakes, so no need to shake his hand."

I fought the urge to roll my eyes and stood there, arms at my side. He stepped forward, reached for my hand, and brought it to his mouth to kiss as he did the first time in the elevator and again on the terrace. This time, I was sorely aware of the energy sizzling between his hand and mine. And he was not letting go any time soon. Unfortunately, the hand kiss did not escape Sheila, and I could see the green-eyed monster bulge in her pale blue eyes. She was livid.

"Mr. Petre," I said, nodding a greeting, pretending to not know him. "It's a pleasure to meet you."

"No, the pleasure is all mine," he said. "I wonder, Ms. Monroe, if I could borrow you for a moment. I have a few questions about the press kit and also the media here tonight."

"Um, well." I looked at Sheila, nervous she would turn into one of those old cartoon characters with steam coming out of their ears when angry, because she looked pissed. "Of course." What could I do? He'd cornered me, with the help of my boss, who was going to throw a shit fit if she realized what he was really up to.

"Sheila, I'm going to steal Ms. Monroe for a moment or two," he said. "You won't mind filling in for her, will you?"

"Absolutely not, Nicolai," she said in a clearly flirtatious voice, sneering at me. She was the Vice President. I was the lowly Account Executive. Even though my father had started the firm, she'd made sure I was forced to toil on the lower end of the totem pole. Clearly, doing my job was a step down for her.

With that, his hand went to my lower back again and he pressed us forward. I hated that I loved the feel of his hand on me. He nodded toward an office door in the near distance, indicating this was our destination. As soon as we got out of Sheila's hearing range, I blasted him. "What do you think you are doing?"

"Getting you out of work for a while." He quickened his pace and rushed us out of her view. "So we can talk."

"I told you I am done with *that* conversation. Are you a freaking caveman?"

"Yes. And I don't give up on matters of the heart."

"Matters of the heart? Do you think it's romantic to tell someone you barely know that you have a destiny with them? It sounds like a line from a bad movie."

He moved us into the office and closed the door, an uncompromising look on his face. As soon as we were alone, he turned his body to me and maneuvered us both so I was backed up against the office door. Next, he was over me, holding himself there by the hand he'd placed above my head. My back sank against the smooth steel. He lowered his head, his eyes hovering over mine, his lips so close. That feeling, the one where some invisible magnetic energy seemed to pull us together, rose between us. It was undeniable, whatever it was, and it was strong. It was holding me against the door as much as he was.

"Hear me out," he said. His mouth was mere inches from mine and his breath was hot and sweet on my face. He pressed his body closer to mine. "Will you listen?"

His lips were close enough to taunt me with the possibility of a kiss. I inhaled the scent of his skin with every breath, detecting the very subtle aftershave. Something about the way he smelled drove me wild. Even his underarm, so close to my nose, was sweet and clean. I could have easily buried my nose into his flesh and allowed myself to be overcome by the primal masculine scents that were dripping off of him and weakening my resolve to not desire him. He kept us there, waiting for my response.

Finally, I nodded in agreement. With his gaze still on me, he lifted his large body from mine and gave me room to move.

"Let's go back into the fresh air." I was glad to put a little distance between whatever just happened and his seductive essence. He walked us over to a glass door that led to another side of the terrace we had been on before. It had an alternative breathtaking view of New York. From this vantage point, the moon hung even brighter over the city.

"Okay, I'm listening." I folded my arms over my chest, happy to find a big pillar to lean on for support.

"I know this may sound a bit unusual, but I am obligated to tell you the truth. I hope you can hear this in your heart, and not just in your head." He took a deep breath.

I nodded for him to continue.

"It's very simple, really. The time has come for me to find my true partner in life and I believe you are the one."

"Just like that?" I said, snapping my fingers, exasperated. "Out of the blue?" I shot him an incredulous look.

"I realize this may be difficult to believe, but it's not out of the blue." His posture was erect and confident.

"It is for me. How could you know this, yet I have no clue what you are talking about?" I shifted my weight from foot to foot trying hard to keep my body from moving toward his.

"I just do." He spoke with conviction, as if it were a fact, but his voice was softer. "I believe you are my *Ves'tacha*."

"Ve-what?"

"*Ves'tacha*. It means beloved, meant-to-be."

"What makes you think I even want my destiny to be with you?" The moon and the sky and the twinkling buildings were romantic, but this was more like a foreign film with hard-to-read subtitles. He was clearly speaking in English, yet the nature of our discussion was foreign to me.

"You don't yet, quite obviously. I have to make you believe in me, in us. I have to win you." He held his head high as if he were proud to be taking on this challenge. "But I do believe you will see me in a different light—perhaps through different eyes—in a short period of time. This is my hope, anyway."

"What if I say, no, not interested?" My mind said, "walk away," but my feet did not want to leave.

"Forgive my impertinence, but I sense you are extremely interested and intrigued, Ms. Monroe." His confidence unnerved me, but he was spot on. "Your kiss, the emotions running through you, the way your body sways toward mine, they don't lie. You're scared because it seems like this is all happening quickly, too fast for your comfort."

"I didn't even know who you were before tonight."

"I knew you. Well … knew of you."

"That's creepy. On so many levels. Did you Google me? Wait, did you investigative me?" This should have been my cue to run as if the terrace were on fire, but I actually was interested in hearing his explanation.

"No, something much simpler and perhaps even less acceptable to you," he said, looking off into the city for a moment, then bringing his blue-green gaze back to me. "My grandmother is a seer and she had a dream about the woman I would marry. You are the one she described to me. She said I would know you when I saw you. And I did, when I first saw you in the elevator. I dared to kiss you because you seemed so familiar. I had to taste your lips on mine to know for sure."

"Wait, did you rig the elevator to stall so you had an excuse to kiss me?" Even I could hear how ridiculous that sounded.

"Of course not," he said. "But once the wheels of destiny start churning, unexpected things happen. Your panic was a chance for me to soothe you. It was my natural response to the circumstances. Can you forgive me for kissing you without your permission?"

"I'm not sure." I pulled my arms tighter around myself. "Maybe I can consider it, if you tell me why you are in such a rush to get married to someone you just met tonight."

He took a deep breath and looked at his wristwatch.

"My grandmother may be dying." His voice lowered. "I don't have time to spare."

"Oh, my God, I am sorry to hear about your grandmother." I could somehow sense that he was telling the truth. "Is all this so she can be here to see your wedding day?" That made more logical sense to me than anything else he was talking about.

"Something like that. She cannot leave this earthly plane in peace until she knows I have found my true partner," he said, speaking softly.

"There are also certain traditions and birthrights that must be passed along to me, formally, upon her passing."

I searched his eyes. "There are dozens of women in that room ready to chew off your underwear, including my boss. Why me?"

"Because you are *the one* ... I am drawn to you by magnetism far more powerful than anything I've ever known or that I can even explain." He reached out to touch his palm to my cheek. "And because you are sincere and..." He stared out at the moon and paused before speaking again. "I followed my instincts to find you, and trust I was led to you, Allison Monroe, for a reason."

A shock of energy moved from my face down to my toes. His touch was electric. My body swayed and leaned into his hand. Yet discomfort rumbled through me at the same time. Either this was *real* but way out of my comfort zone, or my body was screaming at me to leave while I could. Maybe it was both. I wasn't sure so I backed away, out from under his touch, and tried to gather my wits.

"I'm not going to be your insta-wife," I said definitively. "Who does that, anyway?"

"Fine." He paused to give my words some thought. "Then be my fake fiancé or my pretend soul mate."

"You're not serious—wait, are you serious?" Sweat was beading on my neck. I reached up and flipped my hair off my shoulder.

"Yes, very. Let's be practical. You're more comfortable with business than talk of destiny, and I'm willing to be proactive about fate. We'll make a deal. It can work for us both."

"Like, what kind of deal?"

Another gust of wind flew by us. It was so strong that, for a moment, I felt I would lift off the patio. He stepped closer and held my shoulders to anchor me.

"You hang out with me for a few days, get to know me, and help me attempt to fulfill my grandmother's wishes," he said, leaning in. "At the end of a few days, let her see us together so she can be at peace. Along the way, you give me a chance to prove my sincerity. Give me six days.

If you don't care for me by then, you walk away. If you feel something for me, you—"

"Six days? Why?"

"As I mentioned earlier, some things have an expiration date." He let go of me and looked over at the Empire State Building where the waxing crescent moon was hovering. "Our expiration date is the full moon on Sunday."

"Are you going to turn into a werewolf?" I tried to bring a little levity to the situation. But heaviness filled the air when it took him a while to answer.

"My grandmother's intuitive vision specified a window of six days, starting the day we met. It is said that the doors to heaven will open on this full moon, but the door to opportunity closes if I do not step in with you by my side," he said. "I'm not saying she is dying tomorrow, but doctors told me yesterday she may not have long."

"Oh no." My hand instinctively went to his arm to soothe him.

"My hope is that even if you *pretend* there is a possibility that you are my *Ves'tacha*, that you will come to like me in real life. This is important because we must consummate our union by the full moon." He said it as if he were delivering a normal piece of information. "This can only happen if you truly care for me, love me even. True love is the only container strong enough to hold the super powers that are destined to be directed to us both."

"Okay, here's where my mouth drops open because this sounds bat shit crazy." I didn't even try to use polite language.

He appeared to be taken aback for a moment but then an amused smile crossed his face. "So just pretend it is a possibility, for my grandmother's sake. Along the way, give me a real chance."

"Where, exactly, do you hail from that people believe these things?"

"Transylvania." Again, he delivered the information as if it were a normal thing to say.

I tried not to shake my head in disbelief. Or roll my eyes. I was sure he would crack a smile and tell me he was kidding. He didn't.

"Where Dracula lives? That Transylvania? I didn't know it was a real place."

"It's a beautiful place in central Romania," he said. "Dracula did come from there, but not Bram Stoker's version. The people there are known for intuition and a connection to the natural world. It's the world I come from. It's why I trust what I know. I have enough belief to get us both through this."

My heart started racing again. Every time he said something strange, that's how my body reacted. But at the same time, I was drawn to him like we were two neodymium magnets. I worried the powerful force could crush me as it sucked me in.

I tried pressing my back against the pillar and holding on to the rail but on my high heels, I lost my balance. I was about to crumble to my knees when Nicolai grabbed hold and steadied me in his arms. And suddenly, I wanted to be in his arms. There I was, one moment questioning him for pushing this destiny idea on me and the next, in his arms. Silently, he held me, until my vitals stabilized. My face was flush against his shirt. He held my head against his chest.

And when he began to gently caress my head, hair and back while he held me, I was overcome with desire for him. I didn't want it to feel so right, but it did.

Next thing I knew, one large finger lifted my chin up toward his lips and he kissed me. It was a kiss I felt all over my body. Desire moved me to hold his face and pull him closer, devouring his lips, his mouth, and his tongue. I wanted him—more of him, all of him. As if a spell had been cast, I suddenly believed this crazy idea was real. A hunger rose from deep within me, and I did not hold back.

This deep, long, soulful kiss high above the city was the most romantic moment I had ever experienced. He placed his hand affectionately against my cheek, and I rubbed against it like a cat. I looked up at him. There was warmth in his eyes.

"You see," he said, sounding a little breathless. "How could that be anything but the kiss of the beloved?"

As much as I surrendered to the kiss and the urges it stirred within, second thoughts knocked on my brain. This was happening in the middle of a work event. I was neglecting my duties by kissing the client. My boss was going to kill me for this. Listing the multitude of professional consequences in my mind brought me back to the reality: this was all happening too fast.

"That was a good kiss—a really, really good kiss—I'll admit." My mouth tingled where his lips had been. "But still, I don't really know you."

"If I am right, if we are connected by a string of fate, then you already know me in your soul," he said, a smile lighting up his face and making his eyes sparkle in the moonlight. "And my job is now to help you remember."

"Do you realize how weird that sounds?" Weirder yet was that a part of me believed he was sincere. "And, honestly, this is a more than a little crazy."

"You know what they say, my love, fake it until you make it. We have no time to waste."

CHAPTER FIVE

Clearly, Nicolai was convinced of our destiny, but it seemed he was willing to let me sign on for a trial run. The more I stood there with him, the more it seemed to make sense to at least explore the possibilities. All the kissing must have altered my brain chemicals to make me more open-minded.

"Okay, why don't we agree to disagree on the destiny thing but spend some time getting to know each other?" I suggested, getting my bearings again and standing up straighter.

"There isn't a lot of time for that." He ran a finger down my cheek.

"You can't possibly think I'm going to just drop everything and jump into something with you, like, this minute."

"Yes, I do," he said, reaching for an errant hair and twisting it in his fingers. "I need you to give me six consecutive dates."

"I would be crazy myself if I didn't at least wonder if you had some undiagnosed mental illness," I asserted. "Or maybe you're a con artist."

"New York women are so suspicious," he said with a shake of his head. "Do you honestly think I could make this up? Believe me, I realize how unusual this is. But fated romance often is. Haven't you heard all the stories of people meeting their 'soul mates' under highly unusual or synchronistic circumstances?"

Who is crazier, me or him? "I thought love was meant to happen more naturally—a slow, delicious falling in love with a lot of dancing, kissing, and laughing," I said. "Doesn't love need to warm up and simmer before it boils?"

"I can give you that and more." His fingers caressed my face as his thumb stroked my ear. "All of it."

Our moment was interrupted by a new group of guests straggling out to the patio to enjoy the evening air. The sound of ice cubes clinking against glasses and laughter nearby put me on high alert. Glancing at my watch, I knew Sheila would be furious if I didn't return to my post.

"I have to get back to work." I grabbed a bar napkin from a nearby table and tried to remove the smeared lipstick from my face. I handed one to him as well. He just held it.

"Yes, of course, return to your duties. I will not interfere. But may I see you again?"

"We'll set up a date." I started to make my way back into the venue.

"I will take you home tonight." He was close behind me.

"You are not taking me home," I said, over my shoulder. "Don't you think that is a little fast?"

"I *am* taking you home, seeing you to your door, and protecting what's mine."

"Wait a minute." I halted and faced him, hand on hip. "I'm not *actually* yours. This has not been completely agreed upon, proven, or established."

"Nor has it been disproven." He smiled, playfully. "Or unequivocally disagreed to."

"Even if there is this meant-to-be thing between us, I am still my own person." My moxie was coming back. "I don't belong to you. Haven't you gotten the memo in Transylvania? The whole concept is very old-fashioned."

"Fine," he said roguishly, a mischievous look in his eye. He sounded like he was making a fun business deal. "Let's agree to disagree about the term 'mine,' but agree to belong to each other for the next six days. You retain the right to ditch me at any point, and the right to refuse the option to consummate on the full moon. If you decline that option, it means you don't care for me, so the 'mine' part will be irrelevant, anyway. Let's see if you can go along with it for six days. Agreed?"

"I'll get back to you on that." I could play at business too. And I wanted to give some thought to the whole idea, and what I wanted out of this "deal." Should I charge him for my time, the way we do at the firm? Should I get him to buy my father's half of the business back for me? Maybe a cool mil in a Swiss bank account? No, I had no interest in being a whore. The only way I could spend another minute with him was because I liked him. So I had to decide how much I liked him and how much I just wanted to jump his bones. I was feeling a little of both.

"Okay, how about you consider one day at a time?" he urged. At least he was negotiating rather than trying to drag me back to his cave like a Neanderthal. "For now, pretend, for this night, you are mine. And I am yours. Let's see where it goes."

I was impressed with his temporary solution. His words made me tingle all over, in a good way. Since most of my relationships never made it past a few days, anyway, his revised proposal seemed reasonable. I figured he would lose interest the minute I showed real interest, anyway.

"Okay, one night," I said, "and *no* sex." I couldn't believe I brought up the *S* word again and how loudly I emphasized the word no. "You have to stop interfering with my job and let me get back to work."

"Done." He moved closer to me. "Except one more thing."

With that, he bent down and moved one large hand to the side of my head, into my hair, to gently hold me. His lips found mine and he kissed his way down my cheek and chin, finally finding my neck. He caressed my neck, sweetly and sensually licked the skin, sending an erotic charge through me. I melted into his arms. Before I even realized what he was doing, he found a sensitive spot on my neck and began sucking. Hard. Pleasure released into my body and hurried through my system, making me desire him even more. He held his mouth in place for a long time and then pulled away with a look of satisfaction, turning my cheek so he could look at my neck.

"There," he teased. "Mine. For tonight, anyway."

"Did you give me a hickey?" I snapped, reaching to where his mouth had been. "Vampire! That is going to last a lot longer than one night."

He gave me a sly look. "Ms. Monroe, you don't really believe in vampires, do you?"

"Not any more than I believe in destiny." Maybe I wasn't really sure what I believed at the moment with hickey-induced endorphins flooding my brain.

"I've left my love bite so you'd remember the feelings stirred tonight, even if you aren't ready to accept that this is more than a sexual connection we share." He appeared to be quite pleased with himself.

He was right. I had a hard time believing this was anything more than a sexual attraction, and I still thought he was off the rails with all his talk about fate. But I had to admit, it took a person who was self-assured enough to slice through my resistance to letting men get close to me and clever enough to keep my interest aroused.

I was beginning to suspect Nicolai Petre somehow understood this.

CHAPTER SIX

I'm not quite sure how I got to the end of the evening. The music helped. I'd hired a talented piano player and cabaret singer, and they filled the place with classic romantic tunes. It calmed me and opened my heart, the way music does.

Fortunately, I'd already interacted with all the major media guests because after our second encounter on the terrace, Nicolai occupied my mind. My senses vibrated with a heightened awareness of his presence as he circulated through the room, shaking hands and talking to business associates. I noticed the way women looked at him with hunger and desire. *Why was I the one he pursued?*

Several times I felt his eyes on me. His look had changed from intense eye fucking to a sensual, knowing glance. We had been intimate—in our discussion and kissing—and I found myself waiting for the moments when it would come again. His talk about his grandmother's vision was weirdly compelling. Was he really trying to secure my eternal love? Or was he looking for a girl like the one in his grandmother's dream to bring to her sick bed?

I looked up the word *Ves'tacha* on my phone. I tried to spell it five different ways before Google finally delivered the description. It did mean "beloved," apparently in Romani "Gypsy" language. *Gypsy language?* My head filled with images of a caravan of fortune-tellers in my future. *Where did that cultural connection come from?* That's when Sheila waltzed over to the press table. *Fuck.* I'd caught a view of my newly acquired hickey when

I passed a mirror moments earlier. Nicolai had marked me well, and it was in a place where everyone else could see it, too. I quickly moved my hand up to my neck and pulled my hair in front of it.

"What did Nicolai want?" she demanded, hand on her hip while stomping her foot impatiently. "You were with him for a long time."

"He had some questions about how I am pitching the product to media and who had signed up for loaners." I was a bad liar and hoped it didn't show.

"In the future, I will be giving him the details on the account. You can write out a daily status report and I will send it to him."

"Fine."

"I don't appreciate you posturing yourself with him tonight. I was clear about you having nothing to do with him."

"Sheila, you waltzed him over to me. What was I supposed to do?"

"Lie. Just say, 'I'm sorry, Mr. Petre, but I can't leave. Sheila will share the details with you tomorrow.' You stuck me out here doing your job."

She was being completely ridiculous. However, she'd snapped me back into the reality about the precariousness of my job—at the hands of my crazy bitch boss—and I began to remember how crazy Nicolai's ideas were too. I sent an urgent alert to my brain: get some space and get a hold of your sanity.

"My apologies," I said to keep the peace. She huffed away.

Thankfully, she left soon after. And with a little distance from Nicolai, too, I decided not to let him take me home. Oh, there was a part of me that *wanted him to*, but I feared the consequences. What if he was as crazy as Sheila, or what if I started believing him again? What if my boss caught wind I was fooling around with a client? I could not think of one scenario in which this would turn out well for me.

But when the party wrapped up, he headed over with a big beautiful smile aimed right at me. I had to fight my feelings, the ones that told me I liked having him near. Everyone from my office had left, but I still felt the need to keep my distance. Before I had a chance to open my mouth, he stepped in front of me.

"Have a dance with me, Ms. Monroe." He extended his hand and walked me onto the dance floor as the pianist started playing "The Nearness of You." I looked around and realized we were the only ones left. This song was for us only. He must have arranged this final performance.

Even though my heels gave me five inches, he was much taller. He tucked my head under his chin and his breath warmed the top of my hair. When he wrapped his arms around my petite frame and pulled me near, I forgot about reality. I could focus only on the way his body melded into mine. I had never listened to the words of this song before, and suddenly the singer's voice blended into the beautiful instrumentals. The sound was magical. And the magnetic pull was still there as I danced in his arms. It just seemed softer and sweeter. For the first time all night it was not hidden as we danced out in the open. When the song came to an end, he stayed in the middle of the dance floor, holding me close.

When we finally pulled away, he looked like he was the one in a trance. "Thank you for the dance, Ms. Monroe." His voice was softer. "Now, let me get you home."

"Nicolai, that was beautiful, so beautiful, really, but all this attention is conspiring to make me forget that this is not a good idea."

"Hmmm, it felt like a good idea to me." He touched my cheek warmly.

"No, honestly, it's not. Sheila is really on my case. I could lose my job."

"You won't, and if you do, you won't care. You have to trust this. Or at least consider everything will unfold as it is meant to be."

He didn't understand that it was my father's company, and Sheila took it out from under me. My job was all I had left of my dad.

"It's those kinds of statements that have brought down mightier women than me. I think I need to be alone." I stepped away. "This has all been a little overwhelming."

"I think you need to be with me." The voice of insistence had returned and he sounded too controlling for my taste.

"I want to go home, take a warm bath or a cold shower." And get on Google and research all the weird things he talked to me about. "I'm going to grab a cab."

"I have a car waiting outside," he said, stepping a few paces closer to me. "And I would like you to let me drop you off. I don't think it is good for you to be separated from me, either."

Jeez speak for yourself, mister. How the hell does he know what's good for me or not?

"We've only known each other for four hours. I think you may be overstating or exaggerating what is going on between us."

"Really?" He swept me into his arms like a rag doll and kissed me. His mouth came down and his tongue slid in and pressed deep—so deep—it took my breath away. It was more than a kiss. It was a possession. And in that moment, I wanted to be possessed, despite my attempts to steer off this road. He pulled away as I was sinking into his kiss, completely lost to him. I was still out of breath when he spoke again.

"Am I, Ms. Monroe?" he said, setting me back down on Earth, still gripping my shoulders. "Am I overstating what exists between us? Or are you trying to deny what you feel?"

"This is very sudden and..."

"And scary, and different, and I'm your client," he said, curling a strand of my hair in his finger. "I understand."

He pulled me to him again, and this time kissed me gently on the lips. I melted into him. I inhaled him. He was getting to me, and I was stirred up all over. I felt it in every part of my body, including the wetness between my legs.

"You said you wanted kissing and dancing." He grinned. "I would also like to provide door to door service. Please. Mine for the night, remember? I am taking you home now."

I sighed. Deeply. It was a sigh of surrender. Surrender to his wishes—and to my own desire to be near him.

"Take me home." I was excited. I was nervous. I wondered what would happen next.

CHAPTER SEVEN

The elevator ride down from our evening at the top of the world to the streets of New York City was sobering. This is where it had begun, and here we were again. Now we were leaving the oddly safe haven where all this romancing began and venturing out into the real world.

We stood across from each other, staring, like we did the first time we were together in this elevator. However, we'd had what felt like hours of intense foreplay. And it wasn't over yet. Soon enough, our deeply penetrating eye-fucking was captured in the multiple mirrors.

But could this thing, this possibility that had opened between us, survive the streets, the traffic, and the noise below? Would it leave the elevator with us, or would it dissipate like the flame of a candle blown out by the wind? I didn't want it to be over, yet a part of me was scared to death it would continue.

The evening seemed too surreal. A gorgeous man had come out of the blue and insisted I was his meant-to-be. He'd kissed me without warning in an elevator, penetrated my defenses with seductive words, suggestions, and scents. And now he had me leaving the building with him. From seventy-seven floors above the city, so much closer to the heavens, looking out on the magic of Manhattan with our kisses witnessed by the moon, it had begun to seem plausible. I just wasn't sure whatever this was would still be there when we reached the ground floor. I could always still grab a cab.

"That beautiful mind is always thinking, thinking, thinking, Ms. Monroe, trying to sort out that which is only meant to be felt and experienced," he said, with an amused look. "Am I right?"

"You have to admit this has all happened very quickly. Maybe not by Transylvania standards, of course."

"True, but it wouldn't be the first time, in the history of New York City, that sparks flew between two people at a cocktail party and they left together." He grinned as widely as a Cheshire cat.

When we stepped onto the curb, there was a limo and driver waiting.

"A stretch limo?" I had to chuckle. "That's so 1990s."

"I like to travel this way. It's more comfortable for my needs."

The driver stood to let us in, but Nicolai motioned to him to get back in the car and got the door handle himself. He offered his hand and helped me into the plush and roomy back seat. It was built like a classic limo, with two leather couches facing each other, not like the newer versions with seats on the side. It was extremely roomy with lots of space on the blue carpeted floor between the seats. He slid in beside me and gave the driver my address. Then he pushed the button to close the privacy window.

"How do you know my address?" Somehow, I was not completely surprised but I feigned a touch of indignation.

"Your company is employed by my company, remember?" he said. "I have access to all your records. We investigated every person working on our account before we gave the firm our business."

"Again, that's creepy." I pulled my purse into my lap and folded my arms. I was planning to stay like that for the entire three-mile ride.

"It's just business. However, I didn't access employee records to get your address. I Googled you from my phone when we were upstairs." I should have been annoyed by his action, but he was the one who seemed more irritated. "Your address is out there for all to see, and there is also a photo of your building. It's a roadmap right to your door. That kind of access has to be changed."

I wasn't quite sure what he'd meant and was more concerned about what he had in mind for the rest of the evening.

"I suppose you think you are coming home with me?" I sneered at him playfully.

"I would *never* presume that, Ms. Monroe." He took his suit jacket off, expertly folded it in half, and tossed it onto the opposite seat.

"Why not? You presume a lot of other things." I anticipated that he would at least *attempt* to get me into bed and that I would have to somehow conjure all my common sense to turn him away.

"It's not our time." He turned to face me more directly. "And besides, I am quite sure you'd never consider having sex with someone you just met under ordinary circumstances. Then again, these are extraordinary circumstances, no?"

"I guess so, but…"

"Don't fret. As attracted as I am to you, I'm not taking you to bed tonight. I can't, however, guarantee you won't want me to after this ride home."

"Oh, really?"

"Yes, really."

He sounded like such a pompous ass yet there was something appealing about a man who was so self-assured. We stared each other down for a while.

"But you will need more than sex from me," he said, swinging my legs over his lap, and slipping off my heels. I did not see that coming.

"Perhaps." Feet in lap seemed so personal, like something people usually do not do on a first date. I wondered where this was going.

"I'm well aware you need me to prove myself to you," he continued, resting his hands on my ankles. *Damn, why did his touch feel so good?* "And then, I will have to prove myself some more. You need to know I'm for real, and even then, you will have to figure out if I'm worth the sacrifices you think you would have to make, no?"

He looked at me with raised eyebrows, as if he had me all figured out.

"You seem to have given a lot of thought to this in the course of one evening," I said, instinctively pulling my feet closer together while trying not to brush against anything on his body that could get erect.

He smiled and turned his attention to my lower extremities.

"In my country, we show affection through foot rubs," he said, taking my right foot in hand. "It's non-sexual and yet intimate. The skin-to-skin contact allows you to feel the touch without obligation to touch back. It's a way of developing trust. As mine, for the night, can you trust me to pay homage to you through your feet?"

My feet were happy to be released from my high heels, but sitting there with my legs in his lap was peculiar. Was this the part where he declares he has a foot fetish? *Jeez.*

"I guess my trust depends on how well you do with the foot rub." I smirked at my own humor. Then he began to massage my foot in earnest, kneading out the knots and tension, and caressing it with both hands. His touch was heavenly.

"I can see you're not the kind of woman to say 'yes' just because an offer for a relationship is on the table," he continued. His hands were now gently working my ankle and calf. "Despite your protests about the possibility of making love tonight, I would have a much better shot of getting you in bed, I think, then getting you to suspend your disbelief in destiny, no?"

I was suddenly silent. He'd hit a nerve.

In my professional life, I worked hard to develop rapport with people I did business with and kept my panties on at all times. But in my private life, I eschewed attachments. I would rather have hot sex than fall in love. Being in this back seat of my client's car—with my naked legs at the mercy of his touch—blurred the lines between my two, very separate worlds. Maybe he did have some insights about me. It was unsettling to think he might know my secret.

"Am I right?" He took my left foot in hand, and gently massaged it. From the tips of my toes to my ankles, he was rubbing and touching pressure points as his hands roamed my flesh. I was surprised at how much pleasure radiated from that part of my body. I was almost too distracted to answer his question.

"Maybe," I laughed. "Jeez, is that information in my work profile? Or on the Internet?"

"No, this is just what I know to be true about you."

"How, Nicolai? How do you know all these things about me—and about my destiny? Is it your special Transylvanian super powers?"

"Because I know things," he said, working his way up my left leg. My flesh had grown fond of his touch. I wanted him to go higher, to my inner thigh and beyond. "You will too, in due time. And you will come to trust me. You may even come to love me. But we will not have sex. Not until the sixth date because when we do penetrate each other in that way, it will be life-changing."

"You're confident, aren't you." I spoke it as a joke, but his confidence was a turn on. So was his massage. He lifted my foot and sensually rubbed my toes against his smooth beard. Then he kissed it, the way he kissed my hand. I wondered if I would make it out of the limo without jumping him.

"Yes," he said, pulling my legs off of his lap and dropping them back on the seat. "I am confident about things I believe are true. In my heart, you are already mine, and I know this is meant to be. I understand that this is not your thinking right now, that you are allowing me a temporary pass, but I cannot pretend otherwise."

He punctuated the sentence by taking hold of my face. His kiss was rough and erotic, and when he slid his tongue into my mouth I wanted more. Desire took hold of my body. He was right. I wanted to have sex with him, despite all the reasons I should not.

We hadn't even left the curb yet.

As the limo finally drove off, and the kiss deepened, my hesitations lifted as a raw sexual energy filled the space between us. Brusquely, Nicolai pulled me onto his lap so I straddled him. Under my black skirt, I wore only tiny panties. He found this out soon enough when he hiked up my skirt and grabbed hold of my ass.

"There is very little covering you," he whispered. "Isn't that a little dangerous?"

"I did not expect to be sitting on anyone in the back seat of a car tonight."

"Amazing how things can change, and so quickly." With that, he pulled me closer, landing me right on top of his erection. *Holy shit.* He was so hard. And my hips couldn't help from pressing against him. I lifted my skirt more so I could move freely. He got an even firmer grip on my bottom, which made the contact between our lower parts even more intense. I was beginning to think that, under these extraordinary circumstances, I would like to have sex with him. Right here and now.

"Just remember," he said as he angled me even closer to his cock, "I cannot put this in you until date six."

Torture. I didn't know if I should smack him or try to jump him. Arousal was causing me to lose all inhibitions and I attempted to get him to satisfy me. His cock was jutting up from his suit pants and I rubbed myself against it, holding on tight to his neck to anchor the rest of my body. Crazed with lust, I was furiously pressing against him, surprised he gave me free rein to do this. I wondered if he was smirking at me for doing exactly what he predicted, but I didn't care. I was burning up from the contact.

"What about the no sex rule?" I panted. "What do you call this?" I pressed down on him harder.

"It still stands. This is simply frottage, playing. It's not real sex until my cock is buried inside you." He lifted his hips up, maneuvered closer to me, and pulled me in tighter.

"Nicolai, what are you doing to me?" I was losing it to this forbidden passion with a stranger who also happened to be a client. This was so, so bad.

"I am holding you in my arms, on my lap, in my car, as I take you to your home." Even though he was clearly aroused, he was still running the show.

"You know that is not what I mean. I think you've put a spell on me. You're making me want things." I let my head fall onto his shoulder as we ground against each other.

"Do you really think I have the power to put a spell on a woman like you who knows her own mind and body?" He kissed my ear and then circled it with his tongue. His breath was hot and sensual.

"It's all so," I was losing my breath from trying to angle myself close enough to come, "sudden."

"It's not so sudden." He kissed my neck and retraced my hickey with his upper lip. "This has been building up all night. But what if it has been building up all our lives? This is what it's like when you find the one who is meant for you. The attraction is strong, undeniable. It draws you in like a magnet."

"You're seducing me with your words," I said, rocking back and forth on him, too deep into the moment to protest. "I feel so vulnerable."

"I'm not the only one in this car," he said, his voice low and breathy. "You're generating this too. Hop off of me at any time."

As if! I pressed harder against his cock, and gyrated on top of him with the goal of rubbing myself off. If I could reduce the tension and have a release, I reasoned, I would get myself out of his grip. I was gliding up and down his body, my breath loud and fast, so close to coming.

"Have I aroused you, my love?" He was whispering, teasing me with his voice. "Have I increased your interest in me?"

"You know you have," I breathed. "I need you to touch me."

"Yes, I see you do. And I could ... so easily ... rip your panties off and take you." He gently caressed the exposed flesh of my hip and my ass. "But this is not the time."

"I can't stand being so out of control."

"On the contrary, I think you need this. You *need* to feel out of control to give yourself permission to surrender, to stop fighting this. It is the only way you can open to me."

"Don't you need it too?" I sighed, or whined, or panted, as I tried to press closer to him, wanting to feel him inside me.

"Oh yes, I need it too," he said, grabbing my head and pulling my face to his. His tongue drove into my mouth, filling me, making me gasp for breath at first. He held my head close as he slowly moved his tongue in and out until it felt like our mouths were fucking. It lulled me into a hypnotic state and relaxed me so much that with each thrust inward he was deeper. His breathing was ragged when he finally pulled away. My mouth felt raw. "Yes, I would like to take you, all of you, right here and now. But I will hold my arousal and wait for you. This is not just about sex for us. But I think you can tell my desire for you is strong."

His cock was even harder, and it was so close I almost felt I could get it inside me through his pants and through my panties. It was difficult for me to believe he would allow me so much access, allow me to feel him so closely, and not plan to fuck me right there in the car. My whole being was humming with erotic tension and desire in that moment, but he, on the other hand, had amazing restraint.

I sighed and pressed my head to his shoulder. I felt like we should be rolling over and smoking a cigarette from what we had done with our mouths. And that we should follow up with his penis in my vagina.

"Right now, you are just aroused, my love," he said, kissing my head. "Desire is coursing through you, and anyone could satisfy this need. But I want you to truly want me. When I make love to you, it will be because you chose me with your heart. And because you know who I am."

"Holy fuck."

"Yes, it will be, when we finally do."

CHAPTER EIGHT

Just then, the limo stopped and it felt as if it pulled into a parking spot. Sure enough, we were at my apartment building on East 44th Street. I wasn't sure what to do or say next. My legs remained wrapped around him, and my lower parts were sizzling. He also was still quite aroused. Yet, somehow, he had the presence of mind to get us organized for an exit.

"Let's get you into your apartment," he said, lifting me off his lap. He reached over for his jacket and put it back on. Then he pulled my skirt back into place, tucked my blouse back in, and slipped my heels on my feet. He organized my hair so I didn't look so disheveled. I was in a complete sex daze. He, however, was calm as he got out of the car and came around to the other end to help me out. I guess his moment of pulling me together gave him a chance to also let his erection calm down because it was no longer jutting from his suit pants.

"How do you not have a raging hard-on?" I looked down at his pants and back up at his eyes.

"It's my superpower," he said with a grin, offering his hand to assist me onto my feet outside the car.

"You mean mind control?" I was curious how he did it.

"Something like that," he said. "I think about something that is the reverse of wanting to make love to you."

I decided against asking him exactly what that may be.

He strolled into my building as if he owned it, steering me gently with his hand placed on my lower back. There was an aura of sexual tension around us, and I was still dripping with arousal. I said my hellos to the doorman, who looked at me with curiosity but smiled professionally. Nicolai also knew my floor number and punched the elevator key.

"I guess you know my apartment number too," I cracked, stepping into the elevator. "Is that a billionaire thing, or a stalker thing, to know where you are going before you arrive?"

"It's a being prepared thing," he shot back with a smile. "And yes, it's number twenty-seven. You signed as witness to a marriage license in New York City earlier this year and this information is all public domain."

"Jeez." I rolled my eyes. It was my friend Betsy's wedding. I was maid of honor. But why does he know that? Is that what he meant about my address being too easy for others to find? "You had to dig around for that."

"I have my ways." He spoke as if searching my information was merely being a responsible adult. "How else could I properly escort you home?"

I shrugged my shoulders and threw up my hands. "Um, you could ask for my address. That would be a novel approach."

"I took the precaution, simply on the off chance that you had a few drinks or were otherwise too distracted to tell me where you live."

"Or," I said, placing my index finger on his chest and poking him a couple of times, "maybe you figured you'd get me so drunk on desire that I wouldn't be able to think straight."

Looking at me with a slightly wily grin, he playfully grabbed my hand and kissed it. The elevator door opened and how we got here did not seem as important.

We sauntered silently to my door. I pulled my key out and he took it from me. As he stood in front of my apartment, I wondered if I should invite him in or kiss him good night. "What do we do now?"

"I'm not going to come in tonight." The look in his eyes said, "So don't even ask."

"Oh … okay." I leaned against the door. "So how does this work?"

"I will call you." He placed a hand above my head for support and leaned in closer to me. "Please don't be mad at me for leaving. I will give you what you need and want soon enough."

"Okay," I said on a big sigh that did not hide my unfulfilled desire. I smiled, trying to be a good sport. Just hours ago I was storming away from him on the terrace, and now I was quietly accepting that he was dropping me at my door in the throes of passion.

What is happening to me?

He kissed my lips, then pulled me close and held me in his arms in an embrace that made me feel wanted, as if he were glad he'd found me. He opened my door, gently nudged me inside, and looked at me, again, this time with softness in his eyes.

"Tomorrow, please leave the evening free for me."

"How do you know I don't have plans?"

"You do have plans—with me." With that, he kissed the top of my head; actually, it was the space between my brows. He kept his lips there for a long time, and gently circled the skin with his tongue. Then he blew, ever-so-softy. By the time he withdrew his lips, I felt a little tipsy. He whispered in my ear, "Dream of us."

"Okay." This was my mantra for the evening. *Okay. Okay. Okay.* What else could I say? I was under the sensual spell of Nicolai Petre who was offering me—what I wasn't sure—but I wanted to know more.

I closed the door, leaned against it, and took a moment to feel the erotic forces of nature surge through my body. I was about to head for my vibrator when a call came into my cell. It was him. He had that number too.

"Seriously?" I huffed into the phone. "This number is unlisted." But I was glad to hear his voice.

"If you decide you hate me, I will erase all traces of your contact information at your request," he said. "For now, this saves time." Clearly he had made it his business to know how to find me and reach me. A part of me was impressed he went to the effort.

"I was just about to—"

"I will look forward to seeing you tomorrow," he said. "I forgot to mention, please don't touch yourself tonight. I'll know if you do."

"You're kidding, right?"

"I think you know the answer to that, my love. Remember, for this night, you're still mine. Sleep well."

What could I say but, "Okay."

I met this guy less than five hours ago and, already, he is telling me what to do with my vagina in my free time. I'd met lots of men in my life but never one who was so dominant. Not in a BDSM way, but in a take-charge alpha kind of way. And, despite all the reasons why I should not, I was starting to like it. I wondered what tomorrow would bring.

CHAPTER NINE
WEDNESDAY: DAY TWO/ SECOND DATE

"Sometimes you can't explain what you see in a person. It's just the way they take you to a place you have never been."

I once saw that line in a meme on Facebook and it stuck with me.

That's where I was with Nicolai. Oh, he was hot enough to desire under any circumstances, but the rest of it was a big mystery. Obviously, he was rich, charming, appealing—the kind of package most women say they want, but those are the surface things that they see when they gawk at him from afar. In the brief but intense experience I shared with him, I realized it wasn't just the package that called to me. It was the oddly immediate feeling of intimacy with him, the comfort even in the discomfort. He was taking me someplace I'd never been, yet a part of me seemed to think I was supposed to go there. It was probably my vagina talking, but my emotions were also already involved.

I washed off my makeup, tossed off my clothes and slipped into bed naked, as I always do. I was tempted to cuddle up to my vibrator but the minute my head hit the pillow, I fell into a deep sleep. Deep enough, apparently, to have vivid dreams in living color of me and a certain blond, blue-eyed billionaire. But in the dream, he was a knight and I was a lady, tying my kerchief to his arm before he headed off to battle.

"I miss you already, my lord," said my dream self, tears streaming.

"It is my destiny, my love," he replied.

"Then come back to me soon." I pressed my tear-stained cheek against his. With heaving breast, I kissed him farewell and watched as he rode into the distance with the other knights.

Back in my candlelit chambers, with richly embroidered plum colored drapes, I sat in a royal-looking cherry wood chair with flowered upholstery, drinking mead. Probably too much of it. My ladies in waiting came in and found me drunk, helped me out of my garments and placed me in bed. I kicked off the bedsheets and lay there, in my nightshirt, atop the heavy velvet bed quilt and pined for my knight.

My hand found its way to my lower belly and tried to massage the sexual ache within. My medieval double attended to her own needs and just as she was close to the precipice of pleasure in my dream, my alarm went off.

I woke up feeling groggy, but happy and doped up on feel-good hormones. I was also aroused. Seriously aroused. I reached down between my legs. Totally wet, still, and Lord knows what other dreams I'd had overnight. They may have been more erotic than I realized because my clitoris felt engorged.

"Jeez, how will I be able to work like this?" I wondered out loud. I reached for my vibrator. Screw Nicolai's warning. I was close to experiencing the clitoral equivalent of blue balls. I had to have relief.

The phone rang.

"Good morning, my love," said the mysterious man from Transylvania who claimed he was my soul mate. Shouldn't he say, "I *vant* to suck your blood," and sound like Dracula? Instead, his accent was smooth and sexy. His voice resonated through my body, leaving tingles in its wake. "How did you sleep?"

"I think I had a wet dream." I reached my hand between my legs.

"I sent it to you." He laughed, but I was pretty sure he was seriously claiming credit for seducing me in my dream state as well.

"All-powerful, even in my dreams?"

"Yes. I hope so."

I inhaled with a sigh and found myself thinking it would be nice if he were beside me. Why was I thinking that? I barely knew him, and he'd left me completely sexually frustrated last night. I should be angry.

"Do you miss me?" he asked.

I hesitated. It was a weird, egotistical question, and I didn't want to admit it. But I did. "Yes."

"Don't touch yourself this morning, or anytime today."

Jeez, somebody better touch me today. I wished he were here to soothe the need in me.

"How am I supposed to go to the office and walk around so worked-up?" Everything that could be aroused in me was aroused.

"Embrace your arousal." I had to press my legs together at the sound of his voice.

"You Eastern bloc people must have more discipline than us weak American-born girls."

"Yes," he said. "But you are far from weak. If you were weak, you would have never taken the risk of hearing me out last night. You are strong and quite brave."

I kept silent but those last words rolled over my naked body, touching my nipples, my belly, and my lips below.

"We need to renegotiate our status," he said. "We agreed to disagree about use of the word 'mine' and to take it a day at a time."

"Ah, that we did."

"So? Will you give it another try? Pretend we belong together, just for today? And give me a chance to show you I can be likeable?"

Why did that sound so sexy and make me like him, already?

"Okay, but we need boundaries, like, keeping this a secret, for starters." I tried to think of more things, like renegotiating the vibrator use, but his next words dramatically changed my focus.

"No problem, but I will see you at work today," he said. "We have a business meeting at five p.m."

"We do?"

"Yes, I put it on the calendar last night with Sheila."

Oh God. Sheila, my boss, who last night told me in no uncertain terms to stay away from him. *Fuck.*

"Okay." But it was not okay. She was going to know.

Memories of last night's kissing shenanigans and moonlight soul mate chats flooded back to me. Somewhere between the moon and the limo, I'd folded, raised my white flag, and agreed to pretend this was all okay. Work talk was snapping me out of it.

"I'm coming in with my team for an overview of the press response last night at the event, and to review the follow-up game plan for media coverage."

"Excellent." My demeanor turned from smitten aroused woman to professional female who should not have sexual dreams about her client. "I'll work on that today."

"Thank you," he said. "From my perspective, an oral report is fine." He paused and I flashed back to our intense time in each other's mouths last night. "There's nothing beyond that you have to do to prepare for the meeting—except for one small thing."

"Yes," I said, getting up to grab a pen to write it down. I was totally getting into business mode.

"Don't wear panties."

His voice was a blend of dreamy romantic lead and dominant businessman. My legs quivered at the thought of being in the same room with him discussing business with just a thin sheath of my dress between him and me.

"Okay." I can't believe I'd said that!

"After our meeting, I will walk out the door and go to my car to wait for you. Then we will have the night, together. Secretly. As you wish."

"You mean spend the night?" Hope mingled with yearning as I thought of what it might be like to get naked with him. Yet another feeling tugged at me—I was once again to be thrust into a work situation with a client who I was making out with on the sly. The taboo of it all scared and excited me.

"The evening is ours. And then, I will take you home." He paused before taking a deep breath. I could almost feel his breath in my ear, through the phone.

"As in drop me off, alone?" I panicked a little. "Round two of sending me home without sex?

"Yes."

"And, um, remind me why I should be excited about *that*?"

"Because we'll be alone together—after the meeting—and we can make out and feel each other up a little bit," he laughed warm and sexy. "And this will be considered our second date. One down and five to go. I look forward, my love."

I got up and literally took a cold shower. I couldn't believe how turned on I was. The forbidden nature of it all was adding dry wood to passion's fire. Every inch of skin was so sensitive. I had to find something in my closet that was not too clingy—because of the panties situation and the potential for erect nipples—and not too short. I settled on a sleeveless sapphire dress that belted at the waist and had a slightly fuller skirt than most of my outfits. I slipped on my neutral color high heels. No panties. No protection from the elements or the arousal caused by Mr. Nicolai Petre. Hopefully there wouldn't be any strong breezes on the streets of New York today. I figured my best bet was to take a cab to work rather than risk a rush of air blowing up my dress on the subway.

Fussing in the mirror, I noticed one problem with this dress: my love bite was in full display. It was crazy big, but I kind of liked it, as if it were a badge of romantic honor. Nicolai had completely branded me with his incredibly sensual neck sucking. I tried to hide it with concealer, but I should have remembered from high school that there's no covering them up with makeup. Luckily, I found a jacket with a high neck that could possibly prevent everyone in the boardroom from seeing it, if I kept my hair down.

My day at the office was odd, in a hazy, romantic, day-after kind of way.

Yesterday I was a complete professional, preparing for a big media launch party, and today I was an overly-aroused New York woman who, against her better judgment, was now romantically linked to the client for whom the media event was arranged. I was bursting with anticipation about date two with Nicolai and at the same time filled with dread about the business meeting that would transpire prior. How was I supposed to act normal when just last night our big client had informed me I was his beloved, kissed me in to a hormonal stupor, and then nearly made me come from humping him in the back seat of his limo?

Sheila had called me into her office the minute I arrived and revealed the big meeting. I acted as if I had no idea there would be one as she handed me a stack of papers and told me to put a PowerPoint together based on her notes—three lines scribbled on a sticky note—and my notes from last night. Typically, I did all the work and she took as much credit as she could for doing everything. I hated doing her PowerPoints, but this time, I welcomed the distraction. Still, I could not stop thinking about my swelling lower lips and what Nicolai may do or not do to exacerbate, or relieve, the arousal.

My pal, Aisha, passed by my office and poked her head in. "What's up with you?" she said. "Why the scowl? Or whatever that look is?" Aisha's gift with emotional intelligence was admirable. She was able to tune into other people's feelings and moods, and also use her cheerful attitude to uplift others.

"Nicolai Petre is coming in for a follow-up today." It came out on a sigh. But I hoped it would be heard as an, *Oh I have so much work to prepare* sigh, not as an *I am carrying on with this man even though he's our client* sigh.

"Oh goodie," she said. Her dark eyes literally sparkled with glee and she twirled a strand of hair in her fingers, the way girls do when they like a certain boy. "Hope I'm invited."

"Sheila has me working on a PowerPoint," I groaned. And Nicolai gave me a panty task, I wanted to say, but I didn't. I cut and pasted some images from my desktop onto the presentation page. Aisha watched as I struggled to get them sized properly to fit on the page.

"Oh God, why doesn't she have her assistant do that?" she huffed. "You're the account executive!" I loved the way she was always in my corner when it came to Sheila's evil-Queen approach to management, but fretted when I remembered her comment yesterday about Nicolai being on her short list of potential billionaire husbands.

"Because she apparently thinks I am her assistant-slash-slave, too." Finally, I got the photo the way I wanted it on the page. It was one of our hot guys from the e-reader to add a little pizzazz to the presentation with boring statistics.

I had my jacket off, in the privacy of my office, and had forgotten Nicolai's amorous art design on my neck, until Aisha caught sight of my hickey.

"Where the heck … or should I say who the heck did that come from?" She came closer to get a better look. "Wow. Vampire attack?"

"Um, close the door." My hand instinctively went to cover my neck.

Aisha shut the door, situated herself in the chair in front of my desk, and waited for me to speak. I hesitated, debating about what to reveal. I trusted her more than anyone, and she was a true friend, so I wanted to share. But it was still a secret. And what if she really does like him? I didn't want to hurt her or cause her to feel jealous.

"You're killing me," she said, sitting up straight. She placed both hands on my desk and looked at me with rapt attention. Her lifted eyebrows urged me to fess up. Then she gasped aloud as if she'd figured out the mystery. "Wait, was it him?"

"I'm so sorry," I said. "I know you had your eye on him. But he made a pass at me last night. Well, more than a pass. He made a point of telling me that he felt we had a destiny together."

"Oh, my God, Allison." She put her palms together and started clapping excitedly, as if I'd just announced an engagement. "This is amazing!"

"No, it's weird. Can I even take him seriously?" I pushed away from my computer and slumped back in my chair. Next thing I knew I was chewing the nail on my right index finger.

"How can you not take a man like Nicolai Petre seriously?" She stood up and paced. I half expected her to do a happy dance around my office. "He knows what he wants in life and goes for it. And he wants *you*, my friend."

"What about what I want?" I wasn't even sure any more. Yesterday I thought his stories about destiny were crazy. Today, they seemed *less* crazy, and this thing on my neck was warm and tingling with the memory of his lips on my flesh. "I don't *do* relationships. And I'm not looking for love with a client or a billionaire who has complicated family issues."

"Billionaire problems," she laughed playfully. "The troubles of gorgeous, sexy men with money and power can be so tiresome!"

"He told me he believes I am his *Ves'tacha.*"

"Awww. *Ves'tacha* is a Romani term. It means you are his soul mate, his true love, his lobster—you know, like Ross and Rachel on *Friends*." As a lover of pop culture and ethnically diverse romantic movies, Aisha was an encyclopedia of terms of endearments from many traditions and could describe mating and wedding rituals from around the world.

"I know. I looked it up." A tear rolled down my cheek. I didn't usually cry, especially at work. "The moment I set eyes on him I felt a connection, and he came after me and pursued it. But I kept trying to push him away the minute I realized he was our client. He wouldn't let me." As the words left my mouth I realized I didn't want him to. Nicolai came along and had pushed me far out of my comfort zone with his speeches about love and destiny. He challenged me with his sexual dominance and self-control.

"You should be happy," she said, pulling a tissue out of the box I kept on my desk and sliding it over to me. "He would have to come on strong to get your attention."

"I'm confused. He said he is Romanian. Wouldn't the word be *Draga?*" I had done a little more research this morning about his culture.

"His paternal grandmother, Alina Petre, was born in Russia and is also Romani. She's world famous—and quite rich—for her intuitive predictions. I think that's where it comes from. I read about her in *Forbes*."

"Really? Apparently, she is the source of this prophecy that convinced him we are meant to be."

"Well, that makes sense. Many people have sought her out. Royalty and celebrities. I read that he's very close to her. Let me show you the article." Aisha came to my side of the desk, saved my PowerPoint, and clicked over to Google to search. The piece came up with a big color photo of a regal elderly woman. She had Nicolai's eyes.

"He didn't quite mention all that," I said, skimming the article for Nicolai's name. I saw it in the fourth paragraph, where it mentioned she nurtured him as a young adult after his parents died. "Our whole night was him trying to sell me on this idea of destiny. But he told me his grandmother was sick and dying. She looks pretty healthy here." Anger flashed through me and settled in my chest. *Was he playing me?*

"Well, it could be an outdated photo and the article is a couple of years old," she said, leaving my computer and settling back into a chair. "Not to be blunt, but inquiring minds want to know. How good is he in bed? Please tell me billionaires can also be good lovers."

"I don't know. He won't have sex with me." I had a flashback to his erection and my urge to ride him in the back seat but I didn't want to reveal our limo hump.

"Oh wow, does he want you to save it for the wedding night?" She chuckled and I did too.

"He wants to wait. He's got this thing in his mind about the sixth date."

"Holy heartthrob, Batman, he is serious about you!"

"I haven't even known him for twenty-four hours. What makes you think that? It makes no sense to me." My inner world felt like a ping-pong match. On one level, talking about it, and sharing this with Aisha, made it seem more real. But hearing myself reminded me how bizarre it all was. I was bouncing between my desire to see where this was going and my cogent mind telling me it was all ridiculous; that love cannot be rushed to a finish line to make a full moon deadline; that fooling around with a client would mess up my life plans.

"Sometimes things just happen really quickly between couples," she assured me. "I've seen it. You plan your life a certain way, and love shows up and changes things."

"Yeah, you've seen that in all the romantic comedies you watch." I had to chuckle. "I can name about ten right now that had a meet-cute, a crazy conflict, and a big kiss at the end."

"True, but I've seen it in real life. It can happen."

Aisha and her brother were born here, but her parents hailed from India—a culture where arranged marriages were the norm, and they still were in many families. Although her parents would never force her to marry, they felt it was their duty to find a proper Hindu guy for her consideration.

"My mother was promised to my father, and she tried to run away. But her family found her and brought her back," she said, sitting upright in her chair. "Her grandmother tried to tell her they had found the perfect mate for her, and she couldn't believe it. She didn't want to marry."

"Wow, your mother was the original runaway bride?"

"I love that movie!" Aisha continued, eyes lighting up. "She kind of was."

"So how did your grandmother get her back on track?" I moved closer to the edge of my desk, elbow on the surface, and rested my chin in my hands to listen.

"I believe it was fate at work," she said, extending her arms to the heavens in a pose that was part Disney princess and part Vanna White. "She didn't meet him until the wedding day, and when they removed the cloth placed between them at the wedding altar and she looked into his eyes, she says she knew he was her true husband. He had been just as scared, but he knew it too. They married under the pressure to fulfill their family duty, but they ultimately felt destiny brought them together.

That was thirty-six years ago. I still catch them making out in the kitchen when they think no one is around."

"You're so lucky to have good role models for love," I said.

"It can happen, Allison. For you too."

By now I was in a puddle of tears on top of my puddle of arousal. Aisha happened to walk into my office at the right moment. I'd needed to talk to someone about the whirlwind that began on the elevator the night before, to get some perspective. And her tale about her parents was sweet—although it would take more than one love at first sight success story to sell me on the idea of fate.

I thought it was completely possible that a man could want to fuck me on first sight—but it was difficult to believe he'd want me to be his wife after one kiss. My jaded perspective aside, I appreciated Aisha's attempt to win me over to her belief in happily-ever-after. She was a cheerleader for love. "Thank you, my friend. I have no idea where this speeding rocket is going, but I guess I will try to be brave enough to stay aboard."

"Every woman at the party last night, myself included, would think you are insane to not give this a chance, but I doubt anyone would be mad if you threw a billionaire back into the singles' pool," she said with a chuckle. "Especially Sheila. She seemed set on keeping him to herself."

"Oh God, Sheila. She obviously cannot get the memo that he and I are involved. If she catches on that I'm dating a client, all my plans for moving ahead and getting my dad's company back will be fucked."

"You could refuse to take this any further with Nicolai," she said, a mischievous look in her eyes.

"In theory, this is true. But you don't know Nicolai's persuasive ways."

"Yes, I would imagine he doesn't take 'no' for an answer. But I would also imagine that is exactly how it would have to be with you, Ms. Independent. My guess is he'd have to come up with a clever work around to get through your defenses."

Everyone seemed to have my M.O.

CHAPTER TEN

At a quarter to five, I went to the bathroom to freshen up, check my makeup, and confirm that my hickey was hidden by my jacket and hair. I also breathed into a paper bag for a minute in an attempt to relieve some tension. Then I headed to the boardroom to set things up in advance, leaving word with the front desk to have someone show Mr. Petre to the room.

My whole body was on alert as I waited, trying to look busy.

When he came in with his team my heart fluttered. One look at him and I could feel moisture between my legs. The connection from last night, the one he described as the force between us, was still there. It was strong. It was palatable. I hadn't even known him a full twenty-four hours, yet my body seemed completely connected to his.

He was wearing a navy-colored suit that was so beautifully tailored to his form that I couldn't take my eyes off him. No one in the room could. He was flawless. His classic Egyptian-blue gingham dress shirt, with contrasting white collars and cuffs and dark silk tie, made him look like a movie star playing a super-hot businessman. His light beard was perfectly trimmed. His eyes came alive with his body swathed in that color palate, and especially, it seemed, when he saw me. He offered a sexy smile of acknowledgement, just for me, before anyone could see.

"Ms. Monroe," he said, taking my hand and bringing it up to his mouth to kiss. "So lovely to see you again." He gave me that sexy wink, again.

I hoped the fluids of my arousal would not start flowing down my leg.

He bent his mouth to my ear and whispered. "You smell so delicious today. You are happy to see me, yes?"

"Yes," I admitted, struggling to maintain my professionalism. When I looked up, Sheila and two others on her staff had entered the room. The meeting had begun.

I sat by the laptop at the end of the boardroom table, close to the projector screen, to drive the PowerPoint. Nicolai unbuttoned his suit jacket and took the seat across from me. I was painfully aware that my nipples were erect and that Nicolai was looking right at them. The chill from the air conditioning wasn't helping matters. With all eyes on him, I hoped no one would notice where his gaze was wandering.

He gave the directive to start. "Please proceed, Ms. Monroe."

I looked over at Sheila, knowing she thought of this meeting—and all meetings—as her show. It was her habit to position herself, at the start of a meeting, as the person responsible for everything that went well. Her surprised look was quickly replaced with a fake smile but she was not going to be happy about him giving *me* the go ahead.

"Yes, Allison, please get this started." She said it as if it were her plan all along. After that, she kept her mouth shut, but I could feel her displeasure coming in my direction like a million tiny darts of anger.

I proceeded with the presentation. I was focused and got the job done, but it was a twenty-minute blur.

Thank goodness it was a successful launch and we'd had great results last night. Thirty media outlets had attended, twenty had ordered loaners of the product, and a mix of tech bloggers and publishing reporters from *The New York Times* to CNN said they would be reporting on it when the product went live next week. In the PR world, this was great.

The next step was to get the device into the hands of the readers. I outlined our social media strategy for that, and our plan to win favorable reader reviews. I was actually very proud of my work on this product, and I had ideas for making it a success in a very competitive US market as well as other markets. Even though Sheila had told me to keep my mouth shut, I decided to run my idea by Nicolai and his team.

"You know, Mr. Petre, romance readers truly love their alpha heroes," I pointed out.

"Is that so? Enlighten me, please, since this field is new to me," he requested. "What do women love about alpha heroes?"

You could hear a pin drop as he awaited my response with a slight smirk on his lips. I wonder if they noticed he asked about women in general and not just readers.

"Well, of course, they love their heroes to be fully assured of themselves, and to be take charge leaders," I said, sharing the first things that came to mind. "To never worry what others think, and to follow their dreams as they seek achievement."

"And what else," he asked, his voice smooth and low, as if he was in a bedroom not a boardroom. "I'm curious to know, Ms. Monroe."

"I believe readers find eye contact extremely important," I continued. "And when they read, they can almost feel themselves lost in the hero's eyes, or maybe they want to see love in those eyes."

"So, a woman can tell a lot by the way a man looks at her? That's good insight for us to have." His gaze touched mine from across the table. I got lost for a moment before remembering to bring it all back to my point.

"Romance readers are a special consumer, and they especially like when the handsome, sexy men that are featured in the books come alive on their social media pages," I continued. "I wonder if you might consider having one particular model associated with the campaign and with the brand."

"Do you have anyone in mind?"

"Um, well, yes." Him. But I couldn't say what I was thinking of in front of everyone. "We can come up with some suggestions."

"That's a genius idea for social media." His team all nodded and agreed. Sheila looked pissed. "In fact, my cousin is a professional model. Maybe he can help."

I could hear an excited murmur in the room from the other women, and imagined they were all thinking: *Oh, my God, he has a hot cousin too—and he is a model!* I was more excited that he was validating and supporting my ideas.

Aisha, being our official hot man-researcher, pursued it a little further. "What kind of modeling does he do?" I guess she wanted to know if he was Dolce and Gabbana or Macy's catalog material. "Have we seen him in anything?"

"He's in a big high fashion campaign right now," he said. "I'll have his agent send over the details. I can tell you, from observation, women find him very appealing. But you'll have to take a look at him and see if you approve."

"We would all love to meet him," said Aisha, blushing and twisting her hair around on her finger.

"In due time," he said, turning from her and casting a glance my way that made it seem like a personal invitation to meet his family.

Nicolai kept a steady stare on me throughout our meeting, and I'm pretty sure I kept a steady blush. Or was I flushed? I somehow got through it, sounding intelligent about the project, but inside I was melting. Despite my concern that others would be able to sense there was a romance in their midst, it apparently went well.

At least Nicolai seemed to think so, based on his enthusiasm. But I had to wonder if his desire to win me over was spilling into business. Was he pretending to like my ideas?

"Well, Sheila, I am very happy with what you and your team have done. Great start for our launch." He was kissing up to her instead of giving me all the credit. Smart. As much as I was weary of managing Sheila's high maintenance ego, his response showed me he knew how to work her.

"We're so happy to pleasure you," she said. "I mean, please you… Happy that you are pleased."

Jeez, I guess everyone gets flummoxed in his seductive presence.

"That will be all for now." He got up from the conference table. "But I may need someone on your team to come to a meeting tomorrow to share this with the rest of my staff so they are apprised of our success and game plan."

"Of course, I would be happy to—"

"—To send Ms. Monroe. Yes, that would be perfect since she is the lead on this account."

Crap. So much for his treading gently on her ego. I have to admit, it made me hot to see him take control like that. He was so commanding about it, there was no way she could balk. I watched her face turn six shades of red and recognized her disappointment-to-annoyance facial expression, as I have seen that look so many times. But she submitted to his wish. "Of course. Allison, please clear your schedule tomorrow."

I looked over at Nicolai. He tilted his head and cocked an eyebrow, awaiting my response.

"Yes, of course." Jeez, he got me a hall pass out of work. I felt like a teenager cutting school with the high school bad boy.

"I'll send a car for you in the morning." He rose from the table, re-buttoned his suit jacket, and nodded his good-bye to me. He didn't give my boss a second look.

Sheila's glare in my direction let me know she wasn't happy. As he headed out the door, she leaped out of her chair and followed him.

I just sat there, afraid the deluge of lust that could not be contained by my non-existent panties would end up on the chair beneath me. His presence in the boardroom, my lack of underwear, and his public selection of me over Sheila—it all conspired to rev up my passion. I waited until everyone cleared out to get up. Then I grabbed my purse and went downstairs, where Nicolai's car awaited me.

When his driver opened the door, I was surprised that Nicolai was nowhere in sight.

"Where's Mr. Petre?" I asked, sliding onto the back seat. I was anxious to know why he felt the need to get me out of work tomorrow. An act that was likely to bring forth the wrath of my boss.

"He called and said he had to tend to something and will be with you momentarily."

I closed my eyes, remembering the heat that began between us on this black leather seat. I pressed my legs together, trying to relieve some of the sexual tension between them. It didn't help.

Suddenly, the door opened and in came Nicolai. Even though I had just seen him, I felt like a long time had passed waiting. Upstairs, I'd kept myself in reserve and stayed in business mode. The moment he entered the car, every erogenous zone that could tingle started to. Deep longing fired off throughout my body as if on cue.

He sat down next to me and pressed his hand against my cheek.

"You look beautiful," he said. "And you looked beautiful up there. Your presentation was amazing. You've done such great work for us. Thank you."

"Do you really mean that?" I asked. "It's not just part of your six-day wooing plan?"

"Of course I mean it," he said, sitting upright and removing his suit jacket. Again, he folded it in half and tossed it on the seat across from us. "The work you have done on this campaign is nothing less than stellar. It's all brilliant. You're brilliant."

"Thank you." I was never great at taking complements but his comments made me feel good about my hard work. "But why did you get me out of work tomorrow? I have a lot of work to catch up on for your account."

"Bring your laptop along." He gave the driver an address and closed the privacy window. He brought his lips to mine before I had a chance to ask what caused his delay or what we were going to be doing tomorrow. After a moment, I didn't care.

As he slipped his tongue into my mouth I greeted him with my own, and was quickly lost in the heat of the moment. I almost couldn't bear how turned on I was. *Will he let me straddle him again?* I hoped he would change his sex rule and take me right there. When he pulled his passionate tongue from my mouth, I was optimistic he would place it where I burned for him. But his next move was completely unexpected.

"Open your legs."

"What ... why?"

"Open for me."

I did as he asked, feeling incredibly shy, yet also exceedingly excited. I longed for his touch.

"I want to feel your arousal," he said. With that, he lifted my dress, and slowly and sensually traversed my knee, my hip, and my inner thigh with his hand. Then I felt him close to my opening. When he pressed forward and slid one finger between my folds, I gasped. He gently traced my inner lips with his touch.

"Oh. My. God." I shocked myself by so willingly parting my thighs at his command, but I wanted this. I wanted him. His finger felt so good inside. I couldn't even remember why it bothered me that he was a client. I forgot that moments earlier I'd been with him at work, doing a dog and pony show for him, with my boss and coworkers watching.

"Don't move," he commanded.

"I have to." Not only did my hips want to wriggle and writhe beneath his touch, I wanted to force his hand to do dirty things to me.

"No movement," he warned in a sexy whisper. "Or I will have to take away my hand. I'll have to stop right now."

I stilled myself. Immediately.

He slid his finger into me. I instinctively pressed closer, but he used his other hand to hold my hips in place.

"Nicolai, I need you." My breathing was getting heavy.

"And I need you," he said, adoration in his eyes. "Throughout the entire meeting, I wanted to lift you onto the table and open your legs to taste you."

He pressed his finger in about an inch and caressed the sensitive nerve endings at my opening. Then he went a little deeper. Finally, he moved in and out. I clenched around him. Everything inside me was tingling.

"You are even more aroused than I could have imagined," he said. "So beautifully wet and almost ready."

"Almost ready? I would say overly ready. I would say give-it-to-me-right-now-ready. I've never felt this way in my life."

"This is not yet our time for making love," he said. "But your body is telling me you are ready for me to give you pleasure, yes?"

"Yes." Desire and need were winning. Despite all my reasons for not getting involved with him in the first place, my longing for his touch was stronger.

"Even though I am a client, and you don't believe in fate, and you are not sure you want me for more than a day at a time?"

"Yes." The magic of the moment was giving me temporary amnesia about my concerns. My stirred-up passion seemed to have re-routed my logical mind to somewhere in the vicinity of my vagina.

He slipped his finger back inside, moving in and out. My hips gyrated against his hand. After so many hours of arousal I wanted to explode. But he withdrew and brought his finger up to his mouth to taste me.

"Did you know your arousal is like a magic potion that can revitalize and give special power to your beloved?" he asked, licking his finger again. "The ancients call a woman's fluids amrita—nectar of the gods."

"It's not something they teach in sex ed." I smiled at yet another theory from Nicolai.

"This comes from schools of esoteric knowledge, not sex education, my love." He lowered himself to his knees on the limo rug. "To taste the arousal of a woman you care for is to feel her soul and to share her power. But taking without giving creates imbalance."

"I guess that makes sense." I instinctively spread my legs a little farther apart.

He unbuttoned his collar and loosened his tie. "Giving you pleasure with my mouth is a way to share my power with you."

He searched my eyes for permission.

I nodded my consent.

He pulled me to the edge of the seat and lowered his head between my open legs. He kissed my inner thighs, working his way up. When his tongue first reached my most sensitive flesh it was like a kiss from heaven, a rush of pleasure. Just as he pressed his tongue inside me, a slight bump in the road brought him even deeper.

That it was all happening in a moving vehicle was surreal. But one thing was for sure, IFSG: It. Felt. So. Good.

He'd had me in a state of lust for over twenty-four hours and my body was screaming for release. I gripped his head and pulled him in closer, pressing myself harder against his mouth. As I neared the edge of orgasm, he removed his tongue from where he'd buried it and found my clitoris. One lick, then another, and another, and then he sucked with full force. He moved his hands under my ass to pull me closer. The first tickles of orgasm spread through my lower belly as he isolated my pleasure to that one spot. This gave way to a wild eruption. With tremoring thighs, I wrapped my legs around his shoulders as the last of it shuddered through me.

Holy crap. It took a while to catch my breath.

With a tender kiss to my pubic bone, he brought his flushed, wet face upward and all I could do was look at him with affection and appreciation for the best orgasm, ever. We stared each other down for a while, smiles in our eyes.

"I'm not sure what the etiquette is for … well, what just happened. Thank you seems appropriate." I lifted my legs off him and brought them together to get upright.

"You're like manna from heaven," he sighed, lifting off the floor. "I'm the one who should say thank you."

The fact that oral sex was like a spiritual experience for him was impressive.

"Are you still aroused?" He reached over and brushed two fingers against my cheek. They smelled like passion.

"I am." Usually after an orgasm, I completely lose interest in sex—and the guy. But my interest had only increased.

"Good. Maybe you are starting to like me?"

"Maybe." *Definitely.* I could not wipe the smile from my face.

"So perhaps there is hope I can talk you into signing on tomorrow, again, to be mine for the day?"

"There's a strong possibility." I laughed at his daily renewal of his weird be-mine-one-day-at-time agreement. But he seemed to take it seriously.

"Excellent, so now I am taking you out to dinner, and then home."

I looked down at his pants. His cock was jutting out from the expensive navy suit.

"Will you come in with me this time?" Surely he needed some relief from his massive hard-on.

"Only to kiss you good night."

I guess I could not expect an encore of that glorious spontaneous oral performance. Or was it planned?

"Can I ask you something?" Shyly, I looked down at his pants again. "What about, um, *that*?"

"*That* is mine to deal with," he said, looking down at his tented slacks. "But how sweet and caring that you're concerned about *my* arousal."

I eyed his organ. "Shouldn't there be a sexual clause somewhere in our daily agreement that says no erection shall go unheeded?" Most men would insist on it, but he was different.

"Ha, that's not what this is all about, for me anyway," he said, playfully grabbing a handful of his erection. "Believe me, I wish I could fall into you, and give you *every inch* of my affection. But I'm old-fashioned. I need to be loved before I have intercourse with a woman."

I almost couldn't believe my ears. *What adult male says something like that? And who uses the word intercourse?*

"Are you serious? You're saving yourself?"

He gave me that don't ask me if I'm serious look. "I think you know the answer. But I love your concern. You don't have to deal with this right now." He touched his area again, but I could see things had settled back down. Maybe he was thinking of something unsexy to curb his enthusiasm. "I'm starving. Let's go eat."

Somewhere in all the oral sex and oral discourse, the limo had arrived at our destination. Thank God the driver didn't automatically come and open the doors. Nicolai grabbed his suit jacket and then helped me out of the car in front of the Captain's Table, an upscale restaurant on Park Avenue. We were led to a private room off to the side that had its own door. He pulled out my chair in a gentlemanly fashion and took the seat across from me. Somehow, it felt like too much distance between us. I found myself filled with a need to be close.

A waiter came in with ten different dishes and spread them across a long table set up against the wall.

"I wasn't sure what you like to eat," said Nicolai, "so I had them bring a few options."

"It looks like you had them bring everything." And all of it smelled delicious. I opted for Alaskan Salmon with vegetables. He did the same but added potatoes and a salad. The waiter brought over our choices, along with a bottle of wine. He poured our drinks.

"Mr. Petre," he said, handing Nicolai a small device that looked like a doorbell buzzer, "I will keep the service bell in my pocket. Please ring if you need me. Until then, I will leave you in private, as requested." He left the room, closing the door behind him.

"Service bell?" I looked at Nicolai. "Sounds so *Downton Abbey*."

He laughed. "It rings in the kitchen, and, apparently, in his pants," he said. "This is called The Captain's Room and they only venture in here when the captain calls. It's for patrons who like their privacy."

"I see." I wasn't used to hanging around billionaires who could buy private rooms and servers in public restaurants. I raised the fork to my mouth and took a small bite but was distracted by Nicolai's intense stare.

"Eat," he said, picking up his fork. "You'll need your strength. It's just … I can't take my eyes off you."

I laughed and looked down at my food, a little embarrassed.

"In truth, I haven't been able to take my eyes of you since we met yesterday." I lifted my head to look at him. He smiled and took a bite of his food. "And when I'm not looking at you, I'm thinking about you. I'm just so happy we finally found each other."

His gaze stayed on mine as he chewed. He wasn't a shy eater and devoured most of his food pretty quickly.

The salmon was melt in your mouth delicious. I'd barely eaten today, but I was picking at it. I felt compelled to query him about something that had been on my mind, and it seemed like the right moment since he was in a softer mood—unlike yesterday, when he acted like a Neanderthal trying to drag me back to his cave.

"I have to ask you, Nicolai," I said, putting down my fork. "Of all the women in the world you could have, how can you be so sure about me?"

He took another bite of food as he considered my question. Then he downed a big sip of wine and patted his mouth with his napkin before answering.

"Because you're the one." He said it with no *ifs*, *ands*, or *buts* in his tone.

"But how can you know for sure?" I twisted my napkin around my finger.

"Because I have seen you in my future for a long time, I just didn't know your face—until yesterday. I only knew your soul."

His words sent a chill down my spine. My breath hitched. For some weird reason, I started to tear up.

"I know you don't believe in fate, my love." He reached for my hand. "But I propose that you've simply forgotten about it. Life does that. I've grown up with the knowledge that there was someone meant for me, and I've had my grandmother guiding me with her wise counsel and her visions. It's far more natural for me to accept. I realize that."

"But why not find a nice spiritual girl who gets all this stuff?" I tried to pull my hand away, but he held tight.

"Because she would not be you," he said, bringing my hand to his mouth for a kiss. "I have never truly been in love, and I don't date a lot. There's been a part of me missing, and I have busied myself with work and travel, but I've been waiting to find you again. When I stepped onto the elevator it was like a part of me was already there."

I patted my heart with my free hand. His words were touching and sweet yet I still thought his meant-to-be concept was out there.

"Wait, did you say find each other again?" *Paging Shirley MacLaine.* Was he going to tell me we had a past life together?

He paused and took a deep breath, and stared down at my hand. He brushed his thumb over my fingertips and knuckles before looking up to speak.

"There is a Chinese legend called the 'String of Fate' that says when two people who are meant to be together are born, the gods tie a red string to their individual ankles." He was animated telling this story, releasing my hand so he could use both of his to illustrate. "They say that this pair can be born anywhere in the world, miles and worlds apart, but the gods know they are meant to be for each other and tie them together."

I playfully pressed out my high-heeled foot for him to see. "I don't see any red string on my ankle."

"That's because the string is invisible," he said, tapping the table as if he were declaring a miracle. "It is a spiritual string. And it is built to stretch and tangle but never break. And when the two children grow, the string gets shorter and shorter, it pulls tighter, and the couple comes closer. One day, they are standing before one another. And—"

"They cut the string?" I couldn't resist cracking a joke.

His eyes brightened with amusement and he laughed. "No, they recognize each other, and they come to know it was their souls that were united, not their ankles, because they are meant to meet on Earth and fall in love."

It had to be one of the most ridiculous stories I'd ever heard. But my heart felt strange and heavy, and tears, again, began to well.

"That's what happened to us, Allison," he said, moving his chair closer and putting his arm around me. He wiped a tear with his thumb. "The string of fate drew us together. Maybe the recognition was not the same for you, but you recognized *something* in me, when I got in that elevator. I know you did because I literally felt a signal coming from you."

I moved a loose strand of hair behind my ear, and it reminded me of the way we met in the elevator. Was that only yesterday? "Well, maybe I just thought you were hot." *And gorgeous.* I tried to keep it light because this fate chat was still too hard for me to grasp. "But I didn't hear the word soul mate or *Ves'tacha*, going off like an alarm in my head."

"I know. Perhaps we have slightly different alarms or recognition systems. Mine went off in my heart and my third eye." He poured us both some more wine and smiled slyly. "Maybe your alarm went off in your panties first."

"Well, I don't even have panties on today," I shot back, sitting up straight in my chair and reaching for my wine glass. "And I don't recall *that* being my idea." I couldn't resist baiting him but my insides were churning with excitement just thinking about his no-panties rule of the day.

"Maybe I sensed you had to be sexually aroused before you could be romantically interested." he winked as he sipped his wine. "Like the princess who could only be awakened by true love's kiss."

"Maybe I just wanted to jump your bones, before I found out you were my client, that is." Every inch of me was ignited again. "And maybe I prefer sex to marriage on the first date."

"Well, maybe I wanted to press you up against the wall and fuck you, too, even though I was more of a gentleman and just kissed you." His eyes drilled into mine as heat rose between us. He looked as if he wanted to devour me whole.

He stood up from the table, and pulled me out of my chair. Next thing I knew I was near the door, and pressed against it. Pulling my chin toward him, he brought his lips to mine. His kiss was delicious. He gave so much when his mouth was on mine, and our tongues danced. The intimacy reignited the passion below. He was about to place his hand on my cheek when I grabbed it. I placed it on my breast, daring him not to touch me. My body tensed and I swallowed loudly as I awaited his next move.

His nostrils flared and his breathing quickened as he let his finger find my nipple, and slowly caressed it, causing it to become quickly erect. I pressed into him, and felt as if I could come from the way he was touching me.

"I could easily fuck you right now," he whispered into my ear, his breath hot on my skin. "I feel it too." He put my hand on his hard cock. I stroked his length, obsessed with the thought of freeing him from the confines of his clothing.

"You could," I panted, opening my legs to the sound of his voice. "And you should."

"All I have to do is open my pants and lift you onto my cock," he said, winded. "You have no panties on. You're wearing a dress. It would be so easy." His breathing was heavy, getting out of control.

"Yes." My body was writhing with need and desire, my hips pressing toward him. "Very easy." I wanted him to do all that and more. I moved my hand over his pants, trying to get a better grasped of him.

"I could give you all of it, all of me, right here and now." He pushed his hand between my legs and jammed two fingers into me. "We are both physically ready. You're so wet and I'm so hard. I could make you come again. And we don't even have to move. I could raise your hips up high against the door and then slowly bring you down onto me. I just have to uncover myself and bury myself deep inside you, fill you. Right here. Against the door."

"So why are you not doing that, like right now." My words came out on a slow pant. "What are you waiting for?"

When he spoke, his voice was hoarse. "Because I want you to love me when I make love to you," he said, pressing his lips against my cheek as he pressed his hips closer to mine. He gyrated into me, my hand still atop his erection. "I don't want this to be just a fuck to satiate your arousal. I don't want you to lose interest and disappear."

Oh, my God. How did he *know* about my pattern of dropping men after sex?

"Okay, okay." I sucked in some air and then rested my head on his shoulder for a moment so I could think. "I once read an interview with a famous sex therapist. She said it is spiritually wrong to cause a man's erection and leave him hard without release. This is right up your alley of weird beliefs. She said that in the Talmud, in the Jewish tradition, it says when that part of the male anatomy is aroused and there's an erection, the brain flies out if the erection has nowhere to go. You don't want to lose your brain, do you?"

I waited for his reaction before taking in air and exhaling.

He had a crazed look, one I had never seen in his typically calm and take charge manner. His breathing was labored, his mouth blowing hot against me. I thought he'd lift me up and spear me. But, instead, he laughed. And so did I. It gave us a moment to regroup.

"Let me make you feel better," I whispered. "Please. Fuck me."

"I can't," he said, pulling his body off of mine. "Not like this. And I didn't mean things to get out of hand. I'm so enamored with you. You're so hard to resist, but I can't lose control with you."

"It's too late," I pleaded, touching his cock from the outside of his pants. "All you have to do is press yourself against my leg and…"

"You're making me break the six day rule," he said, unzipping his pants. "I did not intend for you to feel obligated to touch me back."

"I don't feel obligated," I said, kissing his cheek. I really didn't. "Besides, rules are made to be broken."

"Not this one, but I may end up in the emergency room with an erection lasting more than four hours." He smiled as he opened his pants and let them slide down his hip. I felt his hardness against my thigh. He took my hand and placed it on his naked sex flesh.

Oh, my God. Touching his body was like revealing a secret, or a mystery. I wanted to make that part of him mine for the day.

"Whatever you do…" He pressed his body fully against mine and urged my hand tighter around him. "Don't let me fuck you."

He kissed my lips, my cheeks and neck as I stroked him. His erection was like steel but the skin that encased it was so soft. He felt so good in my hand. I wanted to lie him down on the floor and straddle him. I want to rock into him and ride him. Instead, I followed his wishes to deny my baser instincts. I focused on his pleasure. Something strong within me wanted to make him feel good.

It didn't take long before he was sliding back and forth into my hand, his hips moving fiercely as need grew deeper. His hand tightened around mine as his pace quickened. He moved his mouth to mine and drove his tongue inside, breathing heavily, wildly. With his mouth still on mine, he groaned. The noise got louder, his breathing more erratic, and his pumping harder. And then, he released. His head fell to my shoulder, as if all the breath had left his body along with his semen. I didn't even mind the way his body pinned mine against the door.

My heart opened just a little bit more to see him so vulnerable.

After a moment, he revived, and his hand slid between my legs. I didn't realize how swollen and sensitive that part of my body had become again—until I felt him on me. His palm went to my clitoris as two fingers slid inside me. I pressed myself hard against them, hips rocking like crazy. When a loud groan escaped from me, he pressed his tongue into my mouth and kissed me as I came. It was my turn to slump against him as the release rolled through my belly and thighs.

We were both sweating through our clothes, which were far more rumpled and creased since our earlier business meeting. Given his thing about female fluids, I guess I shouldn't have been surprised when he took the two fingers that had been inside me and rubbed them along the spot on the center of my forehead, between my eyes, putting some of the fluid from *down there*, to *up here*. Or that he then pressed his lips on that spot and licked. For a moment, I felt dizzy, but he swooped me into his arms, and moved us both onto a nearby chair. I sat in his lap and rested my head against his.

"Holy fuck," I said with a long exhale.

"Actually, holy hand job," he said, cracking himself up. He reached over for a napkin and wiped his fluids off my hand. "This was *not* part of my plan for the evening. I'm afraid I've acted rudely. The last thing I wanted was to ejaculate on your leg and hand over dinner," he said, smiling as his shook his head and looked heavenward, "but thank you."

I stood to get into my own chair but he pulled me back, bringing my face close to his.

"I mean it, Allison," he said, kissing my mouth. "I almost lost control. Thank you for not taking advantage of my weakened resolve."

I pulled away slightly to tease him. "Oh, what wicked things I could have done to you."

"I'll hope to have the chance to find out in the not too distant future." He ran his fingers through his hair and straightened his tie. "For now, I'm starving again. I think we need to finish dinner, just to keep our strength up."

We went to the buffet that had been left for us. He added some steak and pasta to his plate. I grabbed a plate of salad and sat back down in my chair. Crisp lettuce and tomatoes never tasted so good. We ate in silence. I loved that we smelled like sweat and sex.

The notion that I didn't even know Nicolai existed until yesterday suddenly seemed quite impossible. I looked at him across the table and felt a comfort, a familiarity. Once he was done eating, he took a sip of wine, and wiped his mouth with his napkin. His eyes held mine.

"Have a dance with me, Ms. Monroe." He stood and offered me a hand. I grasped onto him and rose from my chair.

I hadn't noticed the iPod and speakers set up on a shelf on the wall. He turned it on and "Make You Feel My Love" played. He looked tenderly at me as he pulled me close to him. I rested my head on his chest and listened to the message in the song, which was about one person who believed in love at first sight and another who had not yet made their mind up. He held me in his arms for a while, after the song had ended. I liked the way his body fit against mine and was hesitant to let go.

"I'll take you home now, my love," he said, nuzzling his cheek against mine.

I suddenly dreaded the idea of being parted from him. "I wish you could stay over."

"Soon."

"When is this sixth date?"

"Four more days."

"It's seven hours later in Romania," I said. "Can't we speed things up a little?"

"You're quite adorable when you desire me," he said, kissing my nose. "I think I will keep you this way for a while. Absence makes the heart—and related areas—grow fonder."

When we got into the limo, he didn't bother giving the driver my address. He put the privacy window up. I rested in his arms as we drove to my apartment.

CHAPTER ELEVEN

The walk past the doorman was much as it was last night, and every night, where a smile and a pleasantry are exchanged.

"Hi, Bill, how are you tonight?" I said, making my way to the elevator, Nicolai's hand guiding my lower back.

"Fine, Ms. Monroe, how about yourself?"

"Doing great," I waved. "See ya."

It was earlier than last night, so the elevators were slower, and there were more random neighbors in the lobby. Some sat on the matching gray couches off to the side. A few women were chatting near the large pieces of local art that lined the walls. It occurred to me that no one had ever seen me in the building with a man, especially one that looked like this guy. It also occurred to me that we looked like we had just partaken in sweaty activities. I felt curious eyes upon us.

The moment the elevator came, I was on it, with Nicolai close behind. One of the women jumped on too. "Hi," she said, smiling at me, and then looking over at Nicolai. I didn't know her name. We'd never spoken before so it was awkward. "Nice night out, huh?"

"Yep," I said, anxious to reach my apartment and get back into my cocoon with Nicolai for a few moments before we parted.

"Well, good night," Nicolai said as we reached my floor, in a voice that probably made her panties wet too. "Enjoy your evening." She watched him grab my hand and lead me out of the elevator.

Alone, finally, Nicolai escorted me to my apartment, but this time, when he opened my door he stepped in. Then he closed the door, pressed me against it, and kissed me. I felt his erection through his pants, big and hard again.

"I want you more than you could know." He pressed himself against me, sounding like he was on the edge of control again. "But I can't stay. I must be patient for that which is worth waiting for, and you are worth waiting for."

He lowered his head, planting tiny butterfly kisses across my neck, until he found a soft spot. His mouth came down, warm and inviting, and he began to lick me softly, teasingly. Then he sucked. Hard. Another hickey. And more "arousal" between my legs. I liked the way he made me feel with those bites.

"You *are* a vampire."

"Ah, Ms. Monroe, if that is true, then you surely would not be able to resist me."

"I think we have established I'm unable to resist you."

"Perhaps on a day to day basis," he said, in a whisper. "I am still hoping that you will want to keep me around for good. The jury is still out on that."

With that, he helped me straighten up and kissed me on the forehead.

"My car will be here for you at eight a.m. tomorrow," he said. "Dress casual."

"And just to clarify, is tomorrow with or without underwear?"

"With. But no guarantees they will remain on your body at all times."

"We're not going to your office?"

"No. You're coming to my home."

"I always thought dating was invitation based, like, 'Hey, would you like to come to my place tomorrow?'" I was excited to see where he lived, and I hoped after the three orgasms between us tonight he might decide to lighten up about his ban on intercourse. "Remember, love doesn't mean taking a hostage."

"How insensitive of me!" He laughed and tapped me affectionately on the nose. "Would you like to pretend you're working but actually come to my house for a play date tomorrow?"

"That would be lovely," I said.

He headed for the door and slipped out. "Tomorrow," was the last thing he said.

Slowly, I stripped off my clothes and took a shower. My lady parts were still on high alert. In fact, my whole body ached—*ached!*—with desire. I had two orgasms tonight. How could that be?

I fell into bed and thought of Nicolai—and this situation that was developing between us. Left to my own devices, I would have gone for the sex and figured the relationship out later. Well, more likely, I would have gone for the sex and then ditched him. But it felt like the roles had reversed—in his approach he was reeling me in with the promise of sex to come if only I give him love. Maybe it was working because I was starting to feel a deepening connection to him. Maybe if we had fallen into bed the first night we wouldn't have had the compelling dialogue of the past two days. I mean, who had conversations like that?

With him out of my sight, I once again worried that sneaking around work in cars, restaurants, and his house would come back and bite me in the butt. He was still my client. I could lose my job.

Finally, I drifted off and my dreams began. Nicolai was there in vivid color. In my dream, he was a Regency era hero, like Mr. Darcy. He reached his hand out to me, helped me out of the bed in the middle of the night, and asked if I trusted his sincerity. He slowly stripped me out of my nightshirt. He kneeled on the floor in front of me and kissed my belly, my thighs, and then he pressed the side of his head against the flat of my stomach and cried. I held him there, tenderly. "I ache for you, too," he said. "I understand your fear and know I can help you heal."

In the dream, he gently laid me down on the bed and brought his naked body over mine. He was hard, and I was ready. He worked himself between my legs, his cock poised close to my center.

"Yield to me," he said, using his arms to hold himself over me. "I will be loving and gentle with your emotions."

"I trust you," I heard myself say.

He was about to have his way with me, but he paused. "I want to take you right now," he said. "But protocol says I must keep you in a state of desire for six days. The erotic force must turn to love. May I have your permission to take charge?"

"Yes," I heard myself say again. "After tonight, I know you are sincere."

With that, he slid himself inside and possessed me. I saw my life flash before me with his first thrust. But it wasn't just my actual life, it was images from the past, and the future, as if I had discovered a new cable channel in my mind.

The dream seemed so real. I thought he was beside me, or inside me.

CHAPTER TWELVE
THURSDAY: DAY THREE/ DATE THREE

When the alarm went off in the morning, my hips were gyrating into the air. And I was totally looking forward to date three.

I spent extra time in the shower, letting the water caress my breasts, washing between my legs with extra care. Everything was on fire. The desire was still fresh.

When I went out to the car, I found Nicolai's driver with coffee in hand. He passed it to me after he helped me inside. I finally noticed he had an ID badge clipped to his suit jacket that read: Sam.

"I will be taking you to a designated location to see Mr. Petre."

"Good morning, Sam," I said, thanking him for the coffee. "I thought we were going to his house. "

"Indeed, we are." He was not much of a talker.

"Where exactly is it?"

He didn't respond. I felt like I was in a political suspense thriller, being taken to an undisclosed location. Maybe it was a bunker in the countryside.

We drove over a body of water and a bridge I didn't quite recognize and into Westchester, passing beautiful, mansion-like abodes. We pulled up to a magnificent, one-level, contemporary wood home with large glass windows. It looked airy and fresh inside. The front lawn was beautifully landscaped and there appeared to be a large property out back.

"*This* is his residence?" I asked. I was expecting a showy mansion or an elegant old house, not something that looked like the vampire house in the *Twilight* movie.

"One of them," said Sam. "The door is open. He says to go in."

I grabbed my purse and headed in, leaving my laptop on the back seat. I wasn't quite sure how much actual work I would get done today but figured I could come out and get it if needed. The vestibule had two small statues of goddess-like women on either side, poised like guardians at the entryway. Inside, the ceilings were high and the walls were bright, with two large scale pieces of art on either side. One looked like a Peter Max, with a red and pink heart entwined. The other was a contemporary painting of a classic statue of Cupid and Psyche. The place was super clean and clutter-free.

Nicolai came toward me from another room. Instead of kissing my hand, his mouth came down on mine in a delicious morning greeting. Then he wrapped his arms around me.

"Did you miss me?" he asked, pulling me in and pressing my head under his chin affectionately.

"I did." His kiss had reawakened all my sexually aching places.

"Did you dream of me?" He looked excited, like a kid about to get a new toy, as he waited for my answer.

"Yes."

"Did we make love in your dream?"

"We did." Recollection flooded back between my legs. "You said you understood my fears and could heal me."

He smiled and caressed my cheek with the back of one hand. I was growing quite fond of his touch. I was growing quite fond of *him*. How could he seem *so* familiar? I'd known him for less than seventy-two hours.

"I'm glad you got the memo," he said with a smile.

"Memo?" Was he trying to intentionally get into my head while I slept? Jeez, as much as I was enjoying my dreams, that was a bit creepy.

"Dreams are a source of information," he pointed out. "Intuitives believe dreams are like memos from the subconscious, or even from those who are close enough to reach you in a dream state. Are your dreams showing you I'm here to cherish you?"

His comment caught me off guard. I expected him to ask if my dreams were showing me how good the sex will be—not if I knew he would cherish me. Tears came to my eyes. I felt silly getting so sentimental but some of the things he said were starting to sound so romantic and sweet, even if they were undeniably weird.

He kissed the tears on my cheeks and gently licked his lips. "I can hold your tears, too, not just your pleasure. I can hold all that you are and all that you feel."

No man had ever offered me both sex and love in one package—well, I never gave anyone a chance too, anyway. I still couldn't completely believe he could, or would, or that this was real and not some strange misadventure. But my heart began to hope.

"It will take some time to trust, my love," he said. Sometimes I thought he could read my mind. He took my hand and led me to the breakfast nook. It was off to the side of the dining room and a kitchen that looked more lived in than the main room. There was a beautiful mural of a mountain range with green forests painted onto tiles against the one solid wall in the room. There was also a small breakfast table. The counters were marble, and there was a work island in the center with a matching top. The aroma of coffee and sweet food filled the air.

"What a striking image." I admired the wall from where I stood.

"That's my homeland," he said. "Beautiful, right?"

"Wow. It's so green." I expected it to be dark and dreary like a classic vampire movie.

"When you step onto the land there it is like heaven. I hope I can show you some day."

It never dawned on me that there would really be a trip to Transylvania in the cards. The idea of visiting a foreign land where I couldn't hop in a cab home was unsettling. Knowing he may have a life there I knew nothing about was suddenly disturbing.

Once we reached the table, he poured me a cup of coffee and one for himself and set them on the table with creamer, coconut milk, and condiments.

For some reason, it triggered anger in me. "Wait, how did you know I use coconut milk in everything?"

He took a seat. Then he sipped his black coffee and looked at me over the rim of the cup. "It's one of those things I know."

Anger rose up in my chest and emptied out of my mouth in words that sounded like accusations. "Oh, it's in my employee file, right? On Google? Or your grandmother told you." Suddenly I was back in that first night, feeling studied and stalked.

"It's just coconut milk, Allison." He stroked his chin, and gazed at me. "You're angry at me for making sure your needs are met?"

"It's not the coconut milk." I spoke a little louder than I meant to. "Thank you, for the coconut milk." I sat down across from him with folded arms. "It's that you seem to know *a lot* about me, and I know so little about you."

He hesitated and considered my words before continuing.

"Okay. What would you like to know?" He sat forward in his chair and pressed his fingertips together in front of him and brought them under his chin.

"Well, you're rich and handsome, so why do you have problems getting women?" I poured coconut milk into my coffee and stirred aggressively.

"I don't have problems getting women," he said, now interlacing his fingers. "I am having problems getting one woman. You."

"What about past relationships? Did you know everything about the other women you've pursued before you met them, too?" I bit my lip.

"No," he said, unlocking his fingers and placing his hands on the table. "I used them for sex and went about my life, not letting anyone in. I didn't know much about them at all. I guess you could say I was bit of a—"

"Manwhore?" I took a sip of coffee. It tasted so good, but I was not about to tell him.

"I was about to say bon vivant," he laughed and leaned in toward me. "But okay, manwhore."

"No girlfriends or wives?" I found it hard to believe there was no relationship baggage.

"I've never had a real relationship," he said. "Not one that mattered."

I didn't expect that. I was sure there would be a broken engagement in there, someone who got away and who he had to replace to appease his grandmother.

"So how can you be so sure ... about us?"

"I'm not sure I can make you understand that this is something *I know*, in my heart, until you feel it in yours." I was tensely gripping my coffee cup, but he reached over and tried to take hold of my hand. "I focused on building my business and on not opening my heart. My parents and grandparents had strong marriages and they told me there was someone special for me too. I took that to be true."

"It's hard to believe no one tried to scoop you up before now." I let him hold my hand but still felt annoyed.

"Hey, I am promising you everything—my heart, soul, riches—and you don't want to be scooped up," he said with a smile, his thumb rubbing across the wedding ring finger of my left hand. "Why is it so shocking that I once favored sex over love?"

"You said you needed me to love you before you would have sex with me," I said. "So, I thought—"

"You thought I was a virgin?" He laughed and stood up, and made his way to my side of the table.

I had to laugh too. "Not exactly."

"Look, my urgency is motivated by my grandmother and her vision, but it's the right time." He pulled me to my feet. "I started to feel very lonely because, in my heart, I believed I was meant for someone. But I never met anyone who was sincere—and who I felt an instant love connection to—until you."

He pulled me into his arms and my body yielded to his.

"Can you forgive the coconut milk?" He gazed deeply into my eyes. "Consider it a rookie mistake. We're on a crash course of discovering more about each other. "

"Okay." Though his insta-love theory was still a foreign concept, suddenly he seemed to speak a hook-up language I was familiar with: relationship-free sex. For most of my life I'd been focused on my career and typically relieved some tension via sex without love. Then I would move on. Quickly.

"What about you?" he said. "What makes you so afraid of love?"

"Haven't you researched me?" He claimed to know so many things about our future together, wouldn't he also know about my past?

"I can't research what's in your heart." He sighed and ran a hand through my hair. "Even in relationships that are meant to be, couples have to do the work of getting to know each other, figuring out how to make each other happy."

"What about happily ever after?" I didn't believe in it, but he did.

"Fate is the opportunity to create a happily ever after, but it's not a guarantee." His eyes sparkled in the sun shining through the large glass window, and there was warmth in his words. "We have to create it, together."

"Well, I hope you enjoy disappointment." I pulled myself out of his embrace, folded my arms over my chest, and stared out the window at the trees along the side of the house. I noticed two red robins nipping at the feed in the birdhouse, and each other. "I have no clue how to create a happy ending, let alone an actual relationship."

"Ah, well, the universe does have a sense of humor," he said, inching back into my personal space. "Maybe that's why you and I are perfect for each other, because we are meant to discover that together." He moved closer. "I really would love to know *your* story."

"I've been hurt by love and loss." I pulled out my chair and took a seat. "Haven't we all?"

"Talking about it is a way to free yourself to move on," he urged, taking the seat alongside me. "I won't bite."

"Really?" My hand went to the hickey on my neck as I shot him a look. "It's very simple. My father left when I was very young. I was raised by my single mom and beloved grandmother. I grew up abandoned by my father, believing if he didn't want me, then no man would. It's text book family trauma, actually."

"I'm so sorry, my love," he whispered. "It pains me to think of anyone causing you distress and heartache."

"You're the first person to care about that," I said. My chest tightened. I could feel the tears rising from deep within and about to reach my eyes again. For some reason, my secret truth about being a loser at love was flowing out of my mouth. "I've had a string of short romances, never lasting more than a few days. I've never wanted to risk falling in love or giving a piece of myself to anyone. So I focused on building my career."

"I understand." I hated that he was feeling sympathy for me—I didn't want anyone's pity—but when he placed a comforting arm around my shoulder I couldn't help but appreciate his touch.

"The thing is," I said, tears streaming down, "when my mother died, my dad *did* show up for me. He took me to live with him. It gave me a chance to get to know him. My grandmother was in assisted living at the time so I couldn't stay with her. He literally got me from my mom's house and moved me into his guest room. And when my grandma died, he said he would take care of me forever."

"Your dad ultimately showed you he cared?" Nicolai's face was filled with compassion as he held out a napkin to me.

"Finally, he did." I took the napkin and blew my nose. "I went to college for public relations and media, and got my first job on my own. After a layoff, my father gave me a job at Berke and Monroe, as an assistant. He showed me the business, how to be good at it. He made me work hard and earn my paycheck, and did not give me special treatment as an employee. He told me it was because he was grooming me to take over when he retired."

"But he never got to do that?" Nicolai asked softly.

"No," I began to sob in earnest. "He got sick. It was so sudden. His partner, Dan Berke, was involved with Sheila when Dad was most vulnerable. Berke brought her into the company. He said her TV news credentials would help the firm. Then my dad died, so quickly, and—" I was totally ugly crying.

Nicolai put his arm on mine and let me get it all out.

"There was no will, no last wishes, and no paperwork leaving his part of the company to me," I said, remembering those horrible days of finding my dad was gone and that there was nothing in place to allow me to have security at his company. "Berke did not want to be bothered running things, so he left Sheila in charge. She barely tolerated me when my father was alive. Now she hates me and wants me out of her way. I have no idea how she gained so much power in the company, but she can fire me, and she is able to curb my advancement."

My body shook as emotions burst forth from within.

The tears just kept coming, but he did not turn away. He listened patiently and didn't try to add in any uncalled-for words or advice. He let me take my time.

"I've been trying to somehow prove myself to Berke and show him I'm not just daddy's little girl," I said, starting to feel a burden had lifted. "I stay at the company for my father, because it was a part of him and I need to keep a part of him near me."

"Thank you for sharing so honestly." He was soft-spoken and almost reflective. "Obviously, I knew there was an issue, but didn't realize how deeply rooted or how painful it is for you. You see, we needed this day out of the office to share about our lives."

We were sharing about our lives and not hiding our imperfections. I'd hidden my secrets for a long time. It felt liberating to speak them out loud. In that moment, I decided to do something crazy and share something that caused me great shame.

"There's one more thing, while we're being forthcoming." I stood and walked toward the window. Looking out at nature was a little easier than being eyeball-to-eyeball with him, but I was determined to get it out of my system. "I pretty much lose interest in men once I have sex. I'm like one of those spiders that mates and then wraps the male in her web and discards him—men become dead to me, I never take their calls and never see them again. In fact, now that I think of it, I've never lasted longer than five days with a guy."

I sucked in a deep breath and blew it out with a sigh as I turned to face him. If anything could prove to us both that I was a lost cause, it was that statement. However, he did not seem to consider my scary truth as an impediment. In fact, he looked as if a light bulb went off in his head.

He lifted up from the table and bolted to my side.

"Perhaps now I understand why I've been given a deadline of six days to work with," he said, taking his chin in hand the way he does when he is contemplating something. "It's not a deadline, it's a lifeline. We have to get past this pattern long enough for me to win your heart."

Apparently, he saw this as a challenge to be met and mastered.

"How can you be so sure you can get into my heart anyway, Nicolai?" I shook my head thinking about how impossible it seemed. "It's damaged."

"Because, my beautiful one," he said. "The spider story happens in some species of black widow spiders, but it is mostly a myth. And myths we have about ourselves can become self-fulfilling prophecies. Or, we can choose a new prophecy. *That* is what is on the table."

Warmth washed over me as we stood in silence for a moment. Then he took my hand and walked me back to the breakfast nook and pulled me into his lap.

Suddenly, it smelled so good. I hadn't noticed before that he'd prepared a spread of yogurt, fruits, honey, juice, and some interesting looking eggs.

"Let me feed you." He smoothed a hand over my hair, to get it off my face. "In my culture, feeding someone is the way you show love and nurturing."

"I'm not really that hungry." Everything looked yummy but I was still digesting our heavy conversation. "And you feeding me—it's weird. Yesterday we used our own forks."

"Today is something new, and you need sustenance," he said. "And I want to hold you close if that's all right. Besides, I think you might like the breakfast I have in mind. It will help you feel better."

I nodded and settled into his lap as he pulled over the breakfast tray.

"There is a Romanian dish called *oua umplute*, which is called here, deviled eggs. I always loved them as a child. My grandmother used to make them. They are, sadly, loaded with cholesterol as they're made with sour cream. But they're tasty. I made some for you today."

"That was sweet, thank you." I smiled, but my mind kept going back to our conversation. *Did I actually admit that I fuck men and pretend they don't exist? Jeez.* And did he pretty much tell me he has done the same with women? This was not a typical third date conversation.

"This will give you the energy you need," he said, lifting the fancy looking deviled egg to my lips. It was delicious and rich. I took a few bites. Then he offered me a spoonful of yogurt with honey. Next, he gave me a strawberry dipped in honey. I opened wide as he slid it in and sensually moved it around on my tongue until I took a bite. And then another. He brought homemade apple juice to my lips and let me take a sip. And after that, he kissed me, his tongue swirling around the lingering taste of sweetness.

"Thank you for breakfast," I said, feeling full from just the small bites. "That was tasty, and very interesting. If you're expecting me to feed you too, I should tell you upfront I know nothing about food preparation. In fact, there is a sign in my kitchen that says, I kiss better than I cook."

"Well, I somehow knew that." He paused, as if thinking twice before stating something *he knows* about me. "I know how good your kisses taste, and I understand you're a working woman who does not have time. But there is a way you can nurture me without food or cooking," he said, helping me out of my chair. "You can feed me with your body. That is, if you want to."

I nodded. I was ready to shake off the intensity of our revealing chat about personal relationship history.

"We can change the mood quickly," he said, setting me on my feet. "Lift your arms up."

In a flash, he had my shirt off. Before I knew it, my bra was off too. This was the first time he'd seen that part of me fully exposed. His gaze moved unapologetically up and down my body, and landed on my nipples. They hardened in response. The deep arousal between my legs reawakened.

"Take off your pants."

"My pants too?" This was becoming more fun. After the heavy talk we shared, I felt closer to him. And I liked that that we were moving in this direction.

"Yes, your pants. Maybe you need some help?"

With a hungry look in his eyes, he unbuttoned the top of my slacks and slid them over my ass and underwear with two hands. His palms brushed my flesh as he sensually moved the material down to my feet and helped me step out of them. "You are so beautiful," he said, standing to touch my face. "The most beautiful woman I have ever seen."

I've never been great at accepting complements. They embarrass me. But his words and the sound of his voice made me smile—and caused desire to rush back in. My body begged for his touch, again. He spread out a plush towel and a soft pillow for my head, and then lifted me up onto the huge Carrera marble counter that separated the breakfast nook from the kitchen.

He lifted the yogurt in a bowl and mixed it up. Then he spooned some out and ever-so-gently he spread the cool yogurt around on my areola. My nipple was throbbing. He did the same to the other breast. Pleasure spread to my lower half and my hips gyrated in the air. He pulled away to survey my writhing body and then closed his eyes as if he were saying a prayer. His lips came down on my right breast. He pulled the nipple into his mouth with gentle force. His warm tongue felt so delicious I thought I could come from the sensations. I squirmed with pleasure.

He walked around to the other nipple, which was still covered in yogurt, and hovered above, gently blowing. Just when I could not take another moment of teasing, his mouth opened onto me, tongue swirling, and sucking me deeply. I never knew breasts could be so sensitive, or that a nipple could be savored in that way. His ministrations made my lower parts swell. I longed to feel his tongue there too.

Suddenly, his mouth was gone from me, and he was standing at the front of the counter by my feet, looking me over. I could hear his breathing getting hot and heavy like mine.

He took my right foot in his hand and raised it to his mouth and kissed it. The look on his face was primal and wild as he pulled my toes into his mouth. He kept his eyes on mine as he sucked them. His gaze was still on me as he ran his tongue along the arch, and licked my heel. He took hold of my other foot and did the same. I could see his hardness springing from his pants as his mouth returned to the top of my foot and he slid his tongue between my toes. I never knew my foot was an erogenous zone, but apparently it was—for us both.

Soft groans rolled out of me on each breathy pant. I felt like a cat in heat.

"Allison," he said, eyes glazed with desire. "Open your legs for me, baby."

I opened. And I fantasized that my female parts were like a magnet, capable of drawing him to me and sucking him inside of me. I wanted him that bad.

He slid his finger up my leg to my inner thigh. He touched my panties.

"These are soaked through," he said, awe and desire on his face. He seemed to be in a bit of a sex stupor.

"I know." I wanted to wrap my legs around his neck and tug him on to me.

"I am going to touch your arousal. Just to feel it. That's all." He closed his eye for a moment as if to get a grip on his own desire.

"Okay," I said, although I wanted to plead with him to make me come.

"Last night, I almost lost it," he said moving his finger to the sensitive flesh where the elastic from my panties rested. "I came so close to fucking you. Too close." He slid under the material and found his way between my lips. This time he touched my clit and hovered over it for a moment.

"That feels so good." The words slipped out as a loud groan.

"Oh my, Ms. Monroe," he said playfully. "Your arousal has made your clitoris very swollen. It must be *very* sensitive."

"It is," I said, panting. I lifted myself up on my elbows, watching his every move. I wanted him to lose his pants and find me with his penis.

His finger moved over my clit. That part of my body had grown fond of his touch. I could only imagine how good it would be if he stayed there and massaged it ever so gently. Now that I knew what his touch could do to me, I craved it even more. I wanted to press into him, but he quickly moved his finger through my folds, reaching my opening. He looked into my eyes as he did this. I bit my lip again, wondering how deep he would go this time.

He slipped his finger in an inch. And then a little more, and stopped. His breath was labored and I could literally see sweat on his brow.

"Oh God, I have to press into you." His control was cracking. But he paused and took a deep breath. "Stay still for a minute."

"Please, Nicolai. *Please.*" I wanted him to plunge into me as if he were making a porn movie. I needed to feel him, deep. My hips began to gyrate as if by their own accord.

He pushed his other hand on my hip to hold me down, but I couldn't help the clenching of my muscles below. It would be so easy for him to make me come.

"Your arousal is beautiful," he said, going deeper. "I can feel how much you want me. I can imagine what it might feel like when you squeeze your muscles around my cock."

I couldn't help it. I forced myself down onto his finger to try to suck him in deeper with my grip. He quickly slid it out of me and brought it to his mouth.

"So delicious," he said, keeping his gaze on mine.

I was so close to the edge. Too aroused. He walked to the side of the counter to help me up. He couldn't even get his hips flush against it because of his jutting erection. I wanted to reach down and free him, and take him out of the confines of his pants as I did last night. What can two people do after such an intimate experience, other than fuck their brains out? I hoped that's where this was leading, but he took control of the moment and broke the sex spell with an announcement, "We're going for a swim."

Was he fucking kidding? "I don't have a suit."

"I know." He winked and helped me off the counter. Then he paused, leaning his back against the cool marble. He closed his eyes again, and tried to calm his breathing.

I reached out and touched his cock. I couldn't help myself. I moved my hand from the base to the tip, and rubbed it through his pants. And, for a moment, he let me. Then he opened his eyes and pulled my body against his. "No matter what, promise you won't try to will *this* inside you," he said, grabbing my hips and pulling me closer to his erection.

"We're here, and you're hard, and I am going to jump out of my skin with hunger for you," I whispered it into his ear. "Why get this turned on just to turn it off?"

"There's a reason we have to wait, and you know it too." He took a deep breath, stood up straight, and, with his knee, gently backed my hips a few inches away from his cock. "I know now that if I lose control I will blow this whole thing with you. I cannot lose control."

Taking my hand and leading me from the kitchen, he swung open the back doors to a gorgeous pool. It was an enclosed and private area, complete with lush foliage, a slide, a built-in bar, and a waterfall. It also had a small grotto area. The pool was like something you'd find on a tropical island resort or on a show about the rich and famous. I expected there to be a floating bed in the middle.

"Keep your underwear on," he said.

I enjoyed the show as he stripped out of his shirt and pants down to a pair of skintight navy boxer-brief swimwear with an orange trim. The drawstring fell from the waist and was set right against the spectacular V of his abs. They hugged his muscular legs and ass. His still-hard cock was pressing against the thin nylon material. Oh. My. God.

The night before I'd touched him in the dimly lit restaurant. This was the first time I had ever seen the outline so clearly, and I couldn't take my eyes off it. If it was ultimately meant to be mine, why was he making it so difficult for me to claim it? Arousal and orgasms without penetration were beginning to get to me. Maybe it was getting to him too? He looked at me with those intense blue eyes and let me see his desire. I wondered if I could somehow make his cock slip inside of me in the pool, even accidentally.

He must have read my dirty mind. "We're going to swim and enjoy the pool together. That's all."

"Why don't we have orgasms today, like we did yesterday?" I pouted. "That was fun."

"Because I almost went too far with you." I took a look at his muscular form, and his physical beauty, and his massive hard-on, and considered the irony of my predicament: we were nearly naked and obviously filled with desire but we couldn't have sex.

"It's never *too far* when you are consenting adults." I moved closer, pressing myself against his hardness.

"You are always so adorable when you are arguing your case for me slipping my penis inside you." He reached his hand out to touch my cheek and kissed me. "Let's get into the pool, shall we?"

He dove in from the deeper end and I waded in from the steps in the shallow part. The pool was warm and the water smelled good, not at all like chlorine and chemicals.

He swam over to me and lifted me in his arms, his cock inches below my lady parts. The sky had gotten a little grayish, but it was warm. The sun was poking through the clouds. I wanted his penis to poke through his trunks and into me.

"Is it wrong that I desire your cock?" I asked it point blank. "And that I am hoping you will have pool sex with me?"

"On the contrary, I am happy this is the case," he said, grabbing my hips and pulling me up a little higher. "Desire is helping us develop mutual affection. I mean, do you feel some affection for me now, whereas you thought I was crazy two and a half days ago?"

"Well, since you put it that way, yes." He had a point. When I first saw him, it was more like blind animal attraction. Now it was conscious, although still animal attraction. But I also liked his personality more than I did that first night. He had a softer side, and he was a good listener when he wasn't bossing me around or charming the pants off me.

"This affection is real, my love. And it is moving us where we need to go."

"Okay, but—"

I was about to argue for insertion, but he winked that sexy wink and took off to do fifteen full laps across the length of his rather long pool. I guess that is how he was going to deal with his concerns about losing control—swim it off. Meanwhile, I stood there watching his perfect form move gracefully and powerfully through the water, and fantasized about pulling his bathing suit off of him. I'd never seen anyone so well-sculpted. If he had the discipline to create a body like that, I guess he had the discipline not to have sex with me simply because his penis was hard.

He came back to me soon enough and seemed a little more relaxed in the lower regions. Well, at least he didn't have that look of crazy desire in his eyes. And I had cooled off a little too. I was touched to think he'd left my side to swim for twenty minutes and I missed him. He took me in his arms, lifted me, and encouraged me to wrap my legs around him, which surprised me as it meant I would be that much closer to his forbidden parts. But I was willing to be close to him in any way I could.

He was taller than me, and my frame was on the petite side, so it was easy for him to lift me and let me wrap my legs around him. That way he could take us to the deeper end; otherwise, the water would be over my head had I been standing on my own. He walked around the heated pool with me and gave me a tour of the lush environment. This was the first time we had true bare chest on chest contact. The feel of our exposed flesh pressed together, and warm water rushing around my lower parts, was delicious.

He moved us in to the romantic grotto area, which was like a cave with built in seats of stone against the walls. I could hear a waterfall just around the bend. This pool went on forever.

Nicolai leaned himself against the wall and held me tight. I relaxed into him and rested my cheek against his. We held that position for a long time. His heart was beating against mine and our breathing was in sync. That, and the sound of the waterfall, lulled me into a peaceful meditation of sorts. I focused on my breath, and the sensation of our beating hearts. I began to feel very calm and connected to him. Maybe we were both throbbing from arousal, but it seemed we were sharing the same pulse and heartbeat.

"It feels good, doesn't it, to be held in the safety of my arms?" He whispered in my ear.

"Yes, but—"

"But it scares you. I know. It's hard for you to believe this is real. And I admit, before I laid eyes on you, there were times when it was hard for me to believe. But here we are."

"I'm still not sure exactly what *this* is, but we have *something* between us. I feel it. And it's not just your throbbing manhood." I laughed and kissed his cheek.

"As uncomfortable as it is to feel turned on around the clock, it is a lot more comfortable than feeling like you might be falling in love. Am I right?" He took my chin in hand and looked at me warmly while still holding me against him with one strong arm.

The waterfall around the bend sounded louder, or maybe it was my heart beating and pulse racing.

"Yes, that is true." I abandoned the idea of ever falling in love when I was young. Maybe he was smart enough to know pressing me in that direction would make me run the opposite way, unless he held my erotic interest. "But it works both ways, right? Maybe sex is your second language, too."

"Touché." He lowered his hand from my face and wrapped both arms tighter around me. Water splashed around us as our bodies slapped together. "Has my strategy been bad? To keep you on edge, filled with desire, and intrigued enough to keep coming back? I sensed it may help you to feel safer and maybe allow you to develop feelings for me in the course of—"

"—Wanting to fuck your brains out?" I blushed a little as I looked into his eyes. "Hmmm, you seem to think you know me pretty well." But it was true.

"Let me ask you this: if I dropped you off home today and said I will leave you alone from now on, what would you say?"

"I would say, 'Like hell you will.' " The idea of *not* being with him was upsetting to me.

He smiled. "Well, at least you've come this far in your affections for me. That's progress. At least you're not tossing my coat back at me and telling me the conversation between us is over."

"Wow, that happened, didn't it?" It seemed so long ago that we were on that terrace. I felt differently now and was invested in seeing how things might turn out.

"It feels like a long time ago, no?" He kissed the spot on my forehead between my eyes and lingered there an extra moment. "I hope things are making more sense. Or at least that you are less mad at me."

"Things do seem a little clearer today." I sighed. "Do you realize we're having the longest, ongoing relationship talk ever for two people who barely know each other?"

"There's much to discuss in any relationship, no?" He laughed and kissed the top of my head. "Ours is just condensed, more like boot camp." It touched me that he thought I was worth so much time and energy.

"You were so smug and arrogant when we met." The words rolled out of my mouth. "Now you seem … nice."

"Oh, I don't want to be *too* nice," he said. "I'm sure you would have no use for a puppy dog."

He was right. I loved that he was an alpha dog, herding our romantic connection along. Left to my own devices, I would have never gotten this far with him. If not for his leader of the pack-type personality, I may have missed getting to know him. I certainly would have never gotten to experience how powerfully I could crave another person. Or how impossibly turned on I could become.

"Whatever this is between us," I said with a sigh, "I remain a quivering mess of sensitive nerve endings."

He pulled me tighter into his embrace, and he pressed his hardness against my leg. "Trust me, you are not alone in that."

I tried to slide down to rest myself against him. He let me get halfway there. Then he quickly separated us.

"Okay, that's enough for date three. I am taking you home."

"I now officially hate hearing those words," I complained, shocking myself with a mini-diatribe on arousal without insertion. "What you mean is, 'I am taking you home and not sleeping with you, once again. I am taking you home wet and wanton, so you can have dreams of me fucking you in the night.' "

That crazed look was in his eyes again. Instead of moving away from me, he pulled me close and kissed me. His mouth opened wide on mine and his tongue went deep. He was thrusting into me, possessing me with his mouth. I had to catch my breath when it was over.

"I've never wanted anyone the way I want you," he said, moving his hands to take hold of my upper arms. "It's torture for me, too. Don't think I haven't had to jerk off for three days, even after you did it for me last night. I want to be inside you so bad, I just ... oh, fuck it."

I was stunned when he quickly detached me from his waist and rolled my underwear off my hips and let them float away. Then he lifted me up against the stone bench in the grotto. Gazing intently into my eyes, he slipped his finger inside me. I moaned.

"Still so fucking wet," he breathed. "You're so endlessly wet and ready. Why am I waiting? You want me to fuck you, right?"

"Yes." I leaned back on the stone, pressing my legs apart.

"Well, I'm losing control," he said. "I'm going to have to give you what you want. If I take you right here, will you promise to be mine, again, for tomorrow? Do you promise you'll still want me?"

A wave of panic rose from within as I thought of my normal reaction to good sex—to lose interest, immediately, and never see the person again.

"No." I pressed my hand to his chest and pushed him away. "Don't do it."

I lifted off the ledge and swam away. He came after me, and with his long legs and arms, caught me almost instantly. We stood in the shallower end of the pool. The water was up to my shoulders and up to his chest.

"What are you saying?" he asked, running his fingers through his wet hair. His gaze probed mine.

"If we have sex, I'll lose interest," I admitted, lowering my head. "And I ... I'm not ready for this to be over. I don't want to ... lose you." There, I'd said it.

He leaned in and held my forearms so that I couldn't drift away. His eyes were still deeply connected to mine. "All right, then," he finally said, gently letting me go. "Let's cool down and dry off."

I grabbed my floating panties and took them as we departed from the pool. I rested them on a patio chair to dry.

As soon as the cool air hit, I realized we had been out there a long time. He wrapped me in a warm, fluffy towel and held me close, tucking my head under his chin in an affectionate embrace. I felt cared for. When he took a moment to dry himself off, I started shivering in the cooler late afternoon air. He grabbed a remote control and pushed a button that lit a nearby outdoor fire pit to warm us up. He pressed another button that turned on music that played from an outdoor sound system.

"Have a dance with me, Ms. Monroe." The night we met I told him I thought relationships should include dancing. It dawned on me that we'd danced every day since then. I guess he did pay attention. Perhaps his attentiveness was not all about control. Maybe he wanted me to be happy?

Keeping the towel around me, he pulled me to him, pressing my naked breasts against his chest. The song was a mellow version of Chaka Kahn's, "Through the Fire." It was a tune about wanting someone and being ready to go for it.

We weren't dancing as much as we were pressed together, seeking more contact. He held my body so close to his. When the song came to an end, we were both still holding on. Tightly.

CHAPTER THIRTEEN

My body was glued to his and I didn't want it to end. He was right. I loved being in the safety of his arms. Moving around to music together was an act of intimacy. No man had danced with me this way. He held me like he meant it.

"So, date four, tomorrow," he said, rousing us both from our dance trance.

"How do you know I am free on a Friday night?" I looked up and smiled, playing it a tiny bit coy.

"I suspect you will consider making yourself available," he said, mock smugness in his tone. "Because you seem to like to be with me now."

"Is that so?" I could not say "no," but I liked being playful, especially after our heavy-duty conversations today. "Self-assured, much?"

"More than ever." He moved a wet strand of hair behind my ear. "And I hope you know how much I like to be with you."

"How much, exactly?" I raised my eyebrows, pretending to be making a joke, but I wanted to hear that he liked me too.

"I love being with you," he said, running his hands through my still-wet hair. "I can't focus on anything but you, us. I just need to do whatever it takes to keep you in my life." He pressed his forehead against mine.

I didn't expect to hear *that*.

"Well, I happen to be available." I no longer felt like playing hard to get.

"Then I consider myself very fortunate." He took my face in his hands and gazed into my eyes, and then he took over my mouth with his. It was like a romantic, lips-only movie kiss. He left me breathless. "Let's head out."

As we went in to change, I picked up my damp panties along the way. In the kitchen I slipped my slacks off the back of a chair and slid them on, commando. He watched every move before he went into another room to get out of his bottoms, denying me a peek. It was his turn to be coy.

I towel-dried my hair. Then I tried to shove my undies in my purse, but he walked back into the room and took them. He placed them on the kitchen counter. "I'll have them washed for you," he said, clearly not intending to send them home with me. He wore jeans and a bamboo green button-up shirt that hugged his body. *So hot.*

"Souvenir?" I smiled. Two days ago I may have argued, but now I liked the idea of my panties remaining close to him, even if I was in a different location.

"It will help me remember you were here … in case you decide not to sign up for another day with me." He pouted. "Unless, that is, *you do* want to give it another go." He lifted his wallet and keys from a ceramic tray on the kitchen table and slid them into his back pocket and looked over at me, hopeful. "So, date four?"

"Yes, I'd like that." I felt a little sad to leave his home. It had been a safe oasis for us, the first time we were not in public or the back of his limo. The pressures of work had been removed for the day and I felt closer to him.

"I'm still keeping your panties." He grinned and we walked out of the door. I always loved the way he gently held my lower back when we walked together, and that he let me walk through doors before him.

As for the panties, I didn't mind at all.

Heading back home, in the limo, I rested my head on his shoulder for a while, exhausted. Sam had picked up lunch and left it for us in the back seat—chicken and turkey wraps and salad, with water and ice tea. After some rest, we ate quietly, both of us famished. Sitting in the car next to

Nicolai was comfortable today. This was the first time there hadn't been humping or oral sex or arguing about destiny. I was at ease.

Until my mind started twirling with thoughts of the real world, namely, my job.

"We got no work done today, at all," I pointed out, sitting up straight and grabbing my computer. "My laptop never left the limo. I didn't even check e-mails!"

"We took a day off," he said, watching me open the computer and try to log on to my work e-mail address. "You can catch up on the ride home. I work from here all the time." He leaned in closer, swiveled my computer toward him, and typed in his user name and password. Within moments I was hooked me up to the Wi-Fi in the limo.

There were a number of follow-up messages related to our launch party, as well as more inquiries from reviewers. I quickly responded to them all, and forwarded an important one to Aisha with a request for her to messenger the product to a TV producer who'd requested it.

"Wow, *The Today Show* wants to do something on our e-reader," I said, my heart leaping out of my chest a bit from the excitement. "Next week."

"That is amazing, Allison." He pulled out his phone to look at some of his own messages, to let me tend to the business at hand. "Congratulations."

"I have to find three fans who love the device," I said, reading the producer's e-mail as I went along. "They want to do a girl talk segment about why women love romance book heroes with the reader as the news hook."

"You're the expert on that," he said. "You should go on as a spokesperson."

"Are you kidding? Sheila is the only one allowed to be in the spotlight at our company."

"Really?" He raised his brows and rolled his eyes. "Good business is about putting the best people in the right spots. Her approach sounds opposite. It didn't strike me that she has any knowledge about the field."

"I'll make it work using fans and a romance author." I quickly went onto the social media pages I had created for the launch and put a call out to the bloggers and beta readers that had received the device before the launch. Reponses poured in quickly, and I sent *The Today Show* segment producer an option of five names with e-mail addresses and phone numbers, with a little bio on each woman. I also sent my cell number. In a matter of ten minutes, she called me, reviewed the segment, and we made plans for the taping.

Nicolai seemed to enjoy watching me in action. He was half-looking at his e-mails, while listening to my chat with the TV producer.

When I got off the phone, I went right back to responding to messages to make sure I didn't miss anything related to the press. I came across an e-mail from Sheila. *Ugh.*

"Hope you had a good day OFF today." It read like she was shouting. "I expect you back in the office by EOD to report back on your meeting with Nicolai."

Fuck, it was already four p.m. I turned my laptop to show him the e-mail.

"What am I going to tell Sheila about our 'work' today?" I asked, making quotation marks in the air on *work*.

"Tell her we had an 'offsite,' at my home." He made air quotation marks on *offsite*.

"And what about getting me back to the office before she freaks out?" I didn't even know where the hell I was, or how far we were from Manhattan.

"We could make it back in time but I have a better idea." He put his phone down, placed his hands on my keyboard and wrote a short message to Sheila: "Traffic. Will be in tomorrow." He might as well have typed, "Fuck you, bitch." That's how she was going to read it.

He pushed send before I could try to talk him out of it.

Her response came zooming back at me immediately with a one word response, "FINE!"

"Oh jeez, you're going to get me fired." Panic gripped my gut. Sheila had dominated my work life for so long that it was my default reaction.

Yet this day had nothing to do with work and I felt bad about lying. On the other hand, my job was way too precarious to let the truth get out.

"Never." He put his phone down. "You obviously can run this project yourself, and work for me directly, without the agency—if you want." He smiled and tried to lighten things up. "You can run it from the back of this car, apparently."

"That's totally weird." I couldn't imagine leaving my dad's business and working directly for someone I was so attracted to. "I don't want to work for you."

"You do work for me already," he reasoned. "Your paycheck is already being covered by the retainer we pay the firm."

"I guess that's true since you are an executive of the investment company."

"I *own* the investment company."

I fell silent.

The first I'd heard about his involvement—and him—was at our launch party. I knew he was in charge, but clearly missed the memo about him being CEO *and* owner. *Fuck.*

"This is an even worse conflict," I said with a wry grin, closing my laptop. "I guess I just broke the ultimate taboo by pool-humping my way to the top echelons of power."

"There is no conflict—only the one in your mind," he said, affectionately tapping my head with two fingers.

"No, no. I believe there is a rule in the employee handbook that specifically says no synchronized breathing or half-naked dancing on the pool deck with a client who is essentially providing for everyone's paycheck." Not to mention the fact that my father would turn over in his grave if he knew what I was up to this week.

"You are not sleeping with me to get somewhere," he said, exasperated but still smiling. "You're not even sleeping with me—yet. You have the business skills, and I have the resources. It's very simple, my love."

Of course, nothing was really simple when it comes to an employee— me—being intimate with a client—him. Even if we never had sex, it would look like we did. He made eyes at me like we already had and he yanked me out of work for a pool party. My job and career were on the line.

But the funny thing was, I was starting to not care as much.

"Sheila has it in for me as it is," I finally said. "And I am pretty sure she wants to fuck you, too, so that puts me in a very vulnerable place with my boss."

He didn't look surprised by either comment. But his response was to go into, don't-worry-I-will-save-the-day mode.

"I promise I'll protect you," he touched my cheek tenderly. "You need to believe that."

But I didn't want him to have to protect me. I wanted to have the inner strength and the outer confidence to deal with that bitch on my own and take back what is mine. "I want to fend for myself," I said, placing my hand over his. "As I always have."

"Some things require the help of a dominant male. And it is time for you to learn that you don't have to do it alone anymore. Besides, it's a law of nature. Man protects his woman."

I had to chuckle. He was repeating what I had told him in the boardroom about why women love alphas, and adding in a little bit of caveman talk. It was over the top, but sweet. And his sexy and warm tone, combined with his offers to care for me, were so seductive. But I had to be able to manage my own work life without his intervention.

The limo pulled up to my apartment and the evening ritual began. He picked up my laptop and carried it out of the car. Once again, he walked me past the doorman, hand on my lower back, into the elevator and then to my apartment. He took the key and opened the door for me.

This time, he came in and looked around.

"You have a lovely apartment." He eyed the small kitchenette, and perused the modern artwork on the way, as he put my laptop on the kitchen counter.

"Thanks." I dropped my purse and turned on the lights.

"Where's the bedroom?"

"Um, over there, to the right." I nodded my head in that direction.

There was a look of steely determination in his eyes as he walked toward it and surveyed the bed from the doorway. Then he entered.

"May I," he asked, sitting down before I could respond. He smiled and looked at the space beside him, urging me to join him

"Are we having date four now?" I flipped off my shoes and got onto the bed with him. "I wouldn't mind a distraction from the image in my head of Sheila yelling at me tomorrow."

"No, I just want to know what it feels like to lie here with you." He stretched out, head on the pillow, and patted the bed cover beside him for me to join. I slid next to him. He took my hand and held it warmly. My arm tingled.

"Have you had sex on this bed?" he asked, point blank. I wasn't sure if I liked his question.

"No, actually, I have not." And would I tell him if I did? It was one thing talking about having had other sexual partners, but it was another showing him where. "Remind me. Why is that any of your business?"

"Because you are my business now," he said, squeezing my hand with affection. "At least for a day at a time, per your agreement. So how come you have not had sex here?"

Because I hadn't had sex in a while. I'd gotten so tired of the way I inevitably lost interest in lovers and having to duck their calls. I'd been on a bit of a sex moratorium—until Nicolai opened the doors to my suppressed passion. But I couldn't tell him all that. I had told him enough for one day.

"It's a new bed, a newish apartment." That should suffice, and it was essentially true.

He sat up and laughed. "So, it's a virgin bed?" He urged me to sit up with him as if getting me out of the supine position would assure keeping the bed a virgin a little longer.

"You could put it that way."

"Good. This is where we will have our consummation date," he said. "That is, if you choose to."

He looked at me and grinned. It made me smile too. I kind of loved seeing him on my bed. It crossed my mind to force him back down and mount him.

"Time to go." He got off the bed and tugged me with him.

His cock was hard. He must have been thinking about the same thing I was—getting back into the bed and fucking our brains out.

When I walked him to the door, I stopped for one moment and did something I had not done during all the smooching we'd shared—had never done with anyone, actually. I pushed him against the door and kissed him hard. Then I pressed my hips against his until his rock hard erection was biting into me.

"Are you trying to cop a feel before I go," he said with a grin, almost daring me with his tone.

"Yes, I am," I admitted.

He lifted me up in his arms so I could wrap my legs around his waist. He turned us around, and pushed me up against the door, his cock stiff against me.

"You know how easy it would be to fuck you right here?"

"Yes."

"Such a thin piece of material separates you from me. You could step out of your pants and I out of mine. I am sure, I would slide right in."

I was wet and I wanted him to slide in. "Please, be my guest."

He pushed me harder against the door and began to slowly grind into me, establishing a sensual rhythm. He kissed me wildly, passionately, roughly. Pleasure bloomed between my legs and grew stronger and stronger as excitement built. I was so, so close, just from the tension of his rubbing against me. I panted in his ear and smashed my hips against his. He pushed back harder.

Our bodies were like two powerful magnets, held together. Then, suddenly, he pulled away.

"Ah, Ms. Monroe, you almost pulled me into your siren song," he smiled but his breathing was rapid. He gently let me down from my spot against the door, and ended our intense humping. "But I have to leave you filled with desire for me. If I soothe it all tonight you may not want me back."

He kissed the top of my head and took hold of my cheek for a moment. Then he found his way to my neck, planting sensual kisses before pressing his lips on my sensitive flesh. Just as he was about to leave a new mark, I ducked out of his reach, and surprised him when I quickly moved my mouth to *his* neck. I licked him. He tasted like sun and a bit of sweat. I gently gnawed at him with my teeth as my tongue flicked his skin. Then I brought the power of my mouth to one spot and sucked, hard, and rough, losing myself in the feel of his flesh. He was at my mercy. And I didn't stop until I felt satiated. When I was done, I held his cheek as I pressed my head against his chest.

When I pulled away to look at my handiwork, a look was radiating from his eyes I hadn't seen before. Maybe it was crazy passion mingled with affection. And maybe I was looking at him the same way.

He seemed awestruck as he leaned against the wall and pressed his hands behind him for support. He closed his eyes, and took shallow breaths, as if trying to center himself.

The hickey was not so big, but it was dark red and pink. I couldn't stop staring at it, mesmerized by what I'd done. And I was stunned at his reaction, as if I'd sucked the wind right out of him. Yet he had this contented look on his face.

"What made you do that?" He was coming back from his momentary stupor.

"I don't know." *Did I do something wrong?* "I needed to…"

"…Give me a love bite?" he asked, his hand moving to the spot where I had left my passion bruise.

"Yes, I guess I did." I reached over to touch it, too.

He moved his hand out of the way and let me feel his flesh. He bent his head to capture my hand between his ear and shoulder.

"You marked me," he said. A huge grin spread across his beautiful face and his eyes were sparkling. "You've made me yours."

"If hickeys are the official Transylvanian symbol of possession, I guess I did." I laughed at how odd it was, him getting so excited about receiving a hickey.

"My grandmother's prophecy stated that my true love would mark me as her own and claim me before others who desired to do the same," he said.

Sheila. She was the only one I knew of who wanted him as her own. And now she would probably notice that, following a day of "working outside of the office," the client returns with a mark that matches the two already on my neck.

"You have to cover it with makeup tomorrow," I said.

"Nonsense, I will bear your mark proudly." He leaned in and kissed me. "This is who we are. We have to get beyond the need to hide things from others."

He pulled me into his arms and held me tight. I melted into him.

"I guess this is good night," I said, a little sad to see him go.

"Temporarily, for now, but perhaps we will meet in your dreams," he said. "Good night, my love."

As he walked away, I realized it was getting more difficult to part. It had barely been seventy-two hours since we'd met, and he was becoming an essential part of my life. How had that happened?

First, my fear had been that he would overwhelm me or try to absorb me into his plans. Now, I worried I could lose him, that he would decide he'd made a mistake. I had tried most of my adult life to avoid getting involved with men. Here I was, three days in, and Nicolai had become my focus—or my distraction, or my addiction.

I stripped off my shirt, bra, and pants before lying down on the bed. I didn't even bother to shower. I wanted to leave his kisses and touches on my flesh, and I was anxious to get to my dreams.

My dream that night played like a dystopian movie, with futuristic sex. In the dream, I was in a super modern, round bed. When Nicolai's beautiful face came onto a screen as big as the front glass window of his house, his voice pervaded the air around me, as if it were exuding from multiple speakers. He was sexy and dominating. His larger than life presence was overwhelming and arousing. I liked him taking control.

"Open your legs for me," he commanded. "Let the air caress your inner thighs. Pretend I am there, kissing you again between your legs, licking you, and tasting your arousal. When a man kisses a woman between her legs he is showing her how intimate he can be, and how much he desires her pleasure. I desire *your* pleasure."

"I want you so bad," I said, opening and feeling the first tickles of need. "Taste me."

"Feel me between your legs." He was whispering now. "Feel my mouth exploring. You have waited patiently for me to taste you again, to make you mine with my mouth."

"Yes." I was squirming, opening to him, as if he were in the room. "Make me yours."

"My tongue knows what to do and where to go to make you feel so good." His words were softer and sexy. "I am on the most sensitive part of you and licking where all the most delicate nerve endings are. I am diving in deep, deep inside you, fucking you, loving you, and filling you with my tongue. You are about to come, so I slide my fingers in you and massage that special spot to make you come even harder."

"Only you can give me that kind of pleasure," I said, hips moving to the sound of his voice. "I open to you."

"My cock is poised at the gates of pleasure," he continued. "I go in slowly, but with enough force to make the first thrust quick and deep. Your muscles contract around me. You're squeezing me, trying to pull me deeper into your hunger. You are properly made love to by a man who wants you and loves you and desires your pleasure more than his own."

"I want you to show me how much you love me," I said, arousal stirring between my legs and in my heart. "I'm ready."

"Each breath is moving us toward a release." His words flowed out in an insistent rhythm. "We press to get closer, to have more of each other. We can't get enough. We cannot tell where I end and you begin. And the pleasure explodes in us both. I empty into you. You empty onto me.

We collapse in a passionate embrace. Everything is so sensitive, so freshly open, that life suddenly feels different. Our loving has opened a door, a portal, to a new place. We step inside, hand-in-hand."

His words worked their way deep inside me. There was a fire sweeping across my body and burning between my legs. My flesh tingled with the promise of him. My nipples hardened, filled with desire. I was wet. Really wet. My hips lurched upward to meet his invisible touch.

Sexual need permeated every part of me. But all these hours of trying not to come had given me some discipline. Before grabbing a dream vibrator and taking charge of my own orgasm, I politely told him what I was going to do.

"Nicolai, I have to touch myself." I was like a dam about to burst and I needed relief.

"I'll watch you, my love," said dream Nicolai, his face hovering over me from the screen. "Show me how to make you feel good."

I lowered my hand between my legs, and, with his eyes on me, soothed the need.

"Come, baby," he coaxed, breathing along with me as my orgasm drew near.

My fingers brought on the release I needed, but I wanted his body buried in mine.

"Next time, it will be me touching you," he promised.

Just then the phone rang in perfect timing with the dream's end. It was Nicolai.

I may have had a subliminal orgasm, but my waking body was hot-wired with erotic need. I couldn't help thinking that these dreams I kept having were somehow changing me. In my nighttime imaginings, I felt freer, and each morning I woke up feeling more liberated.

"Good morning," he said, sounding wide-awake. "I was just admiring your mark on my neck."

"Maybe *I'm* the vampire." It would be humorous to discover that the paranormal person in this equation was me. "Because I really liked the taste of you."

"That's because I taste like you," he said, sweet-talking me before I even had my coffee. "We have extremely compatible pheromones."

"Hey, I have a question." I opened my eyes a little wider and stretched my body out, only to realize I was in need of a real orgasm. "Is there a limit to how much arousal a person can take?" I sighed. "My body is aching for you."

"Aching … for me?" He sounded excited.

"Yes, for you." This was clearly all his fault.

"That's one of the most beautiful things these ears have ever heard," he paused, as if he were being careful not to reveal too much emotion. "That you ache only for me."

I pressed my cheek against the phone as if it were him. Some things he said were corny and old-fashioned, but every little milestone seemed to matter to him. He made it clear I mattered to him.

"It's been three days, and I already feel like you are part of me." It was still strange to utter thing like that, yet it felt safe with him. "How did you get under my skin?"

"Strong desire can transform us so we can embrace our destiny," he said. There was a time when a statement like that would be too pithy, or too full of shit, for the morning, or any time. Now it seemed sincere.

I sighed. "I miss you, Nicolai."

"I know, my love. I will send for you after work, later today. "

"Until then." Even I sounded like I was speaking lines from romance movies.

CHAPTER FOURTEEN
FRIDAY: DAY FOUR/
FOURTH DATE

I got dressed, and this time tried not to torture myself with a long shower. I slipped into casual Friday clothes but packed a small bag with a dress for the evening. I was eager to get back to my desk and finish making the arrangements for *The Today Show* segment before Sheila could insinuate herself into the situation, or sabotage it in some way. She was smart enough to know we had to produce results for clients, but she had a way of adding drama and difficulty to everything. I took a cab to work to get an early start.

When I got into the office, two bad things happened.

One, there was a gigantic bouquet of roses in various colors waiting for me at the front desk. I guessed who they were from. I couldn't get them into my office without passing by Sheila's.

Two, Sheila called me into her office when she saw me pass with the flowers.

This will not go well.

"How was the meeting with Nicolai yesterday?" Her voice dripped with disdain and suspicion. "I expected you back in the office, not emailing me with excuses for your extended absence."

"It was a casual, breakfast and lunch thing. Then a lot of talking." I tried not to lie. "It lasted longer than expected."

"He seems very interested in you," she said, looking up at me from over her reading glasses, a sneer on her lips.

"He's friendly," I said, squirming, and not in a good way. "He tells me it's his culture. It's a friendly culture."

"Those are beautiful flowers, the kind of flowers a romantic man like Nicolai would send." There it was. The accusation would not be far behind.

"I haven't opened the card yet," I snapped. "But maybe you have?" I regretted saying that, immediately, but she'd cornered me and I lashed out.

"From one woman to another, you need to be careful about involvement with clients," she warned, removing her glasses and placing them in front of her. "We don't take kindly to it here. We don't sleep with our clients. And we don't tolerate people who use a client to advance their careers."

"I don't sleep with our clients either, so I'm not sure where you're coming from," I shot. "To advance my career? Are you kidding me?" My blood was boiling, considering how tortured I was when I learned Nicolai was a client.

"I saw you getting into his limo after work two days ago." Her tone was sharp and reproachful. *Crap.* She was collecting evidence against me.

A wave of panic shot through me, but I looked at her and said nothing.

"The account is more important than the account executive," she said. "Just remember that. You could be out of here in a nanosecond if we find out there is something going on with you two. Even if you are the founder's daughter, there are rules." Bringing my dad into it was a low blow.

"Duly noted."

"Besides," she said, "you wouldn't want it to get out in the industry that you slept around with clients. You know that never goes well." After that, she put her attention back on her computer and ignored me.

I went back to my office, hauling my flowers, and closed the door. I stared into space for a while. Now I was really distracted. Not only was this man driving me into a sexual frenzy, he was going to get me fired. I couldn't believe roses were going to be my downfall. *Fuck.*

I set the flowers down and opened the card. It read:

Orange is for desire and passion.

Pink is for romance.

White is for new beginnings.
Lavender is for love at first sight.
Yours, Nicolai.

Damn, why did he have to be so freaking sweet, and, more importantly, why send them now, when he knew it was going to make people—Sheila—ask questions?

Against my better judgment, I called him. I should have known to never call when I'm upset because he was only going to want to come and fix it.

"Nicolai." My voice was still shaky after my early morning experience.

"What's the matter, my love? Did you get my flowers?"

"Yes, they're beautiful. Thank you. But the timing may have been bad."

"Were you upset by the meaning of lavender?" I loved that he made the effort to be so romantic, but was upset he sent flowers to the office. They raised Sheila's ire, and he had to know they would. Why didn't he just send them to my house?

"That's not exactly why I am upset. Sheila's accused me of sleeping with you."

"Did you tell her it's not true—yet?" He laughed. I knew he was trying to lighten me up, but I was too freaked out to find humor in any of this.

"Of course, but she claims to have seen me get into your car outside the office the other night."

"So, what exactly is the problem?" Did he honestly not get that this gave her reason to suspect something?

"It looks like I am fucking you especially when she saw a huge bouquet of flowers for me, a day after I was out of the office with you." I was exasperated that he did not seem to get that the limo sighting and flowers were something my crazy, jealous boss could construe as an affair.

"Well, clearly, *at this moment in time,* you have nothing to worry about. Don't buy into her scare tactics." How could he be so cool? Maybe because he was the one who didn't have to worry about losing his job!

"She threatened to fire me," I said, anxiety running through me. "She said, 'We don't sleep with our clients.' And said I would be out of here in a nanosecond if they find out something is going on between us. She brought up my father. It was mortifying." I felt panicky, as if Sheila could swoop in with a security guard at any moment and remove me from the premises.

"Sweetheart, this is not as big a worry as you think," he assured me. I had his rapt attention now. "She's rattled you. And she toyed with all the vulnerable spots, like your father and your fear of being kicked out of his firm. She is trying to control you and fuck with you. She's not really going to fire you."

"But it's a big, huge, overwhelming worry," I countered. Sheila made me fearful she wouldn't just fire me, but she'd spread the word around. "This is my reputation. People don't like to work with women known for sexing the client."

"But what is happening with us has nothing to do with inappropriate behavior on your part," he said. His tone was caring, yet he sounded like he'd had it with Sheila's meddling. "It's not like that. This is our lives. And it is none of Sheila's business."

"It sucks that a man can have sex with any woman he wants at work, and still go on in the business world without the blink of the eye. Women get labeled as screwing someone to get ahead. People are unforgiving."

"I'm coming over."

"No! To do what?" I needed him to listen to me and agree that this was a train wreck. I didn't intend for him to come running over.

"To work this out." It sounded like he was already walking, leaving his office.

"How can you work this out?" I was panicking twice as much now.

"I'm going to talk with Sheila."

"No. No. You can't. That will make it worse." *Oh Jeez, this is bad.* "She'll hate me."

"I'm sorry to say, that ship has sailed." I could hear from his breath he was walking fast and he was more agitated. "If she liked you to begin with, she'd be taking you out to coffee to discuss this. Instead, she's bullying you."

"I can usually handle her," I said, sucking in a breath and wishing I could go back in time and not have called him. "But I have no defense, really. I broke the rules."

"Let me help. It's my fault this is happening." I assumed he meant sending the flowers and giving her something to use as exhibit A. I didn't expect a new bombshell. "She secretly tried to talk me out of having you at our 'onsite.' She called me into her office when I tried to leave to meet you the other night. She must have had someone watching us. I had no idea she would stoop that far, but I should have told you about her strong opinion in favor of my *not* spending time with you."

I remembered the delay while I waited for him in the back of the limo after the meeting in the boardroom. I should have been furious at him for not telling me she cornered him. But instead, I felt sad. In the few short days I found myself caring for someone, the other most important part of my life was falling apart.

"I don't want to lose my job, Nicolai. Not for this reason. I don't want to get shut out of my father's company."

"Stay put in your office." It sounded like he was getting into his car. I heard Sam's voice and doors closing. "I will be right there."

My world as I knew it was crashing down. I could feel it. I was fooling around with the client. Regardless of how we felt about each other, it was against the company rules and indicated poor judgment on my part, or poor self-control. How could he possibly protect me from the wrath of Sheila, or help shoulder this burden?

I opened my office door so I could keep an eye out for his arrival in the lobby. Within twenty minutes, Nicolai came walking in, cool, confident, and charming his way past the receptionist and heading directly to my private office to come collect me. He wore a light gray business suit, a white shirt, no tie, and had a little more beard scruff than usual. He probably hadn't had a chance to shave and trim yet, but he looked like a model for a *Men's Fitness* article on how to make women fall in love with you at work. He stopped to kiss me and then grabbed my hand, pulling me toward Sheila's office. I was mortified. I felt like a child being dragged to the principal's office. I braced myself for the most humiliating moment of my professional life.

He pressed open the door without knocking. Such an alpha.

"Sheila, how are you, today?" he said, not even trying to smile.

"So good to see you, Nicolai." She greeted him with a fake, plastic Botox smile.

She looked at me with disdain. Or was it disgust? She wasn't happy to see me again.

"I just wanted to clarify something for you." He let go of my hand and walked farther into the room, but kept a slight distance.

"Of course, Nicolai," she said, eyelashes fluttering.

"Ms. Monroe and I are not having sex."

Her mouth dropped open. And mine did too. *Holy Mother of God.* Nicolai, being his typical self, was not mincing words.

"And, if we were, it would be none of your fucking business."

She raised her eyebrows slightly, then sat in her chair as if leaning back to watch a show. An air of arrogance filled the space around her.

"She's still an employee of this company," she countered, raising a manicured red fingernail to her chin. "I am within my rights to discuss areas I feel are HR problems."

"Just a reminder," he said, stepping a little closer to her. "I have a three-million-dollar retainer with this company, a company Ms. Monroe's father founded. And I have an option to opt out before the next payment cycle, at my discretion. It's the biggest account you've ever had in recent times. My money is keeping this firm alive. Don't give me reason to take my business elsewhere."

Holy crap. That retainer was huge. Years ago, when my dad handled the international public relations for royalty and foreign countries, retainers were in the millions. Berke had told me the power of the Internet and the downturn in the economy had changed things and drained the company coffers. Nicolai's retainer *was* paying everyone's salary.

"Of course," she said, clearing her throat, but keeping her calm in the way only mean bitches could in high stress situations. "I think I understand you."

"Good." He stood like a warrior, strong and tall, yet waiting to see her next play.

She shifted in her chair, pulling herself forward. "We are here to serve you, and if you want your retainer to include the personal, um, services of Ms. Monroe, fine. You can utilize her any way you want."

I was flabbergasted. She was offering me as part of the package, like some sort of sexual add-on! Now I wanted to smack her.

But Nicolai took her on like a man. He laughed. Then he walked to the edge of her desk and leaned in.

"No, I don't think you do understand, because you are still talking about her as if she is an adolescent rather than a top-notch professional, and you're looking at her with contempt, yet she has done nothing wrong." He hovered just shy of her personal space and looked down on her. "Ms. Monroe is hardly the kind of person who would intentionally mix business with pleasure for personal gain—unlike others in this company."

I stood there shocked at his line of defense. He was completely defending my honor and my professional standing. He was letting her know he would choose me over the firm. I almost couldn't believe a man would do that for me, but I wondered what Sheila would say, and especially how she may try to retaliate when he was gone. Maybe I should pack my desk up in case.

She tried to respond, but he shut her down. He wasn't taking her crap.

"You, Sheila, are under the employ of my company while you are on retainer, and I am calling the shots on my account," he said, leaning in closer. "Any issues you have with Ms. Monroe's work should be discussed with me. We both know you are out for her, in general, and pissed at her, especially because I have refused your multiple sexual advances."

Whoosh. Bam. I had not expected that. For the first time, Sheila got flustered, as if she'd been smacked. She shifted nervously in her chair, moving her bony butt from one side to the other, holding on to the armrest as if she were afraid she would fall out of the smooth Italian leather and into his wrath. She sputtered out some lame defense, but Nicolai did not relent.

He stood in the same spot and composed himself before he added the final part to his performance. "One other thing," he said, his voice a little lower. "Don't fuck with her. If you fuck with her, you are fucking with me. I'm in love with her."

Sheila looked surprised by his declaration. But she couldn't have been as stunned as I was by his words and actions. He turned, walked to where I stood rooted to the floor, pulled me to him, and kissed me. Deeply, and for a long time—in front of my boss. My heart was beating so fast that the blood must have rushed from my head, making me feel a little drunk.

I must have officially lost my mind. Nicolai, who four days ago had only been a client, had defended me, told my boss she'd better stop messing with me, and then kissed me in front of her. With his hand still on my cheek, he looked at me as if something just changed in the universe. I touched my hand to my lips, still stunned at the force of his kiss.

"Come work for me, Allison." His gaze searched mine for an answer.

My eyes widened. Does he have to do this right now, right here? Jeez.

"Um, can we discuss this later? Please." I wasn't ready to have this completely blow up in my face, with her having me escorted out of the building by security.

He looked over at Sheila.

"Is there anything else we need to discuss, Sheila?" He was more composed now, having gotten that kiss out of his system.

"I think we covered everything," Sheila said, pulling her chair closer to the desk and sitting up straight.

"Good day." He walked out. Thank God he didn't try to drag me out with him.

I stood there, shocked. But I still wanted to maintain some semblance of professionalism with this woman; although, she had never given me the same courtesy.

I stepped toward her desk. "Sheila, I will resign."

"What, and risk the wrath of your boyfriend and cause him to yank his account?" She was fidgeting with her glasses, which were on the desk in front of her. "No way."

"He's not my boyfriend … not exactly." Why was I even explaining this to her?

"Well, you tell him that," she said, putting her glasses back on and looking up at me. "He's fighting for your honor like he is."

I hadn't really thought of Nicolai as a boyfriend but, wow, she was right about that. He was acting like one. How had he just taken off from work to run over here? Doesn't he have more important things to do and a big company to run?

No one else in my company was busy, apparently, either.

When I walked out of Sheila's office there was a trail of people, and a dozen sets of eyes on me. They had all seemed to hear this heated exchange.

Aisha was waiting in the hallway and linked her arm in mine as if to show solidarity after what had occurred. She walked me to my office. As I made my way, I sensed a new respect from the staff who'd heard it all. First off, they were gaga about Nicolai. This was the same bunch that openly drooled over him at our launch party and all week there were whispers that he was the hottest thing on two long, lean legs. Most importantly, they thought Sheila was pure evil. It was part of our office culture to dislike her—although she did have two assistants who were like loyal puppies. I didn't see either of them there.

"Men only do stuff like this when they really care," Aisha said. "This was epic. You may lose your job, but your street cred is unbelievably high right now."

She stopped in front of my office, gave me a hug, and shoved me inside.

Nicolai was in the chair next to my desk, apparently a little calmer than he had been moments before. He held his hands in an almost prayer-like manner, his thumbs resting against his chest and his beautiful bearded chin rested on his fingertips. He looked at me with those gorgeous eyes, a mixture of taking-care-of-business and concern about me in his gaze.

"I am serious," he said. "About everything I said. But most importantly right now, I want you to work with me directly."

"I signed a non-compete agreement," I explained, closing my door. "They have me tied up for a year. They could sue me."

"I will sue them back."

"Nicolai, just let this blow over." Lawsuits weren't the answer, and I did not want to leave my father's company. "I have always believed this was my place, that I should stick it out. I can't let her scare me off."

"I will not stand for anyone accusing or insulting you," he said, getting up from his chair. "And that woman is a manipulative bitch. She has been undermining you to me all week. She e-mailed me this morning to tell me she personally nailed *The Today Show* segment. This, after I watched you do it with my own eyes."

Somehow that didn't surprise me.

"I shouldn't have called you while I was so upset."

"No, you did the right thing." He came closer to where I was standing. "I'm the one you call. I'm the one who is there for you. I can hold your tears and your arousal. I can hold your upsets and your problems, too. Life is not always a pleasant walk in the park. It hurts. I don't want you to hurt—not if I can help you—and if you do hurt, I don't want you to be alone."

"Three and a half days into this and wow, what drama." I rolled my eyes thinking about this morning and everything that came before it. I also marveled at the *concept* that Nicolai was here. For me. With me.

"We will get through this, and many more things, together." He came closer, sliding the edges of his fingers along to the rim of my desk as he walked toward me. He pulled me to him as he turned the lock on my door. His mouth came down on mine. After what had transpired, I owed him at least a thank you kiss, I reasoned.

"Open your pants." He seemed serious.

"In my office?" He'd just had a fight with my boss about his claim that we were *not* fooling around. And I probably still had an audience outside my door waiting to hear what we did next.

"I need to feel your arousal." He bit his lip as his hand went to the top of my jeans and slid over the flat of my stomach. "I need you."

"Are you kidding?" In my mind, I knew this was ridiculously dangerous, yet his desire for me awakened my desire for him. That, along with his hero act in Sheila's office, was conspiring to make me want to give him anything he wanted.

"Have I been kidding you, about anything so far?" He was smiling but his eyes were getting that sex-glazed look.

"No. But if what happened in there doesn't do me in, *this* is definitely grounds for dismissal." Yet it was so hard to resist him. My hips were moving to the feel of his hand on my lower belly. He was working his way between my legs. "What if there are cameras." I didn't actually think there were.

"I had them dismantled." He kissed the top of my head as if that were not a weird thing to say.

"There *were* cameras?" It was chilling to think I was being spied on. "Why? Was she gathering evidence against me?"

"Yes." He looked me deep in the eye, as if revealing a secret. "You must trust me. In a very short time, you aren't going to care much about this episode. But I think you will care very much about me, and about us, and about what we have together. I pray you will."

"But cameras?" I wasn't sure I could shake my discomfort. Then my eye caught sight of the hickey I'd left on Nicolai's neck. Slowly I traced my finger along his collar and caressed the mark. Touching him made me remember how much I'd *wanted* to mark him and how good it had felt. It brought me back to our day together, away from this place. I started to *feel things* again, all over my body.

"There is a great deal of power in two against the world, instead of one fighting battles alone." His mouth came down on mine. Our tongues met. He was so familiar. And there were so many emotions stirring between us. Passion grew stronger and my surrounding disappeared. "Help me open your pants, my love."

I opened the button of my pants and spread my legs slightly. He slipped his hand farther into the front of my jeans and kept his gaze on mine as he found his way to the place that now longed for his touch. He dipped his finger inside me. I bit my lip, as the pleasure of his touch made me tingle and long for him.

"Still so wet, even when upset and angry." He looked pleased to finally be touching that part of me.

"I am. And as long as we are doing this, I'm not letting it go to waste."

Desk sex suddenly seemed like a good idea. Barring that, I grabbed hold of his shoulders so I could maintain balance as I moved. My hips found a rhythm with his hand as I lowered myself onto him. He had his finger deep inside, fucking me, and he let me ride it. When his thumb found my clit, I buried my face into his shirt. I was about to lose it, to come all over his hand, in the middle of a workday, in my office. His finger went deeper and his thumb pressed harder. I had to bite his shirt material to keep myself from making noise. I didn't even care about the lipstick mark I was leaving behind. I moved my body to maximize the pleasure from his fingers. The way they were positioned between my flesh and my jeans made it a sure thing. I claimed my orgasm, with labored breath. I pressed my mouth against his shoulder to muzzle a groan. Then I went limp against him.

The smile on his face made his eyes sparkle.

"You see," he said, kissing my nose. "That wasn't so bad."

He pulled his finger out, glistening with my fluids. He slipped it into his mouth, closing his eyes as he drank in my arousal. He seemed to draw strength from it. "You taste so good," he said. "And you are so beautiful and strong."

He found his way to my neck, licking and teasing and tasting me. Uncovering a new spot on the back on my neck, he sucked on it and marked me again. An erotic force ran through me. Something about his hickey rituals made me feel so desired.

"Do you still have doubts that you belong to me?"

"Yes … but I am starting to think I belong *with* you. Less possessive." I smiled. "I don't want you to have to keep running over here and saving me all the time. But thanks for what you did today." I kissed him on the cheek.

"I can't be less possessive, or less protective," he said. "But who knows, it may be me who needs to be saved by you some day. I think we should keep our options open."

"Options," I sighed, buttoning my pants. "Why does it still feel like some of us have more than others?"

"Because you're not thinking long term." He took hold of my hand and gazed into my eyes. "I know you don't want to hear this because you love this place your father built, but I have money. And resources. And property. If you marry me, you will never have to worry about anything. You'll have everything you could possibly need." He brought my hand to his lips and kissed it, keeping his eyes on mine. "Even if you decide you don't love me, I'll take care of you."

There it was, the *M* word again. He hadn't brought it up since the night we met. But this time he made it sound like he may not disappear if I don't marry him—or did he mean he was more willing to accept the idea of a marriage without love? A nervous flutter went off in my chest at the thought of marriage. I wasn't sure if it was bad nervous, or good, tickly, exciting nervous. Fear and excitement seemed to ride together in my system when he was around.

"I need to work and have a career, Nicolai," I said as firmly as I could to a billionaire offering to lay the world at my feet. "And I would like it to be here." But feeling his nearness, and his breath against my hand, my resolve was crumbling.

"Okay, well consider this," he said, a huge grin crossing his face as he let go of my hand. "I know you love your work and I would never think of asking you to give it up. But if you worked directly for me, or with me, we could have sex on your desk every morning to start the day and no one could say a damn thing."

I laughed out loud. This guy—he was morphing into my perfect man.

"That's an offer that may be hard to refuse," I said, placing my hand on my chest. "Especially if I get fired from this job." My heart felt open. Maybe some of this arousal was moving to other parts of my body.

Stepping closer, he pressed his forehead to mine and closed his eyes. I closed mine too. We stayed that way for a few moments, and it brought me back to the beautiful memory of the experience in the pool. Was it just the day before? I was beginning to see how all our experiences were building upon each other, and every day, we were getting closer and more connected.

"I'll send a car for you at five p.m."

CHAPTER FIFTEEN

It wasn't the easiest day at Berke and Monroe, but I laid low and got my work done. And I started to care less about what everyone thought and more about what was happening between Nicolai and me. Were we becoming a couple? Had I passed the point of no return? Like the famous area in Niagara Falls where, once you step into the river, you are sure to be carried away by the powerful current, unable to come back? He said he loved me, to my boss! How can he love me in three and a half days?

Aisha came into my office and surprised me with lunch at around two p.m.

"You gotta eat," she said, placing a Caesar salad on my desk with a bottle of coconut milk. She was carrying a slice of pizza in a bag for herself. Aisha was a tiny thing, but growing up a vegetarian on Indian food, she had a huge capacity for things made with dough and cheese. It smelled delicious, but after a morning of coffee, I was happy for the fresh greens and chicken.

"Thanks for the sustenance," I said, taking off the lid and digging in. I didn't bother adding in the dressing or croutons.

"So how are you doing?" She closed my door, took the seat in front of my desk and removed her slice from the bag. She folded it, New York-style, and took a big bite.

Maybe it was because she had a mouth full of food, but she had the good grace to not pry into what happened in Sheila's office—although I suspected she heard it—and not to ask what Nicolai and I had done behind closed doors afterward. I decided not to detail our finger sex in my office, but oddly enough, I didn't even care so much anymore if Sheila—or anyone—knew. My amatory exploit was with someone who said he loved me. So it should be allowed in the office, right? Well, In Nicolai's world it would be okay.

"I got *The Today Show* all lined up," I said. "At least there's that."

"You're a master, Allison," she said, still chewing. "I hate to see what Sheila tries to do to you. I'm glad Nicolai stood up to her."

"He also set her off, by sending me flowers," I admitted. It was almost as if he were daring her to show her disdain for me. "There was something weird about it all. Do you think he wanted her to fire me?"

"I think he sees who she is and he's trying to protect you." She used her free hand to flip her beautiful dark hair out of her face and away from her food. "I would love a guy like that. He rode in on a white horse for you."

True. But I couldn't seem to let it set in all the way.

"Do you think it's a little weird that he and I have gotten so, um, close in such a short amount of time?" I sighed. "I mean, how can you know for sure that someone is right if you are swimming in sex hormones—and marvelous tropical pools—and walking around turned on all the time? It's been a whirlwind. And he's so seductive."

Aisha put her food down and sat back in her chair, grinning ear-to-ear.

"Like I said before, billionaire problems—they are rough." She laughed. "But God created romantic whirlwinds to entice people into love."

"What?" I stopped chewing my food so I could hear her loud and clear. "Where did that come from? That's pretty much what Nicolai says."

"It's nature's design to make people attracted to each other so that they want to have sex and make babies," she said, patting her stomach. "I don't have to tell you about the birds and the bees—do I? Man wants woman, woman wants man. Their bodies are drawn together like magnets. They want to be inside each other and under each other's skin."

I pushed my food away so I could focus on the conversation.

"Wait, is this from one of your romance movies?" I asked.

"No, this is how it works," she asserted. She held her left thumb and index finger together in the form of an *O* and she poked her right index finger in and out. "We are designed to want *this*, and do *this*, and do it enough that it makes us fall in love. Attraction is the gateway to love and marriage."

"Holy crap, I feel like I missed sex ed." I rolled my eyes and stood up. "I thought this whole attraction thing was some diabolical plan to make women stop following their dreams because they focus on men."

"Allison, I don't mean to psychoanalyze you, but, well, I have to give it to you straight, for your own sake," she said, commanding me to sit back down. "Your father left when you were young. Your mother never remarried, and she died in your teens. Your grandma lost your grandpa before you were born. You've had no role model for relationships, so of course it seems weird for a guy to profess his desire to want to build a life with you."

"Jeez, like Nicolai, you don't mince words." I took a deep breath. In my heart, I knew she was right.

"And this shit with Sheila," she said, leaning in and putting her hands flat on my desk. "It is all about unresolved issues with your father. He left you, then he found you, then he left you again, and he did not take care of you and leave things in place for you in this company. There was no clear inheritance. That bitch hijacked your birthright."

I rolled my chair away from my desk and turned toward the window. The window shade had been down all day. I reached over and opened it. Sun came streaming in. A tear slid down my face. I sat there, staring at the glass.

Aisha stood and came to where I had rolled myself and leaned over to put her arms around me. I laid my head on her shoulder and cried, until there were no more tears. She reached for the tissues and plopped the box in front of me.

"In my effort to stay connected to my dad's company and his legacy, I guess I never fully grieved," I said, grabbing a tissue. I felt heaviness in my chest. "And I never questioned it when Dan Berke and Sheila told me that my father never intended to leave me the company. My dad was so sick toward the end, and Dan was covering all his medical bills and managing the financial end of things, so I didn't want to rock the boat."

"I know." She was standing now, but had a hand on my shoulder. Then she walked around the desk, to her chair. "Maybe this all came to a head for a reason."

"Maybe," I said, still sniffling. "I can't figure it out right now though. I think I need a warm bath and a drink."

"Or maybe you need Nicolai?" She moved back in her seat, scrunching her face and pretending to duck, as if I were about to toss something at her. "I know this is sensitive, so throw something at me if you want me to shut up, but I think Nicolai is the good guy. He's the good karma coming back to you. And he wants to help you. Let him help you figure it out. I think Nicolai is here for a reason."

It was amazing how she and Nicolai had such similar ideas about romance and gallantry. "Did he tell you to say that?" It sounded awfully familiar.

"Of course not," she swore. "I'm your friend and I have seen you in pain for so long. And you have a chance for something real, even if it seems too fast and too *unreal*. I just want you to at least consider that somewhere in the universe there is a rhyme and a reason for all this."

Aisha's insights were intense, but I suspected she was spot on. I mouthed the words, "Thank you."

"Text me if you need me," she said. "I will be around doing my usual millionaire research."

We both stood for a hug. When she left, it came to me that I had not known Aisha for that long, yet we had become fast friends and I'd trusted her the moment I met her. Maybe things like that can happen with men you like, too.

At five p.m., the energy shifted as I got ready for an evening with Nicolai. With all that occurred in the morning, it seemed we'd already had a date, but I was looking forward to more. In fact, that chat with Aisha made me want to go running to him and jump into his arms. I changed into my dress, dabbed on a touch of makeup and perfume, and went down to the car. Although I couldn't help but wonder if Sheila had her spies out there, I didn't feel my usual paranoia. I just wanted to see him.

Sam stood there with the limo door open. No Nicolai.

"Where is he?" Something felt wrong. Panic set in pretty quickly as I imagined the worst. After all that had been said and done, how could he not be here?

"He got called away to a family emergency," said Sam, taking my small garment bag and helping me into the car. "He asked me to take you home where you can await his call."

Suddenly, I was terrified that he was leaving me. Oh, my God, maybe having to deal with my boss today made him realize I wasn't worth it. I didn't even know who this man was four nights ago, and now I was filled with dread, the kind that only comes when caring for someone.

My mind was occupied running through a dozen different scenarios all the way home, so when I got to my building I was distracted. Sam opened the limo door, and helped me out. Then he carried all my belongings to the doorman for me. He kept his free hand on my elbow, as if he knew I needed a little support.

When he said good-bye, I mustered the courage to ask, "Why isn't he here, Sam?" My voice was clearly shaken. I wasn't sure how this had so quickly turned me into a wreck, but my heart was hurting. It was the first time Nicolai hadn't kept his word. Although he had shown up a little late for one of our dates, he hadn't ever not shown up.

"I can't say, ma'am," he said, warmly squeezing my elbow. It was an uncharacteristic move on his part but he must have seen the pain in my eyes. "But he told me to tell you he will call as soon as he can." He smiled. "He *will* call."

Sam went to the limo. I headed to my apartment.

It was weird making my way on my own. The doorman helped me to the elevator, pushed the button, and handed me my things. Did he know how lost I felt? My mind wandered to three nights ago when

Nicolai insisted on escorting me in, getting me to my door. And now, he was a no show.

There must be an explanation. I tried to fight the feelings of abandonment, but they gripped me. And fear got the better of me. By the time I walked in my door, I doubted everything—again.

My doubts played like an internal audiotape: *Maybe the warm feelings for him weren't real. Perhaps I was falling for him by virtue of my desire for him, which was not the same as love. Could a New York City girl thrive with a sexy alpha from Transylvania? Was it even possible to bring two such different people together? How could a commitment-phobe mess like me even last in a relationship, with anyone?* My mind seemed doggedly determined to be down on love—again. And I had to wonder, what the hell is a soul mate, anyway? It sounded like something made up by greeting card companies.

I searched it online and discovered a few schools of thought. Essentially a soul mate is considered to be someone a person feels a connection to. Maybe there is a natural affinity. Some people believe soul mates are from past lives, or here to teach us lessons. Some say that when they met their soul mates there was a recognition or familiarity. More than anything, a soul mate feels like home.

Holy fuck. These concepts didn't seem so foreign to me anymore. And now that I was hooked, he'd disappeared. I missed the nearness of him and the feel of his arms around me. I thought of watching a movie or making headway on work I brought home from the office, but I couldn't focus. So I called him.

No answer.

Why did it hurt so much? Memories flooded to my mind, like when I tried to call my father the day he first disappeared out of our lives and there was no answer. It broke my heart. It broke again the day I called his hospital room, only to discover from the nurse that he'd slipped into a coma. I never got to speak with him again. The *no answers* of my past haunted me now.

The emotional exhaustion of this morning, the day, tonight, and the week were catching up. It was still early evening, and I could have hunkered down with wine and ice cream, but I decided to lie down in bed to unwind. I drifted off to asleep and into a dream world, but Nicolai wasn't there. The last thing I remembered was saying to someone in my dream, "Something must be wrong."

That's when the phone rang.

"My love, please forgive me for not being there tonight," he began, "especially after the events of the day. I was called into an emergency."

"Nicolai!" I was so relieved to hear his voice. "Oh, my God, I was so worried."

"My grandmother fell ill," he said softly. "It's the only thing that could keep me away from you."

A rush of dopamine exploded in my brain. I shouldn't have felt happy to hear his news, but I had gone into such a dark place that it was liberating to know he had not abandoned me.

"I'm so sorry. I had no idea." I had spent the evening so focused on my own fears that it was just dawning on me that he was in a family crisis. "How is she doing?"

"She seems a little better. But I guess at ninety-eight years young, this is in the hands of the divine." He sounded tired and sad, but accepting. "My grandmother is quite strong-willed, so you never know."

"Is there anything I can do?" I had been through the death of my own grandmother, mother, and father. I knew how much this sucked. Maybe I could be there for him in some way.

"Yes," he said, "Come to me here tomorrow. I didn't want to miss our date tonight, and Grandmamma didn't want me to miss it either, but it couldn't be helped. If you don't mind coming here, we can catch up." I thought it was odd she knew about our date, but I let it go for now.

"Um, okay," I said, nervous that I may be packing for a long flight. "Do I need to bring my passport? Are you in Romania?"

He laughed out loud. "I'm in Connecticut," he said. "But your willingness to travel far and wide to see me warms my heart."

"God, I miss you, Nicolai," I sighed into the phone. I was so glad to hear his laugh.

"You do?" His voice was soft.

"I do." The words flowed out on a whisper, and I realized how true they were.

We held on in silence. As our breathing synced up, it was like we were together in the same room.

"I've had many epiphanies today." I broke the silence. "More on that later. But for now, why don't you take some pressure off yourself and consider this morning, in my office, as our fourth date?"

"Yes, it can hold us for today, but that was a bit of an exception," he said. "I was completely motivated by emotions and my concern for you. Not exactly the plan."

"Well, maybe one of the other lessons of the day is that plans don't always work out the way you imagine, but the results could be the same," I said. I liked sounding like the pithy one for a change. "You did find your way into my pants. Defending my honor was an extra bonus. We don't have normal dates anyway. They're more like episodes." Actually, they were more like telenovelas, but I refrained from saying that.

"You're starting to sound rather Zen, Ms. Monroe." It was good to hear the humor in his voice.

"Maybe you're rubbing off on me." The smile on my face was big and bright. I was floating on a happiness cloud.

"Oh, I most definitely would like to be rubbing off on you." His laugh was so sexy, I wished I could pull his body through the phone into my bedroom. "I'm going to look forward to tomorrow."

"What about your grandmother? I mean, won't it be awkward 'dating' at her home?"

"Grandmamma wants us to be close," he said. "And she wants to meet you."

"So tomorrow?" Nervous butterflies swarmed my tummy thinking about meeting his family.

"Yes. I need to sort a few things out, but I'll call in the morning with a plan so we can be together."

"I'll miss you until then."

"I'll miss you more."

I'd nearly crumbled when I thought he was gone. In my wildest dreams I never thought I would become *that* woman, the one who loses her shit when she thinks she has been left by a man. Then again, I never let myself get this close to the edge of love.

Chapter Sixteen
Saturday: Day Five/ Date Five

I slept so soundly that I couldn't remember any dreams. Nicolai called early Saturday morning.

"Good morning," he said, sounding more cheerful than expected. "So, we're coming into the home stretch."

"Your grandmother? Is she—" I worried she was dying.

"No, she's a bit better today. I meant us," he said, his tone a little sad. "This is the last day I'm going to officially ask if you want to sign on for another day with me. Tomorrow is in your hands."

"Well, if you mean home stretch refers to us *coming* at your grandmother's *home* in the *stretch* limo today, I'm in." I tried to be humorous because I was suddenly feeling a little nervous. But I couldn't wait to see him.

"Then I will send a car for you by nine a.m. so we can have our fifth date on location," he said. "I would have taken you somewhere more exotic but Connecticut will have to do."

He didn't mention exactly where in Connecticut he was, just that it was a bit of a distance. He told me to bring a change of clothing in case. I wasn't sure if that was because I may have to stay over or because something wet or dirty might happen to my clothes. I felt a little bad thinking about sex with his grandmother not well, but then again, he said she wanted us together. And he'd originally asked me to help make her last wishes come true—even if it meant pretending.

Sam showed up with coffee and breakfast in the car.

"It's a bit of a drive to where we are going, Ms. Monroe," he said. "Just let me know if you need to stop for anything. There is a call button on the arm rests."

"Thank you, Sam." I was tempted to leave the privacy window open and pump him for information, but instead I used the time to reflect. I hoped this trip would enlighten me about a few things—like why we were speeding toward this full moon deadline, what his grandmother's role was in all this, and how I truly feel about Nicolai and his proposal.

I was in pretty deep, but was it real love? And how would things change if I were still with him on day six? His words from the first night we met flowed into my head: *"Let's agree to disagree about the term 'mine,' but agree to belong to each other for the next six days. You retain the right to ditch me at any point, and the right to refuse the option to consummate on the full moon. If you decline that option, it means you don't care for me, so the 'mine' part will be irrelevant, anyway. Let's see if you can go along with it for six days."*

He said he was motivated by his grandmother's prophecy, and now she was ill. Would he change his plans or the way he felt about me?

I was prepared to ask Nicolai to clear up my questions before any arousal activities. But when the limo drove up a gravel drive and parked and I heard footsteps, all I wanted was to jump into the arms of my man. Was he my man yet? I was starting to think of him in that way.

Sam got out of the car and Nicolai told him there was lunch for him at the house and to go take a break.

When Nicolai swung open my car door, my heart leapt. He appeared more tired than I'd ever seen him, and vulnerable. He slid into the back seat and pulled me close, so close, and drew my head to his chest, stroking my hair. We held each other in silence. He was clutching on for dear life.

Then he pushed the button that locked all the doors and looked at me with hunger in his eyes.

"How are things going?" I asked, reaching over to touch his hand.

"My love, it's hard for me to talk about it," he said, his voice edged with sadness. "Grandmamma and I are very close, and this is not easy.

But let me spend this time to bring us together again. It felt strange to not be with you last night."

My heart ached for him. When he inclined back against the seat and opened his arms for an embrace, I leaned in and pressed my ear to his chest. I felt his heart pump and sensed his pain.

"I'm here for you," I said rising up to look into his weary eyes. I placed my palm over his heart. I'd never done that before but felt moved to touch him that way, thinking it may make him feel better. "I know what it's like to go through this. Let me help."

"I need physical contact with you," he said, lifting off his gray T-shirt and exposing his chest. "Can we just be close for a while? Is that okay?" He pulled me back onto his upper torso.

"Of course," I said. "Whatever you need." He was asking for permission instead of making a command.

"I need you, Allison." He cradled my head against him and gently rocked. "I can't bear the idea of being separated from you."

"I'm here." I smoothed a hand over his abs and chest. "I came here to the wilds of Connecticut to be with you, didn't I?"

"You are here today, but what about tomorrow?" Pain etched in his handsome face. I felt his body tense. "What if, after today, this all ends?"

I didn't want it to end. I really didn't. But I wanted to know more about where this crazy journey was leading before I made any promises about the next day. Damn that full moon. It was creating so much pressure.

"I need to share some things," he said, running two fingers along the top of my thigh, inching my dress up toward my hips. "That will clear up some questions you may have. But … I need … you … close."

Even in a moment of despair, his sexual appetite seemed intact—or was it his discipline about following through on our dates? He lifted my dress over my head and reached over to unbuckle his jeans. He quickly slipped out of them. We were both in our underwear and he was hard. Suddenly the air around us sizzled with the intensity of need—his need— and I wanted to make him feel better.

He slipped my bra aside and took my nipple into his mouth. Pleasure shot between my legs, making me wet. My whole body was alive with pleasure.

He helped me lay down on the back seat. Moving my knees apart, he lowered himself between them. Next, I felt his mouth on me, kissing my inner thighs until he made his way to the place covered only by my panties. He used both hands to hold my hips down as he kissed me over the thin material. Every gentle caress of his mouth moved me closer to ecstasy. He found my swelling clit, took it in his mouth, and then let go his hold on my thighs so I could rock into him. Even with my panties still on, my lower parts were close to bursting with delight. Suddenly, he stopped.

"I need to taste all of you." He looked up and his gaze searched mine.

I pressed myself closer to his mouth to let him know that was exactly what I wanted him to do.

He pulled my panties to one side and slipped his tongue in deep, sliding in and out until I began to cry out. After tongue-fucking me close to orgasm, his hungry mouth moved to my clitoris and gave that part of me all of his attention—sucking, pulling me in, flicking my sensitive skin—until a torrent of pleasure swirled through me and then released. When every wave had run through me, he put my underwear back in place. My knees were wobbly and weak.

He sat up on the edge of the seat and moved his hand to his face. He gently traced the outline of his lips, which glistened with my fluids, and then slipped his finger into his mouth to taste.

He was wild-eyed, as if in an erotic daze. I couldn't leave him strung out and unsated so I sat up and reached for his cock. He shivered, as if responding to a jolt of pleasure, when I placed my hand on his underwear. I looked him in the eye as I caressed. Then I walked my fingers to the band of his underwear, and slowly slipped my hand inside.

I was ready to free him—bend my head, and take him into my mouth—so I was shocked when he pulled my hand away. I was even more surprised when he pressed me back down on the back seat and brought his body over mine. Holding himself up with his strong arms, he nudged my hips apart with his knees. His erection jutted from within his skintight boxer-briefs. He rubbed himself on my thigh until he was out of breath.

"Nicolai, let me make you feel better, please." I pleaded with him. "You need the release." I angled my hips so that he could slide right into me if he wanted to take off his underwear. I was ready to remove mine.

"No, I don't want to *just* fuck you," he said, pressing the tip of his cock at my panty covered opening. "I mean, of course I want to be inside you, but I want you to love me. Do you think you can love me? Even if you don't love me now, do you care enough to stay with me through tomorrow?"

"You're so upset. Maybe this isn't the time to be making life decisions." I wanted to take him into my body, to heal him and make him feel better. He was so distressed that I wanted to tell him I'd stay, but I couldn't. I didn't know for sure. I closed my eyes, to try to think.

"Please open your eyes and look at me, baby," he said, sounding like he was on the verge of tears.

I gazed back at him and saw his pain, but I couldn't promise.

He pressed his cock closer, the closest it had ever been to that part of my body. I pressed forward, easing him in a little more. He lowered himself, his chest pressing more firmly against mine, as his hips stationed between mine.

"Just do it," I implored, feeling him starting to move in and out, even through the thin strips of material separating us. "Slide into me. I think you need this."

"What I need is for you to choose me, to want me," he said, lowering his lips to mine and kissing me breathless. "I don't want to be without you. This can't be the last day."

"We have to discuss things." I took his face into my hands and searched his eyes. "Like normal adults who do not have a full moon deadline hanging over their heads."

The wounded look on his face was almost too painful for me to bear.

"You don't think you can love me, do you?" He lifted himself from between my legs and sat up, and dropped his head into his hands. He was looking down at the floor, instead of at me, which seemed so out of character for him. "I don't blame you," he finally said. "I had this fantasy that I could make you fall in love with me by now. It was wrong to push you. I'm so sorry."

"This isn't like you, Nicolai." I sat up and tried to soothe him. I urged him to sit upright and look at me. "You push. You go for it. You do what it takes. That's what you do."

"I pushed you to agree to be mine, if even for a day at a time, but I can't push you to fall in love with me," he said on a sigh. He looked lost. "That night, on the terrace, I was on a mission to carry out my grandmother's last wishes."

"I know." I patted his arm warmly. "It was weird, but you were clear about that."

"But I fell in love with you, Allison." His voice was cracking with emotion. His body was trembling. "I didn't realize how much I could love you, or how much it would hurt if you didn't love me back."

"Nicolai, I…" I didn't know what to say. I was unaccustomed to seeing him like this.

He stared at me for a long moment and then moved from where he was sitting, onto the carpeted floor of the limo, and over to the opposite seat. He placed his back against it, and pulled his knees up. Then he wrapped his arms around them and bent his head.

I was taken aback when he started to cry.

I rushed down to the floor and kneeled in front of him. I didn't know what else to do but bear witness to his pain. My heart was aching for him. It was also beating wildly. I wanted to be loving without saying, "I love you." I was terrified that the minute I said it, the feeling would go away. Or he would go away. I remembered how having a good cry in front of Aisha yesterday relieved a lot of pent up stress and how freeing it was when he let me sob in front of him the other day at his house. I had to imagine that part of this reaction was his grief and fear of losing his grandmother. So, I knelt there and let him get it all out. It was one of the most intimate experiences I had ever had with him, or any man, to stay present while he cried.

We remained that way until the sadness seemed to pass through him. Finally, he looked up.

"Nicolai, you're overwrought and with good reason, and you have a lot of pressure on you." I took a deep breath, relieved he seemed to have passed through the worst of it. He kept connected through eye contact. "And on top of everything else, your grandmother is not well. Let's just relax here for a while and figure out, together, how to make this work and—"

Before I could get any more words out, he stretched his long legs out on the floor in front of him, and quickly pulled me onto his lap, facing him. His cheeks were moist with tears, but he was smiling. He seemed relieved too. "You keep amazing me with your strength," he said, moving his lips to my cheek. "Staying here with me through tears is the most beautiful thing any woman has ever done."

"Of course, I want to comfort you," I said, sucking in a deep breath. "You don't have to thank me, and you don't have to go through this alone."

"You must care for me if you did that," he said softly, pulling my face closer to his. "You must feel something in your heart. You didn't turn me away."

"I feel something—a lot of things." Now I was on the verge of tears. "But I … I'm not ready to make the promises you've asked for. Not today."

"Okay." The word came out on a whisper. "I have to accept that. And our agreement was to take it day by day, and maybe even fake it in front of my grandmother. But there is really no faking anything with her. She is highly tuned in. So, you don't have to pretend you love me. I don't want to put you in that position."

His statement confused me. I thought he was bringing me here to put his grandmother at ease and make her think we were an item. Suddenly he was letting me off the hook.

"I thought I was supposed to make her think everything is going according to her plan." I was worried I'd have to pretend I was ready to get married but I wasn't averse to helping her feel her grandson was going to be okay. "If not that, what am I supposed to do?"

"Nothing," he said, kissing my cheek. "Just be your beautiful self. You don't have to pretend anything. She knows you came here for me. That's enough. It's all in God's court now."

He placed his hand on my neck and gently caressed me, but he didn't attempt another love bite. He held me close, his gaze steady on mine. We stayed in that moment for what seemed like a long time. My heart was heavy, but I felt so connected to him. For the first time since this all began, I sincerely hoped he and his grandmother were right—that we were meant to be—and that this crazy week would end on a good note for us both.

"We've come a long way from the Manhattan terrace overlooking the city." I was suddenly reflective and awed that we already had "history" together to reflect on.

"Yes, we have. Because you have been brave to give this a try," he said, handing me my dress from the floor. "And you never once asked me what was in it for you. Do you realize that?"

"I guess I should have asked for a couple of mil, huh," I said, laughing as I slipped off of his lap. Kneeling, I pulled my dress overhead and smoothed it over my curves.

"If you had, it would already be in your back account." He slid on his pants and shirt, tucking it in. "But you didn't. That's because you're sincere, and you're loyal."

"Hmmm, still, I should have made a list of demands," I said, pulling out my brush and running it through my hair to remove signs of our prior activities. "Of things I need you to explain about this week and tomorrow in its entirety." I smiled, but I wasn't exactly kidding. "And I should have demanded to know all of it before we get out of this car."

He looked at me, gaze intensely locking onto mine, and lightly bit his lip. He nodded.

"Things are going to start becoming clearer now," he said, opening the limo door and helping me out and carrying my overnight bag with extra clothes. "I'm taking you to meet my grandmother."

The late afternoon chill hit my face as we stepped out. I shivered a little. He pulled me into his arms to warm me, and brought his mouth to mine. His kiss was urgent, yet tender.

"One last kiss?" Nervousness set in. I didn't want this moment, or this week, to end, but I didn't know if I could meet the requirements for date six. And what if his grandmother didn't like me? I was afraid meeting her could change everything.

"I sincerely hope not," he said, taking my hand and leading me into what appeared on the outside to be a regal estate. "I pray there will be many more."

We passed through the doorway, into a foyer. A round table was set beneath an over-sized chandelier. There were multiple vases of flowers, and, two gold candles burning. It was a bright room, with a wide staircase facing the entrance. The gold trimming on the stairs and banisters was opulent. There were two sitting rooms to either side, each dimly lit and filled with art, antiques and statues, many of them with naked replicas of the kind of things found in museums, or maybe they were the originals. It had a kind of otherworldly feel to it, like an estate in another country.

"I'm going to need to stop in the bathroom," I said. I smelled like sex and sweat and needed to wash up before meeting his grandmother.

"A good idea for us both." He winked and showed me to a big bathroom on the first floor, just below the stairwell. He put down my bag and handed me a towel. "Shower if you like. I will do the same upstairs."

He touched my cheek tenderly, smiled, and then headed toward the stairs. It occurred to me that we had never even been in the same restroom together, or taken a shower together, or gone on a normal date. Yet here we were, meeting his grandmother.

Normally, I would never shower in someone's home upon entering, but I had a strong need to be fresh and clean—and not smell like back seat erotic activities. I also needed some space to collect myself. This entire week had been propelling us to this meeting and my nerves were a little jangled. Locking the golden doorknob, I stripped and quickly jumped into the shower. It was a fancy, glass-encased, black tiled, stand-up shower.

It had many levers and dials on the faucets, and I quickly realized it was to control jets that came out of the tiles. Finally, I found the knob that controlled the showerhead only. It was one of the most relaxing cascades of water I ever experienced. I was tranquil as I washed up, brushed my teeth, and then changed into the clean clothes and underwear I had shoved into my overnight bag.

When I came out, he was waiting for me in the hallway. He had showered and changed into a baby blue button-up shirt tucked into dark gray pants. His wet hair was combed back, and he looked like he stepped out of a *Men's Fitness* article on sexy wet-look hairstyles for men that make women want to shower with them. He reached his hand out, took mine and kissed it. Thinking back to the suave, count-like hand kisses from the night we met, this one was warm and affectionate. His hand smooches had become so familiar.

I stepped in front of him and put my hand on his cheek. I reveled in the feel of his skin and his soft beard and the way he pressed against me like a cat. I didn't pray often, but I said a silent prayer that if this were meant to be there would be a sign. A sign that was clear and easy for me to read. A sign that I couldn't ignore.

"I *do* care about you ... very much," I said, looking into his eyes. I bit my lip and let my teeth slowly roll over the skin before completing my thought. "I just need time."

"How much time are we talking about?" His eyes lit up with hope.

"Enough time to understand things more clearly."

"What if I told you events may unfold to put things in perspective over the next twenty-four hours?" He was suddenly back in his confident warrior stance. "And what if I agree to explain everything I know so far?"

"Then I would say you better start explaining," I said, touching my finger to his lips. "Now."

I hoped the truth would set me free—from doubt.

CHAPTER SEVENTEEN

Nicolai led me to his grandmother's room at the top of the stairs. I checked myself out one more time in the hallway mirror to make sure I looked presentable, and flipped my hair back to get it out of my face. It was hard not to be nervous.

The room was brimming with antique furniture that was likely new when she purchased it. It had a very lived in, yet imperial feel to it. There was a huge armoire, an oak dresser with silver handles, and a portrait of a handsome blond man, whom I assumed was Nicolai's grandfather in his day. The four-poster bed had velvet curtains tied back on each side and she was propped up on five pillows.

As he moved toward her, she opened her eyes and smiled.

There was a nurse sitting by her side in a brocade silk wingback chair in shades of pink and rosy brown. Nicolai motioned to her that it was okay to leave. The nurse got up hesitantly but followed his wishes, regarding her patient with a smile.

The elderly woman was stately, even in her sick bed. With her full head of silver hair and magnificent bone structure, she had clearly been a striking beauty in her youth. She was still lovely.

"Hello, my darling," she said, reaching a frail hand out to him. She spoke excellent English, with an accent.

"I'm back, Grandmamma, with Allison." He took her tiny hand in both of his and smiled tenderly.

"Oh, Allison, my dear one," she said, waving me over with her free hand. "I have waited so long to meet you. Come, let me look at you." She sounded excited and suddenly energized.

"I'm sorry you're not well," I said. Nicolai stepped away, as I moved to the left side of her bed. He transferred her hand into mine.

"I'm fine." She shook her head, as if indicating not to worry. "It's just age. Apparently, it's killing me."

"Grandmamma," Nicolai exclaimed. He clearly couldn't bear the idea of her dying. After witnessing his sadness in the car, I hoped this was not going to renew his angst.

"It's reality, my darling." She looked over at him with a weak smile. "But let's not waste any more precious breath on that. Allison, come closer."

She lifted a hand toward my face. I lowered myself so she could easily touch it. She looked directly into me with her cobalt blue eyes, still so bright. I could tell where her grandson got his intense gaze from. She had the same eyes.

"Da, Nicolai," she said, shaking her head up and down. "This is your *Ves'tacha*."

"I told you," he teased but I thought I saw a tear in his eye.

Then she said something in a foreign tongue and they both chuckled.

"Grandmamma is Russian, but she speaks Romanian too," he explained. "And what she just said in Romanian is, 'Yes, but boys think with their lower parts, so she had to see you to be sure.' "

Her gaze met mine and I started to laugh too. Her joy at making a joke was sweet and catchy. There was something so lighthearted about her spirit that her room seemed sunny, even though she was surrounded by dark colors and woods and the lighting was dim. It was such an uplifting moment.

Yet I cried, too, because suddenly I was so connected to this elderly woman in front of me. And I was saddened by impending loss. My chest began to hurt. It was as if my heart was cracking open. She seemed to have an extraordinary amount of love in her. I had never been in the presence of so much love and acceptance, except in front of my own grandmother.

Yet this was more than just a grandmotherly kind of love. It was universal and all-encompassing.

As she kept her hand on my face, she was imparting something to me. Then she moved her other hand and softly placed it on my chest. I could feel energy moving though me. My being filled up with love and acceptance. And hope. And a million emotions. And I thoroughly understood why Nicolai loved her so much, and trusted her. She was like a ray of light.

My tears fell freely. She touched one that landed on my cheek and pressed it to her mouth. What was it about these people and their taste for bodily fluids?

"Tears of love are healing, my dear," she said, placing her hand back on my face. She softly caught them with her thumb and massaged them into my cheek. "They mean you have a pure and open heart. And that what you feel is real."

Maybe it was the power of suggestion, but at the moment she said those words it was as if a veil lifted, or a cloud dispersed, and I could see through different eyes. My head was not rattling with confusion as it had been for days, and the tightness in my chest had disappeared. In this brief time, I felt changed.

She dropped her hands to her lap and appeared to take a moment to rest. Then she reached one hand to the side of her bed and brought it back to her lap. There was something there now that I couldn't quite see.

Although it surprised me when she asked to see my right palm I did not resist.

"Your heart line is broken from here to here," she said tracing the groove in my palm that ran less than an inch under the fold of my fingers. "These small lines that cross the larger line show you have had emotional trauma. But this," she said, gliding her small fingertip across my hand, "shows that the impact of this trauma ends in this part of your life. You can accept love, if you choose to."

I looked over at Nicolai. He was holding his chin in his hand and tearing up. And he was looking at us both with so much love. Somehow, I could no longer even remember the man who hijacked me during a business event and tried to make me believe we were destined lovers. What I saw was a man who was strong enough to show how much he could love. A man who loved me. *Me.*

"Thank you, Mrs. Petre." I wanted to scoop her up in my arms and hug her. I wanted to keep her alive forever.

"Please call me Grandmamma if you wish," she said, squeezing my hand. Her skin was impossibly soft. My memory flashed back to my own grandmother's skin. "It took some time for Nicolai to be *ready* to find you, but there has always been a place for you in our family. We waited for you."

"Waited for me?" Now I was crying ugly tears. I thought his showing up on the elevator and our meeting had been random. What did she mean that they'd been waiting for me?

"I know you have been through a great deal of loss, and pain, and that it's not easy for you to accept our unusual way of doing things." She seemed to get a new burst of energy as she gripped my hand more firmly, but she was teary-eyed too. "But I ask you to trust my Nicolai. You have only to look into his eyes for the truth of his feelings—but I think you already know this. Only true beloveds can know this in such a short period of time."

"I think I understand," I said. "I'm *trying* to understand."

"Understand with your heart, my dear." She looked away for a moment, as if giving some thought to something, and then she brought her gaze back to mine. "You have not been raised to believe this, but you have a special power in your DNA, same as Nicolai. Tomorrow, a convergence of influences in the heavens will give you both the chance to open to your gifts. But you must do this together."

"What kind of gifts?" Finally, I was getting some answers. "And why must we do this tomorrow, together?"

"In our spiritual clan of seers around the world, a large mass of power passes to the next generation tomorrow," she said. "It is the power to know things before they happen."

She eyed me, as if looking for a reaction, but I kept my face frozen and listened.

"This power is something people of ill-intent would like to use to throw darkness into the world," she continued, shaking her head. "We use our powers only for the best intentions, to help ourselves and others. Nicolai needs his *Ves'tacha* by his side, and you need him. Two are stronger than one."

"But what if I don't want to take on this power," I asked, feeling the edge of panic, and still not sure what I was signing on for.

"It's not something outside of you." She sounded a bit tired now. "The power is inside you. Just as true beloveds are inside each other's hearts before they meet. The full moon will activate it. Nicolai must be with you because he is more spiritually prepared. But then, when you are married and settled, you will be the one with more power—the women folk always are." She laughed. I laughed too, but the weight of the statement—"married and settled"—did not escape me.

Nicolai, being sensitive to my reactions to the *M*-word, brought his body closer to mine and placed his hand on my lower back. I think he knew how much I loved that feeling and wanted to soothe me a little. A great, warm energy came from his hand to my spine.

For a moment, I was distracted. That's when his grandmother pressed something into my hand.

"This is for you," she said, closing my hand around a deep blue velvet pouch. It was a bit heavy, like a stone. "Keep it close to your heart tomorrow—and always."

I was reluctant to accept, but it didn't feel like the right time to refuse her gift. His grandmother's hand was still pressed against mine as she began to fade. She closed her eyes so suddenly I was afraid she was dying.

"She's just weary." He must have sensed my alarm. "She saved her energy to meet you and to share with you. We'll go now."

As I made the move to stand up straight, she reasserted her hold on my hand and looked into my eyes—in the deep, knowing way that was Nicolai's signature look. I marveled again that she had the same eyes—beautiful, blue, sparkling, and expressive eyes.

"My darling Allison, you must not be afraid to meet your destiny," she said in a grandmotherly way, a smile on her lips. "It will all unfold as it is meant to be. You are a strong woman, and now, there is a strong man by your side. Fated love is not always an easy love, but it offers the strong foundation upon which to build your lives, and to get through anything, if you do so together. It gives you a chance to leave the world a better place."

I didn't want to leave her. I wanted to bathe in her magical, loving energy. But I also wanted to know more about her grandson and the destiny she was so sure was mine. She seemed to have the answers. Now was the time to get Nicolai talking too.

"Come, my love," he said, taking my shoulder and urging me away. My hand was still closed around the mysterious item she'd given me.

He said something to his grandmother in Romanian and kissed her forehead.

As we walked out, my attention was caught by a collection of vintage black and white photos in beautiful period frames. She had, indeed, been a beautiful young woman, and the images were from many stages of life—from childhood, to wedding photos, to a photo with two young boys dressed in tiny suits with shorts, sitting on her knees. There was one photo of her laughing with another woman. They sat in front of a house that looked so familiar. I wondered if it was some classic building in Europe, and I could swear I'd seen it somewhere.

Nicolai's eagerness to get us out the door gave me little time to take in the photo, but it stayed in my consciousness.

My head was spinning after that beautiful and unusual encounter. I must have stumbled while departing from her room because Nicolai quickly moved his hands around my waist to keep me from falling. Then he walked by my side, with one hand around my right hip and the other holding my left hand. It seemed he was catching me a lot the last few days. Why did I feel like I was falling so much? Was it a metaphor for falling in love?

"Let's get you food and a libation," he said, guiding us downstairs. "There is something awaiting us in the kitchen."

My right hand began to throb with energy. It wasn't clear whether Nicolai knew what his grandmother slipped to me. I planned to look in the pouch once we got downstairs where he could see it too.

Chapter Eighteen

Just as we began to make our way down the grand staircase, there was a noise below. It sounded like someone entering the palatial residence and chatting with the person who'd opened the door. Maybe it was the nurse? Or perhaps it was Sam or someone who was running the household. A commotion echoed through the very still, quiet halls.

As we reached to the bottom of the stairs, Nicolai looked over to make sure I was okay and he released his tight hold on me. I caught a glimpse of a young maid walking through the foyer to the main room, and there was a gorgeous man with dark hair and blue eyes with her. He looked a bit like a darker-haired Nicolai. The maid was fawning as she escorted him in. They seemed to know each other.

A cautious smile crossed Nicolai's face. He moved to greet the other man and I trailed along. I clenched the velvet pouch tighter in my hand.

"Vlad," he said, kissing the man on one cheek and then the other. "You made it."

"Da. How is she?" Vlad asked. That name! All I could think about was Vlad the Impaler that I'd read about when I was searching for information on Transylvania. I wished Aisha, my walking encyclopedia on men, were here to add historical insights and first impressions.

"Stoic, and determined as usual, but she's weak." Nicolai's eyes rimmed with water. Though he appeared on the verge of tears again, he also seemed to speak with caution, as if he did not want to cause alarm for the other man.

"I want to see her." Vlad looked eager and concerned. "I don't want to wait another minute, man."

"Go. Go see her, and then come and have a bite with us." Nicolai's demeanor was warming up a little more, so I assumed he genuinely wanted to share a meal with him.

For the first time, the other man looked over at me. His gaze linked to mine in an all-too-familiar way. Those eyes apparently ran in the family, yet he was looking at me as if we had known each other for more than ten seconds. Then he gave me a once over, crudely stopping at my breasts, and then the most visible hickey on my neck.

"Ah, your *Ves'tacha?*" he said to Nicolai.

"Da," was his response.

The two men shared a knowing glance. I was still standing there waiting for an introduction. It annoyed me to think this may be *a thing* in the region they hail from—*not* politely introducing the *Ves'tacha* before chatting away—but I gave Nicolai some slack for being distracted and upset about his grandmamma.

"Allison, this is Vlad," he said, tentatively, "my cousin." Ah, the cousin who is the model no doubt. Yes, I could imagine him on the home page of our e-reader as "Hot Guy with Accent." And he would look good on a widely circulated meme in social media—shirtless and windblown on a beach. But there was something off-putting about him. And Nicolai seemed hesitant to introduce us.

I quickly transferred the velvet pouch into my other hand and reached out my hand to shake his. He lifted and kissed it. Another hand kisser! Uncomfortable, I looked over to Nicolai to make sure it was okay. "It's a thing," he explained. "Men in Romania do not shake hands with women. They kiss hands."

"Or they ignore you," said Vlad, with a huge grin. "But who could ignore a woman as beautiful as this." He had the family charm, like Nicolai, but he was more of a pretty boy. I sensed immediately that he could be trouble.

"Yes, cousin, I agree she is beautiful." Nicolai pulled me to his side possessively. I was sure he'd add, "And she's mine." But he refrained. I sensed an unspoken tension between them. Maybe they were both grieving, or perhaps they were so alpha they could not help being competitors.

"Okay, I'll see you in a few," said Vlad, in a statement addressed to Nicolai, but he looked very intentionally at me. His flirty nature would be fun on a photo shoot, where we like to tease out that side of models. Here it was uncomfortable.

When the two men spoke, they sounded culturally western. Yet Vlad also had a slight accent, which I heard again when he turned to the maid and said, "Take me to the countess, please."

That's when the world suddenly stood still, as I replayed what I thought I heard in my mind. Nicolai stood there, looking as if he were bracing himself for my response to overhearing his cousin. I waited for Vlad and the maid to walk away before saying a word.

"Countess?" I asked softly, raising an eyebrow to Nicolai.

"Yes, my love," he said, just as softly. "Grandmamma has had that title for a long time."

"Is it, like, a royal title?" A gazillion questions shot off in my head like fireworks. "From where? What is she countess of?"

"Years ago, it was connected with the court of the Royal Consorts of Transylvania, who were basically seated kings and queens of Romania," he said. "The bloodline was mixed with monarchs being married to Romanian rulers from other countries. My grandfather came from a well-to-do family and fell into favor. Grandpappa was rewarded with an estate, land, and a title for himself and his wife. That is the family legend, anyway."

He took a deep breath and put his hand to his chin before continuing. He appeared to be measuring how much to tell me.

"Oh, please, don't stop there." I folded my arms and shot him a glance that let him know I expected him to continue. I didn't care that we were still standing in the foyer.

"Grandpappa was very young. His family decided they had to work quickly to find him a bride so he could properly claim the rights and deeds to what had been promised." He paused for a moment and looked into my eyes to see how I was taking the information. "My grandmother was born to a wealthy Russian family. She is of Romani blood and her father did not want her persecuted or shunned as a gypsy. He wanted her to have a title and prestige that would elevate her. So, he made an arranged marriage that gave her security and social status. The marriage was put together within a week."

Finally, a clue. Maybe this is a family of fast-tracked marriages—even eighty years ago.

"I guess it is difficult for the family to lose the titles when your grandmother is no longer here?" I placed my hands on my hips and started tapping my foot, eager for his response. From working with my dad, who had executed public relations and marketing for royals, I knew a little bit about people with old money and old titles—they liked to keep everything in the family, forever.

"Well…" He pointed toward a room off to the side. "Let's get out of the foyer so we can grab some food and sit. Family history is always better over a meal and liquor."

"Okay, but, you're not going to tell me you are a marquis or a baron or anything like that, right?" I slipped the pouch his grandmother gave me into my purse, suddenly afraid to look at it. "I mean, your generation is not titled, right?"

"Technically speaking," he said sheepishly, "I do have a title."

"And are you going to tell me this title?" Now I was on edge, waiting for the bombshell to drop.

"Count," he said, taking a breath and looking down before bringing his eyes back to mine to answer. "My title is Count."

"Jeez-us. Does it look like my mouth dropped open?" I asked. "Because it feels that way." *How did Aisha miss this in her research?*

"The older generation likes to keep their titles, and pass them to the next, along with land that has been in the family and certain inheritances a bit more international in scope. It became my inheritance when my father refused it, and later passed away, and my grandfather insisted it continue. And Grandmamma also wishes to keep the titles alive."

"By passing it to a daughter or granddaughter?" I wondered if there were a royal Romanian soap opera about to unfold, with multiple relatives vying for the wealth and legacy of his grandmother.

"No, to you, Allison," he said, calmly, as if it were a logical next step for his family. "There are no daughters or granddaughters. Besides, the title is inherited through primogeniture, meaning through the male heir. Through marriage, you would be the new Countess of Miklosvar."

"The Countess of what now?" It may have come out a bit louder than I intended. "Do I look like I'm having a hard time breathing?"

"It's just a family tradition," he said, putting his arms on my shoulders and pulling me toward him. "But there is an inheritance involved, material and spiritual. If you choose to marry me—someday—that is."

I felt the blood drain out of my head and drop down to my feet as my breathing hastened.

"I think you need a drink," he said.

"Da," was my response.

CHAPTER NINETEEN

We wandered toward the back of the house, into a grand kitchen. The appliances were old-fashioned. Unlike the fancy newfangled bathroom under the stairs and far from Nicolai's super modern abode—with his glass front refrigerator, shiny equipment, and marble countertops—this area looked unintentionally retro. It was something from a time before either of us was born, but it was familiar because my grandmother had older appliances in her apartment when I was growing up.

The refrigerator was a bright turquoise classic Frigidaire that looked like something from the sixties. Nicolai opened it and was poking around inside when he noticed my breathing was still a little unhinged.

He closed the door, leaned against it, and pulled me into his arms.

"Should I find you a paper bag to breathe into?" he asked, trying to be lighthearted. "Or maybe I can use my lips to calm you. It worked once before." I pouted at him in protest, but his mouth came down on mine and somehow, he was right. My body and my breathing began to settle from his touch. I melted into him, remembering the feelings that led me to this crazy situation in the first place.

He took hold of my face and pulled me closer. His mouth moved wildly over mine, his tongue urgent, probing, and moving in an out. Our bodies naturally melded together as we kissed. It was more like tongue fucking each other's mouths—right there in his grandmother's retro kitchen. I got so turned-on that I was about to suggest he do something dirty to me on the Formica countertop. I pulled his shirt out of his pants in the back so I could get my hands on his flesh.

That's when an older woman in a server's uniform came in. She was zaftig and outfitted in a white apron and an old-fashioned hairnet. She had on black work boots. The stern look in her eye indicated she didn't want us fornicating around her food.

"Please, Count Nicolai, sit with your *Ves'tacha*, and I will serve you." She waved us away from the area toward an adjacent dining room.

He glanced over at me quickly for my reaction to the *C*-word. I tried not to roll my eyes and instead stayed very still so I could recover from the kiss—and from getting *caught* kissing and fondling him. He definitely got my mind off the matching titles and taking over the grandparent's legacy for a few minutes—until his scary-looking maid reminded me I had just tongued a Transylvanian count. She apparently was one of his constituents. I still couldn't wrap my head around it. Why couldn't there be *anything* normal about this man and his family? Including the maid?

"There's no need, Helen," he said, straightening up and tucking his shirt back in. "We can grab something."

"Please, sir." She wasn't taking no for an answer, which struck me as odd, since that was usually his approach. I guess he could submit, too. Maybe he was unable to say no to Romanian women who looked like they could kick his ass.

"Of course." He guided me into the dining room. It was the most impressive one I had ever seen in a private home, with a long oak table and magnificent throne-like chairs at either end. The fireplace had beautiful carvings and looked big enough for Santa and his reindeer to descend through. The fire was bright, casting a glow in the soft-lit room. I wondered if he would escort me to one end of the table and then seat himself at the other. I was relieved when we took seats next to each other because I wanted to continue my inquisition.

"Don't think you can kiss your way out of this … Count." I smiled, still feeling the results of said kiss between my legs.

"I had to try, Ms. Monroe," he said, brushing his hand against mine and lifting it to his mouth to kiss. "I didn't want you to faint, after all."

"Perhaps it was not the worst distraction in the world." I ran a finger along the smooth wood of the table. "So, tell me, is this place one of your homes?"

"It is Grandmamma's," he said. "But, yes, it will transfer to me. To us."

"Is the maid negotiable?" I was making a joke.

"She's been faithful to our family for decades, so I wouldn't want to displace her and disrupt her life," he said, quite seriously. "I can set her up in her own place on the grounds, with a cushy retirement fund, if you would rather have a new staff."

My chest tightened. He was still talking to me as if this were happening and that we would be together.

"Is that drink coming soon?" I calculated that I would need at least three shots of hard liquor to loosen me up. "Make it something with vodka, with a vodka chaser."

He left my side for a small bar against the wall and came back with a cool cherry soda with a touch of vodka in it. I took a sip. It was the drink I tasted on his lips the night we met.

"Allison, my love, can we talk about this—all of this—without you throwing that drink at me?" He paced the room and seemed to organize his thoughts in his head.

"Okay," I took a deep breath, and placed my palms down on the top of the table. "But you know this is all very weird, right? And it's weird on top of odd when you think of our unusual courtship rituals. So, I have the right to react."

"Yes, I know it is odd," he said, smiling. "So react away, just don't throw things or storm out."

"I'd be within my rights, with all these late-breaking surprises, on top of you being my client," I reminded him. It seemed like the least relevant part of the story right now, but it would be hugely important again when I returned to work Monday.

"Well, there is something you should know about that," he said, running a hand through his hair. "There's a bit of a back story."

"You might as well tell me all of it." I breathed deeply, trying to pull in as much oxygen as I could, and braced myself.

"Grandmamma had a dream that an offer was coming to me that would bring me closer to my beloved," he said. "A day later, a group of tech developers approached me to pitch the e-reader. I have no business dealings in the electronic world, but it seemed like a sound idea, and I took the meeting. I followed my gut and agreed to back it."

"How did you end up with Berke and Monroe for marketing?" I wondered if he'd seen my photo on our company website, or somewhere, and tracked me down in advance. I was bracing myself to discover he was a stalker, on top of all else, and that he calculated our elevator meet-cute up to the exact moment.

"I brought in other people to work on product development," he said. "People who knew the business well. They warned me it would be a tougher market in the United States because it is saturated with devices here, but they researched countries where we could potentially lead the market. I had the developers adapt products to work in other countries, but we had to have the right international marketing team. I had a short list of three companies."

"I guess I know where this is heading," I said, "but please enlighten me."

"I met with them all. I thought your boss, Sheila, was a complete snake when I met her, but I got a good a feeling about the firm. I didn't know why. I even tried to second guess myself, and brought the names of all three companies to my grandmother so she could tune in."

I lifted the drink to my mouth and took a swig. And then another. "Holy crap," I said. "Are you telling me that you people totally operate on gut instincts and that you paid three million to my firm on a hunch?"

"Yes," he said, stroking his beard as he spoke. "Pretty much."

I took another swig of the drink and rubbed my forehead as if it would take my disbelief away. "You need to get the whole bottle of vodka before you say another word."

He walked over to the bar, snatched the bottle and the cherry drink, with another glass, and brought it over. He poured himself a drink while he refilled mine.

"I wrote the three companies down on a piece of paper," he continued. "When I gave it to my grandmother, she closed her eyes and ran her fingers across the page. This is what she told me: 'One of these has a woman you will hate, but will also have the woman you will love.' "

"Oh, my God," I exclaimed, trembling. The words hit like a torpedo. My stomach hurt and I realized my boss had inadvertently tipped him off to which company to pick.

"Yes, it was Sheila," he continued, nodding his head. "I despised her the minute I met her. I hated the idea of working with her. She was the only one in all the companies who I had such a bad reaction to, so I knew that was the company I had to hire. But I had no idea *you* were who I was looking for. Not until the elevator. Not until that night. I just followed the signs that kept leading me down this path. The only thing I was sure of was that I would know you when I saw you. And I did."

My heart opened when he said that, but my brain shut it down, hungry for more information to explain the crazy ride I had been on for the past few days.

"Why didn't you mention this Count thing?" I questioned. "I mean, don't you think it's information I have the right to know? I asked you if you were a vampire, and you said no. Why couldn't you say, 'I am not a vampire, but coincidentally, I am a count, but not Count Dracula?'"

"Allison, think of how you would have responded *then* if this is how you are taking it *now*." He sounded irritated. "I sensed it would be overwhelming, but I didn't think you would be mad at me for having a title."

"I'm not mad at you for the title; I'm upset to hear about it as an afterthought since it is apparently an important part of this," I said, making air quotes, "'transition of power.'"

"There are a lot of things I wish I'd done better," he said, taking a deep sip of his drink. "I've been trying to figure this out as I go along, trying to keep you interested and aroused. I didn't know Grandmamma was so close to the end, or that you'd be here today, or that we would even make it to this point. I planned on telling you everything on the full moon. But maybe now you can see why I wanted you to love me first, so you were less likely to walk away."

He looked at me with those eyes and took my hand.

"But that's so manipulative, to try to hook me first." My voice was a few octaves higher because of the alcohol. "You know this looks like a setup, right, as if you need a female to put into place to hold the title and inheritance and a breeder to get you some heirs eventually."

I didn't truly believe that, but I wasn't quite sure *what* to believe. I couldn't simply accept this crazy story, could I? My option to mistrust him was like a safety net. He'd topple all my walls if I didn't challenge him. I wasn't ready for that yet.

"I have my own money," he quickly asserted. "A lot of it. I don't need the additional inheritance for personal use."

"But you can always use more, right?" I clinked my drink against his. "No one would fault you for wanting to hold on to family money."

"I wish you would let me explain more about my financial situation," he said, exasperated, grasping his beard. "I want to tell you *everything*. I'll even set up an appointment with my financial advisors so you can review all my holdings, properties, real estate, and other assets."

I reclined a little in my chair as if I were about to see a PowerPoint presentation.

He stared at the fire for a moment. Then he turned his gaze to me with a look that begged me to please listen and let him finish. So I did.

"My father and his brother inherited money from their grandfather and, after the war, established a business in the United States that became worth millions of dollars," he said.

"My uncle, Vlad's father, died suddenly, and my father decided to retire. He sold the company and made sure our mothers, Vlad's and mine, would be taken care of for life. Grandmamma has her own fortune, so when we became of age he gave the rest of the money to Vlad and me. I was twenty-four. Vlad was twenty. My father told us to find a way to invest it so we would never have to rely on anyone else for an income. It was twenty million dollars. We could have lived on it forever, but we turned it into billions, investing in other people and companies. My father did not want me to follow in my grandmother's footsteps. He thought she was wacky, quite frankly. He raised me to become a successful businessman."

"So now I don't feel so bad for my initial reaction," I said, slightly vindicated. "But why are you doing it?"

"My grandmother. She is all the family I have left now, except for Vlad and you, I hope." He seemed sad and reflective. "I've been successful in business, and I want more out of life now. I want my true love. I want my own family. And I want to do things to help others, the way Grandpappa and Grandmamma always did."

"But wait, do you run a business with Vlad now?" Somehow, I did not picture the dark-haired Petre as a business whiz.

"No," he said shaking his head. "My cousin likes to model and party, and not deal with business, so he sold his interests to me. Our financials are pretty much separate at this point. He does his thing, and I do mine. But of course, there will be matters of inheritance to deal with when Grandmamma is, well…" He stopped and took a sip of his drink, savoring it before speaking. "Do you feel a little more informed now?"

"Far more than I was five days ago when you made your first appearance and your first pitch," I laughed. "But tell me again why everything hinges on tomorrow's full moon. I'd like to spend days and weeks talking like this and getting to know you. This deadline feels so rushed."

"It's about the prophecy." He plunked his glass down on the table and stood to pace around the room.

"What about the 'prophecy?' " I made double quotation marks in the air to stress my frustration. I was beginning to understand bits and pieces, but it was still a mystery to someone not raised in the same mystery school as Nicolai and his grandmother. "Why is there such a mad dash to be bound to one another?"

"The full moon tomorrow gives us a window of time when the aspects favor us, as Grandmamma pointed out." He walked to the head of the table and sat on the arm of the big throne chair. "I don't understand all the astrological and spiritual aspects. I simply know my grandmother's dream became part of our family prophecy, and she has guided me toward it since I was young. I wasn't ready until recently, and when that happened, the wheels were put into motion and I was able to enter the world in which you dwelled. I have been preparing for you for many years. I loved you before I met you. This is easier for me. I felt everything I needed to feel about you in that first kiss."

"But were you really doing this for love?" I couldn't let it go. "It seems you were looking for me to fulfill the prophecy or please your grandmother. Isn't it a bit unromantic, trying to rope me in like that?" My mind drifted to Nostradamus' predictions. It dawned on me that Nicolai might also believe there was a bad thing that would happen if we didn't fulfill the prophecy.

"Five days or five months, it has the same end result," he said, sounding practical but annoyed again. He seemed to think I should move on already. "I will make sure there is time on the other end of things for you to adjust and be happy about your choice. For whatever reason, the clock is ticking for us."

"It sounds like a fairytale," I said, nervously draining my glass with a large sip and refilling it with vodka straight up. "Am I going to turn into a pumpkin at midnight tomorrow?"

He looked at me, his beautiful eyes staring deep into mine. He smiled, yet it was a sad smile. "Maybe this *can* be our fairy tale."

"What if I still can't believe in happy endings?" I started to feel a buzz from the vodka, enough to say things I wouldn't normally utter. "Look, you're handsome, rich, tall, titled, own property, and you're a fucking good catch," I said, taking another swig. "I have feelings for you—deep ones. I dream about your penis at night. And even the non-sex I've had with you has been the best sex ever. On top of that, your grandmother is really cool and she thinks I'm great. But I'm pissed." I pointed my glass in his direction. "Do you want to know why?"

"I want to know everything." He came back and sat next to me, but he folded his arms across his chest so I wasn't sure he really wanted to hear it. Liquid courage was helping me along.

"You seduced me and made me fall for you," I said, wielding my drink in hand as I spoke. "At the very least, you created conditions in which I could find you nothing less than irresistible. And once I was hooked and here at your grandmother's house in the middle of nowhere, you people start letting me in on the secrets. Shouldn't I have been the first person to know the important stuff, *before* I was hooked? Before it became almost impossible for me to separate myself from you? Before I fucking fell in … in … fell for you? I mean, who does that to someone?"

He quickly moved his chair so it was sidesaddle to the table and turned me around in my chair to face him.

"Go back to the second to the last thing you said." He took the drink from my hand and leaned in. "You're right. I fucked up. I manipulated everything, but tell me that part again. Please."

"I think I'll wait." My speech was a little slurred and from the way my stomach was rumbling I realized I need some food. And that I probably should have refrained from drinking on an empty stomach. "I should save at least something that you don't know for the coronation or consummation or whatever you think we may do tomorrow to fulfill the prophecy."

I excused myself to go to the bathroom under the stairway. I hoped no one heard me throwing up the last two glasses of vodka. Gross. Fortunately, I'd left my overnight bag in there when I showered and it contained needed supplies. I brushed my teeth, my hair, and washed my face. I reapplied my lipstick. At least I felt sober again.

CHAPTER TWENTY

When I came back to the table, there were three place settings—two in front of where Nicolai and I were sitting, and one across from us. The cook had come in and was apparently getting ready to feed us.

Someone had turned the chairs back and Nicolai sat facing the fireplace. His hands were steepled, prayer-like, in front of him. I sat down next to him and his arm gently brushed against mine.

I gazed at the fire too, waiting in silence for his next move.

"Allison," he said, turning toward me and taking my hand. "My parents were both killed in a plane crash when I was still in my twenties. Vlad travels the globe, doing his own thing. The only person who has given me love and comfort is my grandmother. When you have wealth, everyone wants a piece of you, of it, and you are surrounded by takers, users, and unsavory people—the Sheilas of the world. It is so hard to find someone you can trust with your life. I was lucky my grandmother's dreams helped lead me to you. In my enthusiasm to lock things into place, I may have acted like an alpha. Okay, maybe I was an asshat. But can you let me off the hook for that?"

"Possibly." I wanted to let him off the hook and return to his arms, but I felt there was still a missing piece of information.

"I hope you can," he said, squeezing my hand. "Because there is only one person I want, need. Deep down, in a place where there are no words. Don't you feel it too?"

"Crazily enough," I sighed. "I do. But I need more words. Tell me one more thing. What is the spiritual component you mentioned?"

Nicolai looked at me as if he was about to reveal something I might not like. Just then, Vlad wandered in. Nicolai stood, seeming relieved, and walked to his cousin. Together they were like a matched set of dark and light gorgeousness. Was it possible there could be two human males as handsome and hot, not only in the same room, but in the same family? Well, maybe the Hemsworths.

"So, what did I miss, cousin?" Vlad said with a grin, slapping him on the back. He was much more jovial in nature.

"I was just catching Allison up on some family history." Nicolai opened a new bottle of vodka and poured Vlad a drink.

"Ah, you mean *The Transylvania Saga*?" He gave me a sly, sexy look. I folded my arms over my chest. He had those sexy Petre eyes too, but more mischievous. "There should be a book on it."

"Vlad," said Nicolai. "Please, go easy on the TMI. I don't want Allison to run screaming out of here. She's had enough for one day."

I realized Vlad, who was younger and seemed much more easygoing, may have some family secrets to share. I intended to pump him for some.

"What do you know about this prophecy?" I insisted, looking him square in the eye.

"My grandmother hails from a long line of seers, and healers, and has the gift," he said. "Her father was also rich. He saw her destiny with a man who had favor with a branch of royalty and somehow made connections to find him through a Romanian family. Grandpappa came into his land, title, and money at seventeen. He needed a wife and heirs to his title and estate. Our grandparents accepted their destiny, no problem. Grandmamma gave birth to Nicolai's father, and then mine, but they are both deceased. This is where my dear cousin comes in. He's the oldest grandchild."

I massaged my temples. Their stories checked out, but Vlad put in more nuances. Now I knew Grandmamma's father had a vision about her husband-to-be before they physically met.

"For the elder ones, it is all about continuing forever," said Vlad, "So it is up to my cousin to keep the line going. This requires a wife and heirs. Also, he has to tend to that Godforsaken area of the homeland, and the people, that my grandmother loves so much."

Nicolai jumped in. "Don't make it sound like a cold business deal," he said, scowling at his cousin. "Grandmamma has given us both insights into our romantic destiny for the purpose of helping us find true love." He turned to me. "Allison, I've found this week *extremely* romantic."

I stayed quiet as this new information rolled out, trying to wrap my brain around what that really meant in terms of day-to-day existence and a lifetime commitment. Vlad broke my concentration. There was something very charming about him, maybe overly charming and bordering on devious. When he spoke, I was compelled to listen.

"Allison, you look a little troubled," he said. "Most women want to jump on this guy and take him home to their mothers. He's quite a catch, as I understand it."

"It's just that the marriage thing, in general, was not high on my list. And now..." The love thing had been off my radar until Nicolai maneuvered his way in there. And the count and countess thing—definitely not on my wish list.

"Ah, you haven't had the sixth date," said Vlad, surprised. He looked at his cousin with a raised eyebrow.

"Tomorrow," Nicolai explained. "Grandmamma got sick and we are trying to work things out here. And now, I am afraid I may have given Allison bigger doubts about me than the day we met." He grinned, trying to make a joke, but he seemed unsettled. "I fear this day will make her run from me."

Looking in my direction he mouthed, "Please don't run."

My heart sank a little, to see this softer, needier side of him, but I was sure it was part of his strategy to make me sympathetic to his needs.

The maid came in with the first course: soup. She must have gone out and foraged for the vegetables somewhere because it had taken forever for her to bring any food into the room. Everyone sat down and ate in silence. I pushed the spoon around in my bowl, but could barely lift it to my mouth. I still felt crappy from boozing it up and then barfing in Grandmamma's bathroom. I felt Nicolai's gaze on me the whole time. He looked worried.

He and his cousin exchanged glances. They appeared to be as close as brothers, but brothers who possibly had a bit of animosity. I couldn't tell what their issue was, but if I had to guess, the younger cousin was more of a ne'er do well and Nicolai was the responsible one. That did not stop them from being in each other's business. Vlad seemed to know more about my destiny with Nicolai than I did.

"Vlad, tell me more about that 'Godforsaken area of the homeland' you mentioned before, the place your grandmother loves." I placed my spoon in my soup just as the cook arrived to collect the bowls. Then she returned with a dish that had a yellow covering and red peppers on top, with small pieces of beef, and a dish with potatoes, peas, and lots of mayo or sour cream. The food temporarily stalled my information gathering. It also made me a little nauseous.

"Oh, Salad de Boeuf, thank you, Helen," said Vlad, smiling at the older woman. "Just the way you used to make it for Grandpappa." It was apparently a favorite dish.

"And here's potato salad," she said, setting it close to Nicolai. "Exactly the way you like it." Nicolai smiled at her like a kid on Christmas.

She spooned out a big portion for the men and some for me. I was touched when Nicolai asked her to also bring me a regular salad and the coconut milk in the fridge. She brought both out and set them at my place.

The hot cousins both dug in to their food as she waited for their reaction. She seemed pleased to see them enjoying her Romanian classic cooking so much.

"Helen, you're the best," said Vlad, grinning at her and his full plate, and then singing her praises to me and Nicolai. "Man, I'm starving, and I can't eat this stuff when I'm doing fashion shoots. But how can I resist Helen's cooking? Never! She's been cooking for us since we were little."

She blushed and headed back into the kitchen. I realized how fond of them she was and that there was a lot of history between them. Maybe she was just *different* and not so scary.

"So, Vlad, what were you referring to before?" I drank the coconut milk to soothe my stomach and began to slowly work on my salad, while continuing to probe. "The Godforsaken place?"

He looked over at Nicolai, who nodded to go ahead to explain.

"Grandfather was able to get back possession of his manors in Miklosvar, which is in Transylvania," he explained, chewing as he went along. "He also began the project of restoration to his family's old lodge on the land there. But part of the deal was that he would also make renovations in the village and on the roads. The place has not changed much in the last hundred years, and the people still live off the land. Rebuilding brings income into the economy and provides jobs."

He jabbed his fork into a serving plate to scoop up more food.

"Grandmamma has kept it going all these years since Grandpappa died." He took a sip of his drink and paused, eyeing me for my reaction. "She wants Nicolai to take over, and to build a place for the people she considers her tribe, so they can come and chant or meditate or something. She has money in a foundation to cover it."

"That's sweet," I said, looking at Nicolai. It sounded like a good cause, in that moment.

"Sweet until you have to drive on those crappy roads or you crave Starbucks," Vlad said with a laugh. "It's antiquated. And as the Countess of Miklosvar, you will have to reside there."

Nicolai dropped his fork with a clank. He cleared his throat, as if trying to get my attention, but I kept my gaze on Vlad.

"Seriously? Like move in?" I stopped chewing for a moment. And stopped breathing, too.

"Just for a few weeks each year," Nicolai interjected. "It's beautiful there. The Prince and Princess of Wales bought a home there. There must be worse things than being stuck in a foreign country alone with me, no?"

I stared down at the plate and played with my food. Having to live in another country for an extended period of time was a deal breaker for me. I mean, I was no Grace Kelly jetting off to Monaco to be a princess. And this was Transylvania. Why would I want to go there?

"Please look at me, my love," said Nicolai, pulling back his alpha powers of seduction and serenading me with his sexy voice.

I looked up. His gaze captured mine, the way it always did. Holding me, pulling me in, making me feel things—even if the circumstances now seemed overwhelming.

"This was not entirely my choice," he said. "To carry around all the baggage of my inheritance."

"Then why carry it at all?" I finally looked at him.

"Family honor and duty. Tradition. Grandmamma." He put down his fork and wiped his mouth with the linen napkin. "And you. I didn't really understand it until I got to know you, but this could be an adventure, if we share it together."

He did it again. He made me want to cry and melt into him. Although there were a million reasons my red flags have been flying all week and all day, there were two things I believed in this moment: Nicolai truly cared for me, and I cared for him.

Maybe we could work this thing out? Every time he said something that touched my heart, it made me want to have faith in him.

"I'll tell you one thing, Nicolai," I said, regaining my sense of humor. "On top of everything you and I have to work out, if we make it to date six, you are going to have to deal with my boss. I don't even want to think about her reaction to this whirlwind of insanity. And God forbid I take any time off for a trip to Romania."

"Oh, we will deal with Sheila," he smiled at me and laughed. "So, what's the verdict? Have we sufficiently welcomed you into the family?"

"More like sufficiently hypnotized me with Romanian folk magic," I laughed. "But I guess that's how things roll in this family. So, I suppose I feel welcomed."

Vlad just sat there quietly, finishing his food, watching my expressions.

Nicolai stood and took our plates into the kitchen. "I must stay with Grandmamma, tonight," he said when he returned to the table. "So, I think it is best to get you home. I will come to you tomorrow and you can let me know your decision."

"Nicolai, maybe I should stay here with you," I said, apprehensive. Perhaps it was separation anxiety. I had a weird feeling that something bad might happen, maybe that his grandmother could pass away and I would be so far away. "Maybe we shouldn't part."

"I don't want to be separated, either, but I am needed here and it's only fair that you have this time to go home and give some thought to all that was discussed," he said. "And that you rest."

Vlad stepped over to say good-bye, kissing me on both cheeks, acting extremely friendly. "I hope you will be my cousin, soon," he said, bending in a little too close to whisper in my ear. "Keep in mind, this intensity will blow over when Grandmamma is gone. Many of his choices stem from his desire to serve her wishes."

What the hell did that mean? That Nicolai's professed feelings for me would blow over too? That he wouldn't care as much about us or family responsibility if Grandmamma were gone? Or that we would be freer, and less pressured to follow family protocol? I smiled at Vlad but felt a new kind of angst brewing inside of me as I headed for the door.

Nicolai walked me back to the car, where Sam patiently awaited. He seemed to have his communication system with Sam tightly orchestrated.

"I love you," Nicolai said. "*Poti sa ma iubesti?*"

I searched his eyes for the translation.

"It means, can you love me?"

I wanted to say yes and throw caution to the wind, but every time I turned around there seemed to be a new obstacle to face down or discuss.

"Ask me tomorrow." I pressed my cheek into his shoulder. He held me tight.

"If you find it in your heart to take the chance with me, then we can do this, Allison." He kissed the top of my head and pulled me closer.

"I hope so, because this looks like a hot mess right now." I didn't want to tell him the comments Vlad made on my way out, but I couldn't shake it from my mind. Those comments, combined with our intensive family information session, were weighing on me. Nicolai was right. I needed to go home and chill out from the day.

"I think what we have is *hot,* but not a mess," he said optimistically. "Any problems that come along with this have solutions. I promise you."

"You never answered me about the spiritual part of it all." I was probably too weary to take this on, but it was one of the last pieces of the jigsaw puzzle.

"The Count and Countess of Miklosvar have traditionally maintained leadership of a spiritual community of seers in Transylvania who are devoted to using their gifts to help people toward the betterment of humanity," he said. "They confer on many foreign affairs and current events. It was a secret society, forced underground during communist rule and still not part of the mainstream. My grandmother, being Russian-born, expanded the circle to healers around the world. At ninety-eight years old, she is still at the helm. She has always used her gifts and her title to do good works."

"And this gets passed to you as well?" There was a gulp that followed the words. If I met him at a social event and dated him for six months, this might all seem like an impossibly charming romance. But he wanted me to say "da" to it all tomorrow.

"Yes." I expected him to be uncomfortable, but he seemed happy.

"But I don't have any second sight or healing powers." I shifted from foot to foot trying to find words that didn't insult those who do. "I search everything on Google. The Internet. That's my superpower."

"You do have these powers, you just don't know them all yet," he said, kissing my forehead. "Haven't you noticed more gut feelings about people and things lately? I've been kissing your third eye every night to try to help open your sight."

That's what that was? He even licked between my eyebrows. I flashed to every time he touched that part of me. "Why didn't you explain?"

"I was giving your natural abilities a little prodding," he said. "But you can develop these if you choose, with or without me. It's just that the full moon has special powers. Man is like the sun, but woman is part of the moon. And the full moon increases powers of intuition. It brings things to fruition."

He was making sense again, in his own offbeat way.

"Is there anything else I should know?" I was slightly terrified to ask because, frankly, I'd heard enough for one day.

"Only that having more information does not change real feelings." He looked up into the darkened sky at the nearly full moon. "When you strip away the layers and look at the purest essence of it all, what I'm offering to you is love. If you take away the baggage and family drama, I'm just a man asking a woman to love him."

Did he know he was kind of lifting that line from one of my favorite movies, *Notting Hill*? I didn't even care. I heard that louder and clearer than anything else. I wanted nothing more than to believe him with all my heart.

"Come to me soon." That was all I wanted to say.

He helped me into the limo and kissed my hand.

CHAPTER
TWENTY-ONE

On the way home, restless and edgy, I tried to sort through the multiple revelations that had dropped like tiny bombs all day. Especially the last one, which could be construed by a jaded mind like mine as Nicolai trying to enlist me in some kind of cult. Was this secret spiritual society filled with Moonie-like followers led by Grandmamma? She didn't strike me as being that devious, but then again, she sent her eldest grandson on a quest to find true love based on dreams and intuitive hunches. Has she sent hundreds of others into the same wedding abyss, with a deadline to consummate these spiritually arranged marriages beneath the full moon tomorrow? Jeez.

I pulled out my smart phone and searched for Miklosvar in Central Romania. There was no information, obviously, about the secret spiritual society, but I was surprised to see that it had a small population and was a place where people traveled by horse-drawn carriages, tended homegrown crops, and baked their own bread. It sounded like *Doctor Zhivago* meets *Little House on the Prairie*.

I read that after the collapse of the Berlin Wall, families were able to go back and claim estates that had been seized by the state. There was another count mentioned who had turned his family home into a Bed and Breakfast, so I figured there was a paper trail somewhere to back up what Nicolai and Vlad shared.

Based on what I found, it was a fairly common belief that that Transylvania sat on one of Earth's strongest magnetic fields, a vortex of sorts, and the people who lived in the region had extra-sensory perception. Maybe the small town of Miklosvar was filled with intuitives who could predict the future without being touched by the real world?

I looked at photos of some of the homes and estates, and they looked like summer bungalows as compared to Nicolai's other family home. Where was Nicolai's family property? It seemed like going to Romania would be like taking a camping trip in the deep woods.

I read about a nearby city called Sighişoara, which seemed livelier. It was considered a medieval Saxon village but had a population of over 26,000 so there were more castles and churches and things to do. It was also the location of the home of Vlad Tepes—Vlad the Impaler—who was credited as the inspiration for the Bram Stoker character, Count Dracula.

Why was Nicolai's cousin named Vlad? Oh, my God, was this a secret society of love-biting, arousal tasting, rich vampires I was being courted into?

Fuck. Aisha had told me to reach out if I needed her, so I texted her.

Me: "Did you know Nicolai's Grandmother is a countess?" I added five exclamation points.

She texted back immediately.

Aisha: "Yes, I heard that … I also read somewhere that the title had no power or status in her country anymore, but that it had street cred around the world. Let me check. I think an interviewer asked her about it."

She returned with a quote pulled from an online publication:

Aisha: "My title is authentic, and we do have the Incorporeal Hereditaments in the lawyer's vault, but after the war and the dissolution of the monarchy, it meant nothing. But a title is a title. I am used to it. And it adds a status that helps open doors to do my work in the world, and occasionally, to get a theater ticket to a sold-out show or a better seat in a restaurant."

Me: "You're slipping up lady. How did you forget to mention that?"
Aisha: "Oops…"
Me: "Well, better late than never. Thanks for the info. Today I discovered Nicolai is a count! Did you know that?"

I sent a smiley face rolling its eyes.

Aisha: "I didn't know that part. Billionaire problems are such a drag—said no one ever."

She added a smiley face with a heart emoticon.

Me: "I met his grandmother today, and I kind of fell in love with her."

Aisha: "Did she sell you on marrying her grandson?"

Me: "She tried."

Me: "I also met the model cousin. His name is Vlad Petre. Is he on your list?"

Aisha: "Oh no, that's a new one. How did he slip through my radar?"

Me: "Maybe he goes by a different name professionally."

Aisha: "I will get on that as soon as I can and let you know what I find. Meantime, you enjoy your evening."

Me: "Thanks, Aisha. See you Monday. Don't forget we have The Today Show *early in the morning."*

I suddenly remembered the item Grandmamma had given me. I rooted around in my purse, where I'd dropped it, but couldn't seem to find it. I decided to look under better light once I got upstairs.

When Sam pulled up in front of my building, I sat staring into space before I made the move to get out. I tried to absorb the energy of the back seat, and all Nicolai and I had shared there earlier, before reality started to rain on my parade. If things did not go well tomorrow, I may never see this car again. Or Nicolai. The thought of that made my heart hurt.

I was reflective as Sam opened the door and helped me out. I looked at him thoughtfully. "Thank you for everything, Sam."

"My pleasure, Ms. Monroe." He seemed concerned, like the night he dropped me off at home after Nicolai was a no show for our date. Was that *last night*?

"I hope I see you again." I wanted to hug him and thank him for always treating me respectfully, despite my obvious messing around with his boss in the back seat.

He looked puzzled. "I am sure I will see you soon." Why was everyone sure but me?

With that, he tipped his hat and got back in the car. I made the long, lonely walk to my apartment. I didn't know what to do with myself. I wished it were Sunday and I worried it would come too soon. Finally, I opted for a warm bath and a glass of wine.

I filled the bath with sea salt instead of bath salts, because I heard it cleansed spirits and cleared "auras." I hoped it would clear my head, but it actually activated a review of many of the questions I had rolling around in my mind all night.

How much could I love him in only five days, or even six? Did I feel bad for him because he said he was lonely? Was his grandmother making him think he loved me? Do I care about him enough to accept a destiny so far from the life I had planned? Would I have to run a household in Transylvania?

I was completely lost in my head, drying off and getting into my robe, when the pouch from Grandmamma flashed through my head. I reached for my purse on the kitchen counter and turned on the light. I found it wedged between my wallet and makeup case. As I was about to take a look, the buzzer rang. *Who could that be?* Something told me to slide the pouch into a hidden zipper compartment in my pocketbook and look at it later.

"Mr. Petre is here, Ms. Monroe," my doorman said. My heart leapt. Nicolai had come to me early. But how did he get here, if Sam dropped me off a little more than an hour ago? Maybe he took a helicopter to the 34th Street Heliport. It didn't matter. I was glad he was here. Somehow, when we were alone, it was easier for me to believe.

"Thanks, Bill," I answered. "Please send him up."

I waited anxiously by the door. When I opened it, I was stunned to see Vlad standing there, leaning against the door frame. I pulled my robe tight around me.

"Vlad?" I said, not hiding my shock and disappointment. "I thought you were Nicolai." I really wanted to ask what the hell he was doing here, but I tried to be polite.

"My cousin sent me." He looked at me with a come-fuck-me look in his eyes, so I had to wonder why Nicolai would send him. Had Grandmamma died?

"Why?" I sensed trouble. Something in the pit of my stomach didn't feel right. "Is your grandmother okay? Is Nicolai okay?"

"Relax, Allison. I want to help you." With that, he strolled in, stopping to kiss my hand. *What the fuck?*

"Help me with what, exactly?" What was it with these Romanians and their hand kissing, and why did they know my destiny—and my address? I wondered if I should put my grandmother's crucifix on.

"Please, sit. I want to talk to you," he said, motioning for me to walk ahead of him.

He followed me into the living room. When I sat on the big beige leather couch, he joined me. It was inappropriately close since I was in my robe, so I moved to the chair across from him.

"Please, how is your grandmother?" I asked, feeling nervous that he might be there to deliver bad news about her. "Is she all right?"

"She's holding her own at the moment, thank you. Nicolai is spending precious moments with her as we don't know how many more she has." He sat forward on the couch, elbows leaning on knees, like he was about to watch a soccer game. I didn't want to be rude, because he was Nicolai's cousin, but I couldn't understand what he was doing here, sitting on my couch, with me in a bathrobe. I debated about whether I should excuse myself and get dressed, or try to get to the bottom of his visit and escort him to the door.

"So, to what do I owe this visit?"

"Aren't you going to offer me a drink?"

"I don't think that's a good idea." I couldn't help feeling he was up to some kind of mischief. Maybe he was sent to test my devotion to the count. Maybe he *was* a vampire.

"Have a drink with me and I'll explain." He eyed me as I got up to go to the kitchen and get the bottle of wine and another glass. My wineglass was sitting on the coffee table already.

I came back and poured him a glass. I didn't feel right being in my robe, so I excused myself to put back on the dress I was wearing earlier. When I came into the room, he had taken off his jacket and was sipping his wine.

"My cousin adores you," he said, holding his glass up in a toast. "But something has come to my attention today at Grandmamma's, and since I know you are concerned, I think you deserve to know."

"And Nicolai sent you to tell me this?" Now I was getting nervous.

He ignored my question and pulled out his phone, flipping to a photo of something. He handed it to me. "It came to my attention, through my grandmother's staff, that she put a spell on you and Nicolai."

"A spell?" I refrained from laughing but, honestly, that would have been my first natural response. "What kind of spell?" Was this the part where the hidden cameramen jump out to tell me I'm being punked?

"A love spell," he said. "Read it."

The words were written in cursive, and they looked to be part of a book made with parchment colored pages. It read:

To help a man move heaven and earth for love, show him a ticking clock and tell him he has six dates to inspire a woman, to see that she loves him, and to make her his. And repeat this prayer:

Bring these lovers together soon,
When the moment is opportune.
Let fiery passion them consume,
And bring consummation at full moon.
Stir arousal, so romance can begin,
Melt resistance and invite love in.
Give him strength to penetrate her shield;
Give her desire to fully yield.
Tho' she may not know they are meant to be,
Let awareness grow and become reality.

"Is this a joke, Vlad?" I took a big sip of wine and followed it with a deep breath. "You came from Connecticut to show me this?"

"My grandmother is a very powerful wi ... woman." Was he about to say witch? He leaned back on the couch. "It's only that I know you have concerns about whether these feelings you both have are real, so I thought you should know."

I was starting to lose my patience, but I realized that his odd visit might be an intervention. My heart was once again filled with doubt.

"Why would this matter, anyway?" My tone started to reflect my aggravation. "I don't believe in spells. I don't even really believe in fate. Why should I care?"

"Because my grandmother tried to influence my cousin and control your future," he said, wiping his mouth with the back of his hand. "I think she made this whole thing up to manipulate him to take over her crazy legacy and to suck you into her plans. There was no dream. There was no prophecy. She knew your grandmother, and she's trying to hijack your life for her own purposes. And my cousin? He never stands up to her. He simply does her bidding."

It felt like my throat was burning. I couldn't find words. My head was pounding too. I wrapped my arms around myself, and rocked, trying to tune out his voice.

"Oh, don't worry, my cousin is the marrying kind now," he continued. "He will take care of you, but you will never know for sure if he truly loves you, or if he was manipulated to believe he does. I mean, who falls in love so fast?"

That was like a knife in the heart. I took another sip of wine and suddenly felt so sleepy. Too sleepy to ask any questions or talk anymore. I wanted to curl up in a ball and disappear.

Abruptly, a wild downpour of rain started beating on my window. Lightning and thunder followed. A flood warning came through on my cell phone saying there was a hurricane watch with strong winds. He got the same warning on his phone and looked at me.

"Well, we are not quite family yet, but can I stay on your couch?" He seemed to think it wasn't an unusual request.

Are you fucking kidding me? I wanted him to go away, but somehow in my tired, pain-filled haze I couldn't find my words. My voice was swallowed into the deep pit of despair. Vlad's words echoed all my fears and insecurities that I was being played. And I could never really *know* if Nicolai loved me.

"Don't you have friends in Manhattan?" I asked. My words were slurred. The day must have been catching up with me.

"Nope. I just have you, Allison." He sounded so creepy, but I didn't care. Was he the bad cousin, I wondered, or the good one? Perhaps he was here to bring the words of truth to save me from making a mistake.

The last thing I remembered was tossing him a blanket and pillow and going into my room, locking the door.

Every instinct in me told me to call Nicolai, but I was too freaked out. And so tired. I was afraid to disturb his time with his grandmother. I didn't want to bring up the Vlad thing and start a war between them. I was confused about all that Vlad said. I didn't know who to believe. I reached into my night table for my grandmother's crucifix and grasped it in my hand. What did I do with my purse? And the velvet pouch from Grandmamma. I couldn't remember. Exhausted, I drifted off to sleep, still in my dress.

CHAPTER TWENTY-TWO
SUNDAY: DAY SIX/ SIXTH DATE

I woke to a beautiful day. I guess this was the day my destiny would unfold. I automatically put coffee on and slipped into the shower and then back into my robe. I forgot Vlad was there. And I didn't even notice he had apparently taken his clothes off or that he was naked on my couch, dead asleep. Not until the door buzzer drew me out of the shower.

"Mr. Petre is on the way up," said the doorman. "He said you are expecting him."

Fuck. He's early. I brushed my teeth really quick and then I panicked. I wanted to run over and wake Vlad up, but Nicolai was at my door in no time. I opened it and he scooped me into his arms, happy to see me. He looked so handsome. He could have been the photo illustration for a story on why a billionaire boyfriend would be perfect if he didn't have many family issues.

"My love, Grandmamma had a remarkable turn-around so I rushed back to you as soon as…"

His gaze caught his naked cousin.

"What the fuck is he doing here?" He was in full warrior mode, standing up tall and surveying the environment. "Why is he naked?"

"He said you sent him." My head was pounding. How much did I drink last night? It was all a blur. But I also wondered why Vlad was naked.

"I did no such thing." His tone was incredulous and his eyes filled with suspicion. "I would never…"

Nicolai stomped over to Vlad and shook his shoulders. Then he rolled him off the couch with one hand. The younger man hit the ground with a thud and a groan, his skull just missing the coffee table.

"Hey, man, what the fuck?" he shouted but seemed groggy. It took him a minute to realize Nicolai was in the room.

"Yeah, what the fuck?" Nicolai sounded menacing. "You're naked. She's in a robe." *Did he actually think I had sexy times with his cousin? Ugh.*

The two men stared each other down. This could be the way all their family gatherings ended up for all I knew, but I felt like I was in a bar brawl. I had a hard time watching it, fearing it would turn violent. I also didn't want to cast my eyes on Vlad's man parts.

Nicolai stood over his cousin, who was now naked all over my rug. *Jeez.*

"I came to talk to her." He was still on the ground and he sounded pissed.

"I told you not to." Nicolai was being so aggressive. Seeing him so furious was troubling.

"I was trying to help, man!" Vlad wiggled away, pulled the blanket off the couch, and wrapped it around him. He grabbed his pants and ran into the bathroom to dress.

Nicolai turned his attention to me and lashed out like a controlling father reprimanding a teenager. "Why did you let him in?"

"I thought it was you," I said, agitated that he'd turned this into my fault. "I took a warm bath, stepped out, and the doorman said Mr. Petre was here and, thinking it was you, I let him in. He said he wanted to help us."

"How did he want to help?" Nicolai ran his fingers through his hair and took a few breaths. Then he moved from the living room toward my kitchenette and leaned both hands against the counter.

"Maybe he was trying to save me from making a mistake," I shot at him. "He told me about your grandmother's love spell and her control over you, and he said my grandmother knew yours. Is any of this true?"

He cupped his chin and lips the way he does when he is thinking. I could tell he was trying to control his breath and measure the words that came out of his mouth. "Why did you even let him near you to tell you these lies?"

"Excuse me? He's your fucking relative." Now I was shouting. "Why did he even have my address? You brought him into my life. Don't you dare blame me for this family drama."

"But you let him in the door." He was insistent that I did something wrong by opening my door.

"What are you implying?" Now I was incredulous. My heart was racing, and not in a good way. I wanted to smack someone.

"That maybe you wanted to let him in, maybe find comfort with my younger cousin. He's good looking and rich, but not as loaded with baggage." He looked like he was the wounded one.

"That is one of the most offensive things I have ever heard, from anyone." And hurtful too. It was surreal that he was accusing me of cheating or, worse, gold-digging. He had pursued me, professed to love me, asked me to be with him, and gotten me involved with his family. He'd broken down my wall with his promises to love and honor me. And now this? "I can't even believe you would consider that as a possibility after all we have been through. You don't know me at all." My heart was aching.

"What would you think if you came to my house to sweep me off my feet and found me with your cousin, naked in my living room, and me with a towel around my waist?" He spoke a little softer now and looked into my eyes this time.

"I see your point, but he practically barged in here last night, saying he wanted to help. He filled my head with some story about how I would never be able to tell how you truly felt about me because your grandmother had cast a powerful spell on us both." Tears were close behind my words. "He showed it to me on his phone."

Nicolai reached for his cousin's jacket and pulled out his cell phone. He clicked it open to the photo gallery and looked at it in disgust. "My grandmother told me about this spell," he said, shaking his head in disgust.

"She said she was *thinking of* doing it and on the same day, I called to tell her I had met you. She never did a spell. Her nurse told me she didn't have the energy to complete it on her own. He doesn't have his facts right."

"Oh, my God, why did he do it? He's your cousin!" I was appalled and confused. How could he come here and hurt me like that? Hurt Nicolai?

"Da, he's my cousin who squanders money, can never stay true to a woman, and isn't able to handle the responsibility." He started pacing around the kitchenette. "I guess he'd rather sabotage his own family than see me happy with you. He was fucking with you. With us." His face was etched with pain.

"How I was I supposed to know?" I dropped my head into my hands. A sense of gloom filled my heart, and my apartment, as I realized I had been messed with by another Petre. "I only let him in because he is *your* relative."

He walked to my front door and played with the lock.

"The locks have to be changed now," he said. "No, I have to move you out of here."

"You're not moving me anywhere." I was fuming.

"Vlad has started an attack." He reached in his jacket for his own cell and started dialing. "I have to alert my security team. You have to be in a secure location."

"No, I don't want you keeping me safe," I shouted. "In fact, I don't care if you have a title and all the money in the world. I'm tired of you spending every hour of the day seducing me and trying to get me to be your wife. I would never marry a man who yells at me, fights with his cousin, and has one insane idea about relationships after another. This day will change both our lives because this chapter is now closed. I *am* aroused … with anger."

"Allison." He sounded like he was calling after an angry teenager.

I turned and headed to my bedroom, locked the door, and got dressed. When I heard the two men speaking loudly at each other, I sat on my bed to gather myself. When things quieted, I walked into my living room, hoping both of those crazy cousins were gone.

Nicolai was still there, with Vlad's phone in hand, looking dazed. Vlad had apparently left. I looked at my open door and realized he must have bolted.

"I'm going out, Nicolai. Lock the door when you leave." I grabbed my purse and keys.

"You're not going anywhere." He moved to block the door.

"Are you serious?" I said, pushing him aside. "I said I'm going out. English translation: I am going somewhere, and you are not invited."

"Don't leave." He looked dejected. I'd seen that pained look before. I turned away before his sadness swayed me to stay.

"Don't you dare try to control what I do." I was starting to crumble inside, feeling his emotional pain in my own heart. But I had to get away. "I am furious with you."

"Let me come." I felt those words in my body. A part of me wanted to go to him, but I fought it.

"No. We're done here." I kept walking out the door so he wouldn't see my weakening resolve.

"This is not done." He was pleading more than bossing me around. "It's a stupid mistake. We can fix it."

"Whose stupid mistake? Yours? You accused me of tempting your cousin when you gave me no indication that there was anything to be warned about. I don't need this soap opera. You said it was my choice, and my choice is this: I decline date six."

I couldn't bear seeing the angst deeply etched on Nicolai's face. But I also could not accept his bad behavior.

I raced out of the apartment, down the stairs, and, started jogging down 44th Street toward First Avenue and the United Nations building. I had no idea where I was going until I recalled the house of worship on 47th Street. I'd been to the beautiful garden outside the rectory but had never been inside the church. Ironically, it was the United Nations Parish. I sprinted there, went through the garden, and found my way into the side door. I needed sanctuary.

Although the garden was green and filled with beautiful foliage and a cozy bench, the church was high tech inside. A tall, modern, metal sculpture of Jesus took up most of the wall behind the pulpit. Next to it was a smaller, sculpted cross. Even the stained glass windows and etchings on the walls had a contemporary look.

I was grateful to find it completely empty.

When I got in the door, I bent over, completely out of breath. I could barely get my wind back as I walked up the aisle, holding on to the tops of each green, velvet-covered pew as I made my way to the last row. I slid in and sat for a few moments, huffing and puffing as I recovered from my run. Once the oxygen returned to my brain I decided to take this time to figure out my next steps.

I needed to light a candle. Lighting candles always made me feel good for some reason. Maybe it was because my grandmother used to take me to light candles and say a prayer when I was a little girl. I hadn't been inside a church since then. I approached the altar, in the middle of the church, with its rows of red glass candleholders. All but one was in use. The "flames" were electronic. It took me a moment to figure out how it worked. With the push of a button I turned on the light of the last candle, in the top row.

"I know I don't come here often," I murmured, watching it flicker. "But I need help figuring out what to do."

I searched in my purse for my wallet and grabbed a few singles and then folded and slid the bills into the metal donation box. When I returned my wallet, I felt a pen and it gave me an idea. Walking the aisle back to the last row of pews, I noticed a flyer for an upcoming service. I turned it over to find the other side blank and decided to write a list of Pros and Cons about Nicolai. I made a column for each on the paper and hoped it was not bad form that I used a Bible on my lap as a surface for writing.

My first thought was that I must be desperate for love. How else could I fall for this gorgeous, sweet-talking Transylvanian and get involved with this peculiar family situation? And what about Nicolai's anger and jealous streak? Suddenly, I felt I didn't know him at all. I wrote down all the bad stuff under the "Con" side of the page.

1. Possessive, controlling, and jealous.
2. Too into my business.
3. Possibly delusional.
4. Driven by mission for grandmother.
5. Dysfunctional family relationships.
6. Withholds important information.
7. Tells me important things on a need to know basis.
8. Pushing me to make big life choice on deadline.
9. Distracted me from work and endangered my job.
10. I didn't ask for him to find me.
11. I never wanted to have feelings for him.
12. It never feels like he is giving me enough time to get to know him.

I felt horrible when I finished but was compelled to write the "Pro" list to try to feel a little better.

1. I like to be with him.
2. He seems to care about me and thinks I am important.
3. Our long, unusual relationship talks are interesting.
4. There is an ease of intimacy and a desire for more.
5. His hand kisses are sexy as well as all his kisses.
6. His touch, on the curve of my back, feels so right.
7. My body always leans toward his.
8. I've never desired anyone the way I desire him.
9. The way he looks at me.
10. Making love with him would make me happy.
11. I always wish we had more time to get to know each other.

The lists were neck and neck but I had to choose the one with the most entries. That would be the "Con" list with twelve even. I re-read it and thought back to what had happened earlier in my apartment. Even with all I loved about Nicolai there were too many problems—especially for someone who had no interest in being in love in the first place.

I reconfirmed my decision: date six was not happening. This relationship was not happening. Nicolai was not taking over my life. I took a deep breath and walked out the side door, checking my watch. I had been there for thirty minutes.

I breathed in the fresh air and squinted in the sun. I felt relieved.

Nicolai was waiting for me in the church courtyard, sitting on the bench in the garden. I guess the vampire in him could not risk coming in and getting near the crosses. Or maybe he was just giving me some space.

The minute he saw me, he stood from the bench and planted his feet on the ground. He looked shaken and, for a moment, a little shy.

A deep, deep sadness came over me for what I had to do, but I knew it was right. "This won't work, Nicolai," I said softly. It was hard to face him, but I looked directly into his beautiful eyes. It was painful to see the sadness reflected back.

"It will work, and it is already working." He was insistent, and suddenly channeling the Nicolai I first met earlier in the week. "Don't throw our relationship away."

I didn't want to be dismissive, but I didn't know how else to part.

"This is not a relationship." I raised my head high and straightened my posture. "This is six days and two lives, rushed together, with one party not feeling comfortable with the ride."

"Will you ever be comfortable with someone loving you?" He shot back, moving closer to where I was standing.

"Maybe not." I took two steps backward, and contemplated returning to the church.

"You're out of your comfort zone." He inched closer. "I know I am far from perfect and I lay a whole new set of challenges at your feet. But what about *your resistance* to love?" A sudden wind blew through the garden, lifting my hair off my shoulders for a moment. He reached for an out of place strand and gently tucked it behind my ear. He was so close I could feel his breath on my skin. "I suspect you would find any excuse to get out of taking the risk of giving your heart."

"You may be right, but it's my prerogative. I'm entitled to decline love," I said, summoning my courage. I grabbed a few leaves off of a nearby hedge and rolled them between my fingers as if it would give me strength. "You came into my life and threw me into a tizzy with your demands and plans. Then you come to my house today and act like a scary Neanderthal. And now you are stalking me outside a church. Why can't you be a normal boyfriend?"

"Because your normal boyfriends," he said, edging his body closer, "are gone in five days. I want more from you."

"This," I said, pointing from him and then at myself, "is not all about what you want."

He tilted his head up to the sun and pursed his lips as he took a deep breath. His exhale was loud, impatient. "I want to spend the rest of my days making *you* happy, giving *you* what *you* want. It's been like wrestling with demons to get this far, and I am still fighting to simply spend this day with you." He put his hand to his temples and massaged them for a moment.

"How am I supposed to know, in six short dates, who you really are?" Now I was irked. "How do I know you won't be a horror show on day seven or turn out to be a raging narcissist who will try to control me the rest of my life?"

"By this," he said, grabbing my hand and putting it on his heart. "This is pure and it beats for you." He gazed deeply into my eyes and held my hand in place inside his suit jacket and over his shirt. As it pumped beneath my touch I remembered when our hearts beat so close together, and how good it felt. I knew how much he wanted me to believe he was sincere. But I couldn't believe this was a fairy tale with a happy ending. Real life, my real life, was crumbling. Even if we did get together, he would leave me some day. There was only one way to bypass the pain.

I pulled my hand back as if I'd touched a hot stove and turned on my heel to leave. I speed-walked out of the church garden, onto the tree-lined street, and made a left toward First Avenue. Out of the corner of my eye, I noticed Nicolai's limo. Turning, I saw Sam, following me slowly in the car as I moved on foot.

"Are you kidding me, Sam?" I shouted at the car as it pulled alongside me. "You're following me?"

"You should know by now I never kid, Ms. Monroe." I heard the voice behind me. Nicolai was following me too, on foot.

It made me melt when he said my name that way and reminded me of the command he'd had on me all week. But I had to resist him. *Don't even look back!* I didn't want to turn, but I did.

"Just let this whole thing go," I pleaded, moving faster. "Let me go."

"I cannot." He was resolute. The look on his face was focused and determined as he pursued me.

"Because you need a wife, an heir, a replacement for your grandmother, another dependent for your income tax? What?" I kept walking fast, though my head was tilted, looking back at him. "What else do you want from me?"

"I want you." He was moving faster, breathing harder. "It's you. Please believe me, Allison." Now he was back to my first name, which always seemed so intimate.

"I don't know what to believe anymore." I tried to move faster, get far away from his grip, but his legs were longer than mine. My heart was thumping wildly. "I don't even remember how I let myself get so involved with you."

"I will have to help you remember." He closed the space between us with one huge step and moved in quickly. He took hold of my face and pressed his lips to mine. Then in came his tongue, kissing me deeply, reminding me of the things he could make me feel. My body went along with him until my mind snapped out it.

"No, that's it. No more." I pushed my hands against his chest and backed away.

"Please don't run," he pleaded, reaching for my hand. I remembered him mouthing those words to me last night and it broke my heart. "We've made it past the fifth day. We can break this pattern, together."

"No, I'm not built for this. I'm not built for … love." I bolted.

I headed down the street, running toward—anywhere. He chased me. Even though it was weirdly romantic, I kept going and going until I felt him alongside of me again.

"We need to talk," he said, scooping me up in his arms like a fireman carrying someone to safety. "Now."

"You're a freaking caveman." I tried to squirm away from his strong grip, but it was too tight and he was holding me hard against his chest. "And a vampire!"

"Yes, perhaps. But we still have things to discuss," he was trying to catch his breath, but it didn't stop him from capturing me. "You leave me no choice but to take a caveman approach to having a conversation. So, I will ask you in advance to forgive me because this is going to piss you off."

He carried me to the corner, where the limo was now waiting. Random people, mothers with carriages, and a group of Japanese tourists were watching from the park area across the street as if this romantic drama were a theater performance.

"This is kidnapping," I snarled at him.

"This is claiming what's mine." He kept moving with my full weight in his arms and still kept his gaze on my eyes as he spoke. "This is me not letting you get away because I … I love you."

His words scared and excited me.

"I told you before, love is not about taking a hostage." I looked away, avoiding eye contact. I didn't want to melt beneath his gaze.

We reached the car and he put me down, keeping one arm on my side. I suppose he was afraid I might bolt again. Perhaps he read my mind.

"Maybe we are both love hostages," he said, opening the limo door. "Join me, and we can talk this through like adults."

I slid into the limo, too tired to run. A part of me no longer wanted to. "I'm so mad I could scream," I said, folding my arms. They heaved up and down over my chest as I tried to catch my breath. Anger boiled beneath my skin, but I couldn't figure out what made me madder—his behavior and tactics or the fact that I was having trouble letting him go.

"Let me be the one to make you scream." He leaned across the seat, his mouth angled close to my ear and breath so close. "Or scream your anger at. But please, don't run away from me. I lost my temper this morning. I screwed up. I'm sorry."

He pulled me into his arms. I tried to resist, but then, all of a sudden, it felt so good to be close. "This is too much for me." It came out on a huge sigh and a shaky voice. "I am a New York girl who loves her city and her independence. I am not wife or countess material."

"You don't fully know what you can become yet and neither do I," he said, affectionately rubbing my right arm and pulling me closer. "A few days ago, I loved the concept of you, and the promise of you, but now I'm in love with *you*. I am becoming the man I'm meant to be. Maybe my love can help you grow. I've been so busy trying to win your affection that I've not showered you with the love you deserve. All I want is to show you how deeply I can cherish you."

"There you go with that sweet talk, again," I said. "It fucks with my defenses."

"It's supposed to," he laughed. "Courtship is supposed take down defenses and build affection. Fights are supposed to inspire make-up sex and closeness. You are looking for guarantees of perfection. Relationships aren't perfect, even after ten or twenty years."

He hit a nerve. It dawned on me that we had experienced more intimacy in this limo in less than one week than many people do after long periods of time together.

He waited for me to react.

"Penny for your thoughts?" He paused but I kept quiet. "Maybe we can share more over breakfast? Will you agree to a meal with me?"

I lifted my chin upward to look at his face. He looked relaxed, now that he wasn't running in hot pursuit of me. He looked happy to have me in his arms. It was so easy to fall back under his spell.

"I guess a girl's got to eat." I was starving from all the exercise and emotional drama.

"Good." He sat up straight and pulled out his phone. "While we're there, I need to send my security team to your apartment to make sure there are no cameras or recording devices hidden by the scoundrel or anyone else he may have allowed in during the night."

I leaned deeply into the back seat and sighed. I was finally feeling calmer and didn't want to remember the weirdness of last night and this morning. But there was no getting away from it. My mind flashed to the pros and cons list I'd shoved into my purse after writing it in the church. Despite all the good things on my pros list, this moment was reminding me that, at the end of the day, they will probably still be outweighed by the bad stuff.

"Security people at my house?" I hated the idea. "That's creepy."

"Unfortunately, he's betrayed my trust." The look on his face was serious, but I could tell he was also disappointed and saddened. "I have to assume the worst and protect you. He's family. This is hard for me, but it's unacceptable to leave you vulnerable again."

Nicolai called his head of security. When the call ended, he asked me for my key.

"Don't they have a way of changing the locks without me even knowing?" I didn't hide my sarcasm. "Isn't that your usual approach?"

"Very funny," he said. "It may seem hard to believe but this, and everything I am doing is about protecting you."

With his gaze on my eyes, he held the palm of his hand open. I placed my keys in it and gazed right back at him. Surrender. That's what this was.

But ultimately, did I want a life in which there was a need to be protected? I didn't want him to have to save me in order to survive in the world.

He opened the privacy window and handed my keys to Sam to take to the team. Then he instructed him to head to the next location. We sat in silence the whole way there.

I kept reading the list of cons in my head. It was running through my mind on an endless loop, reminding me what a mess this was. The motion of the car coming to a halt roused me from my thoughts but I sensed that the energy between us had changed. I was sure that breakfast would be our last time together and I was sad. Very sad.

CHAPTER TWENTY-THREE

When he opened the limo door for me I immediately recognized the location. We were in front of the building where we first met.

He placed his hand on my lower back and guided me inside, to the elevator. As we waited, he reached for my hand. When the car arrived, we stepped in together. And there we stood in the overwhelming hall of mirrors where his kiss had activated the chain of events that led to this moment. He didn't kiss me, but he made love to me with his eyes the whole seventy-seven floor ride.

We were back at Club Kismet.

I raised my eyebrows and looked his way. "Why are we here?"

"They have Sunday brunch on the outdoor patio," he said, apparently excited to return to the scene of his first seduction. "Let's share a meal and a little bit of conversation, and see how things go. If you still hate me afterward, I will let you go—and never bother you again—if that is what you wish."

I didn't hate him. I wished I did or could. Just being with him in this place was instilling quite the opposite feeling. Clearly, he knew bringing me back to the scene of the first incident would remind me of how impossible it was for me to resist him that night.

"I reserved a private area, outside the office," he told the maître de. He looked over at me and winked. I remembered the way he leaned over me in that office and took me out on this terrace to discuss his crazy family prophecy six days earlier. It seemed a lifetime ago.

"Of course, Mr. Petre, follow me." We moved on the familiar path we'd walked before, on the night we met.

We were led out to the little area of terrace where he first told me he wanted to marry me. And here we were, on the day that would decide it all. He was setting things up so it would be hard for me to walk away, but I had to be firm in my decision. I braced myself for saying good-bye. My heart was heavy, like lead, and I could barely breathe.

He pulled out my chair and sat across from me, and then, taking my hand, he kissed it. Once again, I saw that look in his eye. The one that was meant for me, only. A look he would never share with Sheila, or Aisha, or anyone. He held my gaze for some time before he finally spoke.

"I love you," he said, squeezing my hand. "And with everything that's happened in the past twenty-four hours, I have come to a big decision … that I would be willing to step down from the 'family business' if it meant I could have your love."

My mouth dropped open. This stunned me as much as his first declaration of our fated love on the night we met. "What about your promise to your grandmother? How could you betray her wishes?"

After Vlad's accusations last night, I didn't know what to believe any more about the legitimacy of the 'prophecy,' but still, Nicolai adored his grandmother.

"Because they are her wishes for continuing a legacy," he said with a sigh. "My wish is to be with you no matter what. Even if it means forgetting about this tradition I have been bred to carry out. If I were to bail, I could stop pressuring you to marry me, unless you want to, of course. If I knew you would at least love me and stand by my side as my partner, I could leave the rest."

He lifted the water glass from the table and took a big sip, looking at me over the rim. Then he set it down and awaited my response. He seemed dead serious.

"But you're the count, and you have a destiny," I said, panic rising in my chest. "I could never interfere with your life like that." The idea of

Nicolai *not* fulfilling his calling, after knowing how important it was to him, did not make sense.

"Believe me, if I lose you, it will interfere with my life," he said, his fingers now caressing mine. Tears rimmed his eyes. "If you run from me and are so scared of this life that it makes you not want me, then I will not be in much shape for my so-called destiny. You are my destiny. I am clear about that one hundred percent. The fact that you even engaged me on this journey speaks volumes about who you are, my love."

We looked at each other for a long time. It all flooded back to me. And the emotions felt deeper, stronger, and more solid than anything else in my life.

"But you can't not be who you are," I said, tears welling. "Not for me. You can't do this for me."

"Allison, I will still be who I am, but without the baggage." He let go of my hand and brought both his hands to his chin, fingers in a prayer-like pose. "Let's face the facts. You have disdained everything I have presented to you this week—fate, marriage, prophecy, legacy, leaving your company to work with me, becoming my countess, my offer of financial support—everything. And I realized I had bought into a belief that you would want these things if you wanted me."

My throat constricted. I was on the edge of sobbing. He finally seemed to understand how overwhelming it had all been for me.

"I'm sorry," he continued. I could tell he was trying to hold back his emotions, but the tears in his eyes broke my heart. "I was wrong to try to sell you on this, and to try to change you into thinking you wanted these things." He dropped his hands in front of him and sighed. "But I don't think I was wrong about one thing. I believe you truly care for me. And that's really what I wanted from you today, to just care for me. And even if nothing happens with us, I will carry that in my heart."

He reached across the table and I placed both my hands in his and felt the warmth between us. He looked at me through tear-rimmed eyes and all I saw was love. I realized all I felt in that moment was love for him as well. My heart was suddenly wide open. And it was beating so fast that my chest tingled. A rush of awareness spilled into me so quickly and powerfully that it tickled the top of my head. I almost couldn't speak. I removed one of my hands from his grip and placed it to my chest to calm myself as I searched for the words. I observed him and his warm expression.

"Nicolai," I finally said, my face scrunching with tears. "I think … I'm in love with you."

I bent my head, lost in a swirl of emotion. I heard him get out of his chair and walk around the table. He got down on his knees in front of me and lifted my chin. His other hand went to my cheek and softly caressed it. His eyes were changing colors in the sun, but they held my gaze in a loving embrace. We stayed in that moment for what seemed like a long time. Then he put his forehead against mine. The tears finally stopped.

He took a huge breath and let it out on a sigh, "Da, my *Ves'tacha*, I love you, too."

Our private revelry was interrupted when two waitresses delivered an onslaught of food to the table. Nicolai lifted himself up from his position leaning into me on his knees and kissed me on the forehead before returning to his seat. When he sat, he folded his hands in front of him and looked at me. He didn't quite seem to know what to do next.

"Food!" I exclaimed, louder than I intended. I suddenly felt excited, as if a weight had been lifted. I was so relieved that this had not turned out to be a break up meal. I didn't remember even putting an order in—he must have made it in advance—but the classic Sunday brunch of omelets, goat cheese, toast, assorted baked goods, and coffee all smelled good. "I guess we should eat something."

"I think we have earned the calories today," he said, unrolling a napkin and placing it on his lap. He ate a few bites but did not seem that interested in the food. He still could not take his eyes off me, and I couldn't take my eyes off him, either. But my gaze caught the coconut milk on the table. He remembered to order it for me. It got me every time he remembered little things that were important to me.

"Nicolai," I said, pouring my special milk and stirring. "There is something I want."

"Anything." He put down his fork. "Let me know, and it will be yours. Do you want me to order you something different to eat?"

"No, this is delicious." I dug into my omelet and savored the taste. Then I tried the cheese and a fresh-baked muffin. I suddenly felt like we had options before us and not just in the medley of food. "I want you to ask me on a date."

"A date?" He shot me a roguish smile. "One in which I do not have to carry you off caveman-style?"

"Exactly. I want to turn back the hands of time, and start out with something normal," I said, taking one last bite. "As if we had a new start."

"Okay, Ms. Monroe," he said, leaning closer onto the table. "Will you go out with me?"

"Yes," I said, smiling coyly. "I would love to."

"Where can I take you?" he asked, eyes aglow. "Anywhere you want. Have you been to Paris? Or how about the Swiss Alps for a ski date? Or we can be on a beach in the Caribbean by lunchtime."

"That's sweet." I had no interest in travel, or even dinner and a movie. I wanted a sex date. "But I want you to take me home. That's where I want our date to be."

"Of course." He raised one eyebrow. "And, what did you have in mind?"

"I want to make love." It was the first time I said those words and felt as if they may actually come true.

"I think I can handle that." He hailed the waiter for the check. "I don't even need to finish eating. I'd rather feast on you."

"Good." I started to gather my things. "And here's the deal: you have to deliver on your promise to give me everything I need and want."

"Fair enough. And, what if in the course of the experience, we decide that the Earth moves and our destiny is sealed?" he teased, or pretended to be playful at any rate.

"I have no idea." I shook my head and bit my lip. "I just want your body for now."

"You drive a hard bargain." He winked playfully. "I surrender to your wishes."

My mind was in my bedroom where I wanted to be free and naked with Nicolai but when the check came I was a little surprised he signed but remained seated.

"Are we leaving any time soon?" I tapped two fingers on the table as if it would get us out of there faster. "You don't want me to change my mind, do you?"

"God no," he said, checking his phone, "just waiting to hear from my team ... and here's the text." He read it out loud. "All is secure."

He grabbed my hand, and rushed me to the elevator. This time, he kissed me, hard, for seventy-seven floors.

CHAPTER TWENTY-FOUR

The limo ride, entering my building, and opening my front door—they were a haze of events. The next thing I knew, we were inside my apartment with soft romantic music playing and champagne chilling in the kitchenette.

I eyed Nicolai suspiciously as he closed and locked the door behind us, and I popped into the bedroom to make sure there wasn't a maid fluffing the pillows. I found the curtains drawn and brand new linens and blankets on my bed. Apparently, his team did more than secure the premises. They set up for the sixth date.

When I returned to the kitchen area, he'd poured us both a glass of cold water. Apparently, he was saving the champagne for later. I picked up my glass and took a sip, looking over my glass at him. Placing it back on the counter, I walked slowly to where he stood, in the walkway area that connected the kitchen and living room in my smallish, one-bedroom apartment.

"You must have been pretty sure we'd end up back here," I said, loosening his tie and slipping him out of his jacket. I kept my eyes on his, pretending to be miffed, but smiled as I unbuttoned his shirt. I decided not to make a fuss about the sexing up of my apartment and to instead enjoy the sensual energy percolating in my home, and inside of me.

I helped him out of his shirt and tossed it on the floor. That body. I could not resist the urge to let my hands roam over his chest and abs and to feel the V-shaped lines on the side of his body. Oh my God, his flesh and muscles—so sexy and smooth to the touch.

"So here we are," he said, taking me into his arms and pulling me in close enough to feel his erection through his pants. "Just you and me."

"Yes." I melted into the warmth of his naked upper body and reveled in the way he held me. My heart was beating fast, excited to finally have this moment. "Two consenting adults, fresh from six days of drama and foreplay."

"Maybe it would be nice to make this a completely naked date, no?"

I nodded. A part of me was surprised we didn't just rip each other's clothes off upon entering the apartment. The idea of all of our clothes off, at the same time, in the same room, excited me.

He lifted off my shirt over my head and looked at me, studying my breasts and face. He reached out and touched the skin on my arm with the backs of his fingers. A look came over his face. He was wild-eyed and his smooth chest heaved. Stepping closer, he pressed my body against the wall. Then he leaned against me with his erection, as he used both hands to take hold of my face and pull my lips to his for a kiss. He plunged his tongue in and out of my mouth as his hips took on a sexual rhythm of their own. His motions urged me to move with him to the beat of a primal dance of love. I got lost in the erotic tension that was building inside me.

When he slowed his kiss and withdrew, my lips were sore—in a sexy, hot kiss kind of way. Hunger for him tingled in every part of me.

"Do you want me to love you today?" he whispered it in my ear, still holding my face in his hands. His breath on my flesh made my body tremble. He slid his hands over my neck and shoulders, then down my arms, and caressed my exposed upper body. "Tell me I have your permission to make love to you."

He could have easily thrown me down on the couch and fucked me until I couldn't remember my own name, and that would have been hot. I was ready, but his polite approach was even hotter.

"Yes, you do," I agreed, squirming and pressing my legs together as he removed my bra and took hold of my breast. His hands roamed over my flesh as he focused his mouth on my nipple. It registered like a full-body kiss. I felt it between my legs.

"So many things I want to do with this body," he said, moving his lips to my other breast and kissing every spot of sensitive skin he could find. "Would that be okay?" He unzipped my skirt, sensually moved it over my hips, and let it fall to the floor. He held me as I stepped out of it.

"That would be very nice," I panted, unbuckling his belt. "As long as it works both ways." I yanked the belt from the loops and let it fall to the floor.

"Then any pleasure I see fit to bestow upon this beautiful body," he said, lifting my leg alongside of his hip and grinding into me, "is fine with you?"

"Absolutely," I said, reveling in the feel of him against my soaked panties. "As long as that goes the same for your body? Anything I want?"

"Of course," he said, sucking my lower lip into his mouth. "This is an equal opportunity date. Both sides have full erotic power."

"Good," I murmured, unzipping his pants and slipping my hands over his underwear. "Because I want this particular appendage, the one you've been teasing me with all week." I grabbed his cock. "And I want it right now."

I had to taste him. I needed to take him into my mouth.

I kneeled in front of him, reached into the fly opening of his briefs and set it free. His pants were undone and still hanging on his hips; there was no need to remove them yet. I loved the feel of his baby soft flesh, covering that massive hard-on. I brought him into my mouth and let my tongue explore. Then I took him in as deep as I could. He groaned and pressed in deeper, his hands instinctively on my head, but he let me find my own pace. My hunger for him would not extinguish. My desire was to give him pleasure, to make him explode in my mouth, but he stopped me.

"I don't want to lose control, not yet." He sighed and ran his fingers through my hair, twisting a strand in his fingers. I put my cheek against his length, and pulled him closer. I craved closeness with that part of him.

Then he lowered himself to the ground and kneeled before me. He pulled my face to his and took me over with a kiss. Yet his lips and tongue were so familiar now. I felt it was my own mouth, a part of me.

Slowly he moved us back into a standing position as his mouth stayed on mine. Then he leaned me against the wall and stepped away.

"I have never taken a moment to just admire you, knowing I could have you," he said, stepping out of his pants. "I want to soak in this moment."

And I wanted to soak in the sight of his beautiful body, too.

Another time in my life, I would have been embarrassed to stand and gape at a man and let him look at me the way Nicolai did. I would have been too shy to allow his eyes to lay claim to my flesh. But I felt so close to him, I had no shame. In this moment, it was like a reward.

I wanted to see the rest of my prize, so I stepped over and sneaked my hands into the band of his underwear. I slid them completely over his hips, along with his pants, and dropped his clothes to the floor. He leaned his hand on my shoulder as he stepped out of them.

His gaze roamed my body and focused on my arousal soaked undies. "Can I set you free from the material that stands between us?"

"Yes," I whispered, my lower parts throbbing.

He lowered me to the plush rug and parted my thighs ever so slightly with the back of his hands and kneeled before me. I expected him to remove them quickly, but instead he kissed me through my underwear, starting at my lower belly and working his way down, until his lips found the drenched center of my panties. My knees trembled.

He slid his hand under the elastic. He gently spread me and entered with one finger—going in an inch, then two, then more, until he was all the way inside. He plunged in and out of my wet inner flesh. It felt like all the blood in my body had flowed to the area between my thighs. I longed to be filled up by him.

"So, so wet," he said, inserting a second finger. He moved around in me, making wider strokes, going a bit deeper. "You're still so aroused. All these days and you have stayed so wet for me."

"I have, Nicolai, all for you." I pressed up against him.

"Those words," he said, smiling at me. "They are music to my ears."

He removed his fingers slowly, keeping his gaze on mine. I didn't want him to leave that part of me but was excited when he moved his hands to my belly and softly stroked my heated flesh. He caressed his way to my hips and, sliding his hands inside my panties again, this time gingerly removed them.

I lifted up slightly as he moved his hands over my ass and the tops of my thighs and helped me out of my last piece of clothing. Sliding the panties down to my ankles, he freed one leg and let it drop to the floor. Then, after dragging the panties over the other foot, he raised my leg and brought my toes to his mouth. Pleasure shot through me as he kissed my foot and slowly returned my leg to the floor.

"Now there is nothing to come between us," he said with a grin, but I suspected he was talking about more than my underwear.

I smiled as I felt his fingertips traveling up my inner thighs, his soft touch tingling on my skin.

"Stay open for me." His command excited me. I spread my legs even farther apart. He bowed his head just above my pubic mound and kissed me there. He breathed me in. I gave myself over to the moment.

"You are so beautiful," he said, whispering into me, so close I could feel his breath on my lower parts. His mouth traveled downward and brushed lightly over my public hair. So close. But instead of visiting my aching center, he licked and kissed my inner thigh. He kept finding a new area of flesh with his mouth, closer to my center, but teased the place that ached for him most.

"I want so badly to taste you," he said, his voice vibrating between my thighs. "I want this part of you to be mine. I want you to be mine."

"That's what I want, too." I was open and raw, and he was the only one who soothed the burning need. I craved him. I needed him. I wanted him to take me.

He brought his mouth close to my clitoris and grazed it, ever so gently, with a puff of air. And then another, and another, until my hips bucked wildly. I hungered for his tongue. I wanted to shove myself into his face, to force him to lick me.

But he had other ideas and brought his hands to my hips to stop the movement. I was burning for him. "Still, my love," he said, his words hitting my sensitive parts as he spoke. "We're going to take this very slow."

I relaxed and sank into the ecstasy of arousal that had formulated between my thighs for six days. But I couldn't help from moaning for "more."

He opened me with his hands as his mouth found my center. Burying his face deeply between my legs, he pressed his tongue inside, overwhelming me with pleasure. His tongue found a rhythm and he released my hips so I could rock them back and forth. An erotic tickle began in my lower body and thighs and moved through me. And it got bigger and more intense until finally, with several sweeps of his tongue at just the right moment in just the right place, I came. Hard.

Sounds I'd never heard before rose from within me like a love call. He stayed on me until my hips stopped quaking. Then he dipped his tongue inside me, tasting the fluids he'd teased out of my body.

He crawled his way up my body and lay flat out on the rug beside me. He took my hand in his.

I felt drunk on sex hormones. It felt as if parts of my body were singing with joy. I felt loved. And I realized I had never, ever, been this intimate or this close with a man.

Silently, we stared up at the ceiling. He caught his breath as I caught mine. I became aware of the instrumental music playing in the background. It was a karaoke version of "I Can't Help Falling in Love with You."

When the song was over, he reached out a hand to help me to my feet. As I rose from the floor, passing his cock on the way, I had to admire how perfect—and perfectly hard—he was. Once I was standing, he moved his hands to my butt and pressed me close. He jutted up against my stomach. Flesh to flesh, we stood. Complete contact. No clothes in our way. Finally, he was all mine.

"I need to feel you inside," I whispered, grinding my hips into his.

"It's about time, right?" He laughed, caressing my hip and butt. "Now is our time, my love. We are free to…"

"Fuck like bunnies?" I took hold of his hardness and rubbed him back and forth in my hand.

"Exactly." He moved out of my reach and playfully smacked my ass and massaged it. It sent a rush of erotic energy back into my lower parts. "Now I have to do something caveman."

He picked me up off the floor and lifted me in his arms like a man about to carry his bride over a threshold. I wrapped my hands around his neck as he walked us into the bedroom. He placed me on the new sheets. They were elegant, probably four hundred count Egyptian cotton, and smelled fresh. I couldn't wait to cover them with sweat, pheromones, and sex. I moved my limbs like a snow angel, to test out the material. It was cool and smooth on my heated skin.

I left my legs open. He accepted the invitation.

Nicolai pulled himself over me. His cock pressed against my skin as his long torso traversed my body. He brought his face to my lips and kissed me, sweetly. Then he rested his forehead against mine for a moment and stilled his movements. We lay there, melded together by this invisible force. How could this power be six days in the making? It felt ancient, primal.

"I don't think I can wait another minute," he finally said, breathless. "Is that okay? Do you want me? All of me?"

"Yes," I whispered.

He felt around the bed and grabbed hold of a condom. His security team comes prepared. He kneeled between my legs, ripped it open with his teeth, and looked right at me as he slid it on.

"Open for me," he said, bringing his body back down between my legs. He kissed my lips and cheek as he nudged my thighs farther apart with his knee. "Just for me."

He looked deeply into my eyes as he moved to my opening. I saw warmth, passion, and need. Then he paused before entering me, searching for permission.

I nodded. In a moment, he was inside me. So deep. His first thrust sent sensations through my whole body. He did it again, slowly bringing himself out and pressing back in. Then in and out, again. *Holy fuck.* My hips picked up the rhythm and moved with him until I greeted him thrust for thrust.

"Oh, my God," I groaned, my hips thrusting wildly. "I can't believe you are here, making love to me."

"Baby, I've been waiting for you for so long." He panted, his hips bringing him in and out of my body, firing off every nerve ending. "I'm going to lose myself." He leaned his head on my shoulder, his breath hot against me.

"Don't hold back," I said, clawing at his shoulders and pulling him deeper. "No more holding back. I want you."

He grabbed my hips and plastered them to his, filling me and staying deep, while still managing to move in and out, creating delicious friction. Our bodies and lower parts were sweaty and swishy as we pumped into each other. I wanted so bad to make him come, but suddenly, I was swirling off into a tingle that spread from my toes to the top of my head and then circled through my internal organs. I surrendered myself to pleasure, letting it wash over me. I lost myself to the moment, to him, as I came again. And it felt so good.

He slid his tongue into my mouth and kissed me deep enough to take my breath way. My still-quivering love muscles clenched around him.

"Allison." He groaned and shuddered as he released. He brought his mouth down on my neck and sucked, hard. Another hickey. "I love you. I really do."

I couldn't stop the tears that flooded into my eyes, and he couldn't stop his either.

Gently, he slid himself out of me and kneeled between my legs. I was surprised when he lifted me up to kneel with him.

"Thank you for trusting me," he said, pulling me close. He brought his mouth to mine and we both cried. Then he kissed the tears streaming down my cheeks.

I placed my arms around his neck and looked into his eyes. "I think the Earth may have moved," I whispered through my tears. "Something has changed."

"We're changed." He was smiling now. He pulled my body tightly against his so we were chest to chest. "Today we danced with our hearts."

"I love you," I said. Even though I'd said it earlier, I knew it now with complete and utter clarity.

"My *Ves'tacha*." He kissed my forehead.

"Da," was my response.

CHAPTER
TWENTY-FIVE

Sometime in the evening, around midnight, we rolled out of bed. He tossed on his underwear and I put on his shirt, and then we made our way into the kitchen. We were satiated, finally, from our time together, but starving for actual food.

He went to the refrigerator and pulled out all sorts of small dishes, apparently left by his team, and grabbed a couple of spoons and forks from the counter. He lowered himself onto the kitchen rug and sat.

"Grab the champagne and a couple of paper cups," he said, opening all the containers of various organic salads and other stuff. "Now we really have something to celebrate."

"So your security team caters," I joked, thinking about his earlier request for my key.

"They do whatever I tell them to, my love, and they will do the same for you." He handed me a container and a fork. "Eat." The first thing I tried tasted like a chicken salad with herbs. Whatever it was, it was good.

We stared at each other, for long stretches, as we nibbled on the food. It was like being a couple of giddy kids, sharing the containers, passing them back and forth, and giving everything a try. The past week seemed like years of waiting. And, in the moment, everything seemed perfect in our world.

He popped open the champagne, expertly capturing the cork in his hand.

"I did something I'm hoping you are happy about," he said, pouring some bubbly into a glass and handing it to me. "And I would have done this regardless of how things turned out between us, for purely business reasons."

"Uh-oh," I said. "Luckily I'm in a very good mood, Mr. Petre." I had no idea what he was going to reveal.

"I hope this puts you in a better mood," he said, pouring a glass for himself, and taking a sip. He paused to savor the taste, or stall, before speaking. "I bought your father's company."

"You bought Berke and Monroe? As in *you own it?*" This was not a piece of information I expected to hear on the heels of all that had unfolded tonight. I was stunned.

"Da," he said, taking another sip and eyeing me with caution as if I may have a bad reaction. "Remember, this is happy news."

"What if I decide I don't like you tomorrow, and I then am stuck with you as my boss?" I rolled my eyes and laughed. Even by romantic comedy standards, this was a pretty bizarre development.

"The thing is, I want you to be the boss," he said, holding my gaze in his as I adjusted to the idea. "I've invested in the e-reader, and I need someone to market it. I don't have the time or skill to nurse that company along, but you do. So you would really be doing me a favor if you continue to service my account."

"I could continue to, um, service your account." I smiled, jokingly batting my eyelashes. "But how did this happen?"

"I've been working on the deal for a while," he said, taking a bite of bread. "I looked into the company before we signed. I heard your father's partner wanted out, and he was keeping that Sheila there because he couldn't hack it. I prefer to own small companies that can work on my business interests rather than paying big retainers to companies that may not be as vested as a loyal staff would be." He took a moment to finish chewing.

"I guess that makes sense from a business perspective." I picked up a different container, feeling the need for comfort food as I processed this new development.

"There's something else," he said, sipping his champagne. "More recently, Grandmamma had a vision that certain dishonesty and greed had stolen your rightful place in the company, and your rightful inheritance, away."

"What do you mean exactly?" I put down the food to listen. There was a part of me that always wondered how things went down in the business when Dad was sick.

"We never know exactly how Grandmamma gets her insights, but based on her warning, I did some investigating." He took my hand into his. "I learned your father was the financial brains of the operation and he was a pretty organized guy."

"Very. He did run the business end of things for all those years," I said.

"Something didn't make sense to me about that." He squeezed my hand. "Why would a man with business acumen not have a will, or at the very least leave directions and an inheritance to his only child?"

I bent my head. The pain of being abandoned by my dad again, in the end, flooded back. "I was so concerned about being cut off from his company I never rocked that boat."

"Allison, around the time of your father's death, several large transfers were made from the company to offshore accounts." He leaned in and lifted my head. "We think they diverted money from your father's share of the business."

"Oh, my God." I stood up and grabbed the kitchen counter for support. "They stole my father's money? I thought they used it for his health care costs. I just wanted him to be taken care of. I never questioned."

He stood and put his hand on my back for comfort.

"My finance team and my legal team are looking through the books and bank statements, as well as your father's medical bills." He kissed the back of my neck. "We will get to the bottom of it."

"Nicolai, I can't believe you would do this for me." I turned and threw my arms around him.

"This company was always meant to be yours, and I believe at least half of it legally is," he said. "I am simply restoring what is meant to be. I get the added bonus of a top-notch firm putting a new product on the map."

"I don't even know what to say. Somehow this all feels right."

"There's just one executive decision I'd like to make, and that's to fire Sheila," he said. "Especially since she is now part of an investigation. As is business protocol, we have locked down her computer and removed files from her office so she could not get a chance to go in there and hide her tracks. As of Monday, after we're finished with *The Today Show* segment, she will be called into the boardroom to meet with the new owner. And you, as the President of the company, can fire her."

"That's intense." I should have felt vindicated, but I was oddly sad. Sheila was the bane of my existence at work; still, I didn't like the idea of hurting another person. "Shouldn't you do that?"

"No," he said. "I think you should. Or at the very least, we can do it together. Your team already loves and respects you, but this will seal your place as a leader of the company."

"Okay. I'm ready to do that," I said, looking deeply into his eyes. I saw love and warmth. I saw a man who cared enough for me to invest his time and money in winning me back something that is close to my heart.

"And I am glad you are ready, Ms. Monroe," he said, retrieving our champagne from the floor. He clinked his paper cup against mine "Here's to bringing in the new. And to having what is rightfully ours."

He put our cups on the counter and leaned against it, pulling me onto him. He wrapped his arms around me. Over his shoulder, the bright glow of the full moon hung outside my window. And when Nicolai kissed me deeply, the moonlight seemed to fill my kitchen. And my heart.

CHAPTER TWENTY-SIX

Suddenly, there was light all around us. And something moved me to reach inside my purse on the kitchen counter and open the secret zipper compartment. My hand touched the velvet pouch Grandmamma had given me. I'd forgotten all about it. The item inside felt heavy and cool. I pulled it out and held it in my palm.

"What's this?" Nicolai traced a finger along the soft material. "Are *you* going to propose to me and give *me* a ring?"

I laughed out loud but wondered if he hoped I would.

"I forgot all about this." I was super curious now about what was in the bag. "Your grandmother gave it to me when I met her. And she told me to keep it near my heart on the full moon."

"Really?" I could tell from his face he was surprised. Apparently, he hadn't seen her hand it to me or noticed me slip it into my purse. "You didn't mention it."

"I meant to, right after she gave it to me, but your cousin showed up at her house and I stashed it in my pocketbook before I had a chance to look," I said, remembering how something had told me to hide it from Vlad. "When I rediscovered it later that night, I hid it again, moments before he showed up at my door."

I thought he might get mad at the mention of Vlad, but from his expression, he seemed intrigued. "Interesting," he said, nodding. "Whatever is in there seems to have protected itself from his eyes."

I hadn't even thought of that. "Seems we were meant to open it together," I said.

I opened the pouch and let the object slide out on my hand. It was some sort of blue stone, almost like a dark crystal, and smooth to the touch. The stone was attached to a pendant with diamond-like gems at three points. Maybe it was a piece of antique costume jewelry.

"Is this a family heirloom or something?" I walked to the window to look at it under a lamp. Nicolai followed. "A piece of jewelry Grandmamma used to wear?"

He lifted my palm in his to take a closer look and seemed astonished.

"Oh, my Lord," he said out loud. "This is Queen Marie's sapphire pendant." He took a deep breath and looked more closely. "It's been in the Romanian and Greek monarchies."

"It's a replica. Right?" I searched his face. "Like from a museum?"

"No." He eyed it more carefully. "I believe it's the real one." He was shaking his head in disbelief, but there was a huge smile on his face.

"Seriously," I said, taking a closer look. "This can't be real."

"It most definitely is," he insisted. He whistled, as if making a catcall. "That's some piece of jewelry. I believe it is a four hundred and seventy-eight karat sapphire."

"How do you know so much about it? Was it in history books or part of the country's folklore?" My breathing began to get heavy.

"Grandmamma had me look into this a while ago and I discovered it was with private owners and she didn't ask me to pursue it any further. She must have had her clairvoyants' community figure out where it was and then had her lawyers get it."

"How do you just go 'get' something like this?" I had no idea how people could buy and attain royal jewelry.

"Private deals are made, things come to auction." He stared at the jewel. "You never know with Grandmamma." He had a devious grin on his face.

"Why … why would she give me this?" I was flabbergasted.

"She must have felt you needed to be the keeper of that stone," he said, running a finger over it. "She probably charged it with special protective energies, her energies. Clearly, she wanted you to have power. Look in the bag, is there a note?"

I slid my hand into the pouch and found a small folded card along with a key. I handed it to him to read.

"My Dearest Allison." He read it out loud. "The authenticity papers for Queen Marie's Sapphire Pendant are in a vault (key enclosed). Perhaps you will step into the role of countess and wear this. Most importantly, my hope is you love my Nicolai. But this jewel is yours alone, whether or not you choose to be by his side. I don't want you to ever be dependent on a man. If you hold this to your heart, it will help you know your truth. It has been blessed especially for you. With Love and Great Affection, Grandmamma."

"Holy crap." I rushed back over to my purse, pulled out my phone and searched online. I found photos of Queen Marie and several other royals wearing the jewel I was holding in my hand.

I looked at Nicolai but said nothing. I was too stunned to react.

"She's passing along her power to you, Allison." He looked happy, but he also seemed a little sad. "But she is apparently making me optional. You could buy the business from me outright with that rock. She's made sure that you don't *need* me."

Without even thinking, I placed the jewel against my heart. It warmed my skin. Within a moment, a burst of energy moved through me. My mind's eye filled with colors and images. It was some sort of telepathic slide show of photos and videos. But they weren't from my past. They seemed to be in the future sometime. In every image, Nicolai and I were together.

"No," I said, placing my free hand on his heart and looking into his eyes. "Not being together is no longer an option."

I gently pushed him onto the couch and climbed on his lap. Within moments, he was hard, I was ready, and the scant amount of clothing we'd had on was quickly tossed to the floor.

He kissed me like he really meant it and I kissed him right back. We made love like long lost lovers finally reuniting. I'd never felt so close to anyone in my whole life. Life seemed filled with pleasure and new possibilities.

Once we were wildly satisfied and spent, we clung to each other for a long time, flesh against flesh.

"Let me be your family now, Allison," he whispered, kissing the top of my head.

"Da." The answer came flowing out, as if it were the most natural thing in the world.

ABOUT A.C. ROSE

A.C. Rose is a sex and love journalist who also loves to write very steamy romance books.

As a former editor of an iconic women's magazine, sexy stories and beautiful men have long been her beat.

She has written extensively on sexuality, relationships, female desire, and the "kissing book" industry.

Has real life provided fodder for her fictional worlds? She'll never tell.

She is a member of the Romance Writers of America (RWA), Passionate Ink (PI), and the Author's Guild (AG).

Connect with A.C. Rose here:

Hot Romance Column: http://thethreetomatoes.com/category/love-sex/
hot-romance
Website: http://www.acroseauthor.net/
Blog: http://acroseauthor.com/
Facebook: https://www.facebook.com/AuthorACRose
Twitter: https://twitter.com/ACRoseAuthor

Subscribe to my newsletter here and join my VIP list.
http://www.acroseauthor.net/newsletter.htm

YOUR NEXT STEAMY
READ FROM A.C. ROSE

Amanda Slade has a major crush on her sexy art professor and wants his help with an important extracurricular activity: Project VirgEnd.

Professor Jem Nichols knows falling for his beautiful student is a bad idea but he just can't say goodbye as the semester ends. However, the professor refuses to hastily take her virtue. Instead, he wants to slowly teach her the most important lessons of lovemaking.

As she experiences first-time pleasures and passions, love blooms.

By the time they're done, he'll know every inch of her body. But with the pressure building around his show and her sexual debut, will Jem be the one to take her all the way?

Read Other Books and Stories by A.C. Rose